Praise for

Truth and Other Lies

"Twisty, timely, and rivetingly thought-provoking, Smith mines the intensity of competition, the duplicity of the human psyche, and the terrifying knowledge that with one wrong decision, your life can be changed forever. This author knows her journalism—the pressure, the stress, and the compulsion for the big story—and deeply understands the tension and conflicts women battle when their professional and personal lives are set on a collision course."

—Hank Phillippi Ryan, Emmy-winning investigative reporter and *USA Today* bestselling author of *Her Perfect Life*

"The political skews personal in this debut, which focuses on the bonds of powerful women in the rough-and-tumble world of politics and government. Smith's characters sometimes do each other in, more often do each other proud, always with an awareness of the fragility of reputation set against the abiding strength of spirit. Smith leads with boldness and heart from the first page."

—Jacquelyn Mitchard, author of *The Deep End of the Ocean* and *The Good Son*

"*Truth and Other Lies* is my favorite kind of novel—one that tackles tough topics in a breezy, compulsively readable way. Maggie Smith is a welcome new voice in fiction."

—Camille Pagán, bestselling author of *Don't Make Me Turn This Life Around*

"Expert storytelling, and a sharp exploration of the complex relationships between women—mothers and daughters, mentors and protégés, best friends and frenemies—are at the heart of Maggie Smith's compelling and savvy page-turner. Good thing books are calorie-free, I gobbled it down in a single afternoon."

—Karen Karbo, author of *In Praise of Difficult Women*

"Keenly observant, tense, and smart, Smith unravels the complexity of being a journalist in a time where loyalty, motherhood, and the medium itself are in a constant state of flux. *Truth and Other Lies* has everything you want in a book and more."

—Ann Garvin, *USA Today* bestselling author of
I Thought You Said This Would Work

"This ambitious debut tackles not only mother-daughter dynamics and family secrets, but also the workplace and real-world politics affecting modern women. Written with an engaging, conversational tone, the story conflicts are both realistic and substantial."

—Jamie Beck, *Wall Street Journal* and
USA Today bestselling author

"*Truth and Other Lies* promises three women, two secrets, and one lie, and boy does it deliver. Smith deftly weaves serious social issues such as abortion, sexual harassment, and toxic social media with the more typical women's fiction themes of female friendship, mother-daughter conflict, and romantic relationships, resulting in a taut and timely story. The surprise ending will leave you wishing for a sequel."

—A.H. Kim, author of *A Good Family*

"Complicated mother-daughter relationships, fierce professional ambition, and questionable journalistic ethics all interlaced with hot-button issues, internet trolling, mystery, and romance . . . *Truth and Other Lies* captures the essence of newsrooms, political campaigns, and Chicago itself with specific, sensory language that brings you right into the scenes."

—Catherine Johns, professional speaker, former broadcast journalist for 25 years, primarily at WLS Chicago

"In the thrilling novel *Truth and Other Lies*, a young reporter works to uncover the truth, which could have ruinous implications for others."

—*Foreword Reviews*

"An engaging and topical tale of politics and journalistic ethics with a feminist slant."

—*Kirkus Reviews*

"Smith's characters have complicated histories that overlap and interweave as they navigate the complex worlds of politics, journalism, and social media. Smith does a masterful job exploring the interplay between these issues with wit and compassion all through the lens of a strong female protagonist."

—*Windy City Reviews*

Truth and Other Lies

—•—

Maggie Smith

Ten|16
PRESS

www.ten16press.com - Waukesha, WI

Truth and Other Lies
Copyrighted © 2020 Maggie Smith
ISBN 9781645382621
Library of Congress Control Number: 2021942514
First Edition

Truth and Other Lies
by Maggie Smith

For information, please contact:

www.ten16press.com
Waukesha, WI

Cover designer: Kaeley Dunteman

To my father, who died too young. You deserved more.

There are two ways to be fooled.
One is to believe what isn't true.
The other is to refuse to believe what is true.

Søren Kierkegaard

ONE

July 2018

The media coined a term for people like me: boomerangs. Young adults launched by relieved parents with great fanfare into the world, finely tuned missiles brimming with lofty dreams, only to turn around mid-flight, tail tucked between our legs—out of a job, out of money, and out of options.

God, I hated being a cliché.

When I phoned from New York, my mother said she'd be out of town until tomorrow night, but of course I was welcome to stay as long as I wanted. By the time I landed at O'Hare, it was dusk, the height of rush hour, and traffic was a snarl, so the trip out to Evanston took a good forty-five minutes. I drummed my fingers against the seat cushion, wondering if the house would be different.

If *she'd* be different.

Once the Uber driver unloaded my bag and drove off, I retrieved the key from under the fourth flowerpot on the right. Not the most original hiding place, but this was the northern suburbs. Most of the crimes here happened behind closed doors.

I punched in the alarm code, flipped on the lights, and was stifled by my mother's signature gardenia fragrance. Nothing had changed. The mahogany banister still gleamed with polish, the brass sconces on either side of the fireplace sparkled, the white carpet showed fresh vacuum lines. Straight out of *House Beautiful*. Mother was still the dyed-in-the-wool Martha Stewart acolyte she'd always been. Everything clean, tucked away, not even a scrap of mail scattered on the hall table.

Now her only child was back, messing it all up.

I stopped in the kitchen where I scarfed two peanut butter and banana sandwiches and washed them down with a glass of chardonnay. Then I hauled my bag upstairs to my old bedroom and did a double take. There was no trace of the twinkling tea lights I'd strung across the ceiling. The corkboard with my movie stubs, prom corsage, and track medals had disappeared. So had my posters proclaiming *Support the Dreamers*, *Occupy Wall Street*, and *Feel the Bern*. Instead, I faced a stage set of off-white walls and sleek Danish furniture.

She'd erased my childhood.

Except for my old pal Jocko, the sock monkey, a long-ago gift from my grandmother. He sat propped against the pillows on the bed as if he'd been expecting me.

I'd been in such a hurry to leave New York, I'd only packed one suitcase. The rest of the boxes would arrive in a few days and I'd store those in Mom's basement for now.

It didn't make sense to unpack all my stuff since staying here was a stop-gap until I got my own place. I hung a few clothes in the closet, stripped to my underwear, and went to the bathroom to brush my teeth.

The phone rang. I waited for the answering machine to kick in, but when it didn't, I walked to my mother's bedroom at the end of the hall, debating whether to answer. After two more rings, I picked up the handset and plopped onto the elegant satin duvet. "Helen Watkins' residence."

"Megan? When I didn't hear from you, I decided to call and make sure you were okay." Mother's voice was a mix of concern and exasperation. "Your cell's going straight to voice mail."

Not this again—checking in, coordinating schedules, a barrage of questions. I should set ground rules right away or we'd wind up not speaking to each other before the week was out. "I was getting ready to turn in. I've got a busy day tomorrow."

Truthfully, my agenda was short. A good long run, a good long cry, and meeting my best friend Becca.

"I'll let you go then. There's leftover lasagna in the fridge if you want some. See you tomorrow night. Be safe. I love you."

"Love you, too," I parroted back, the autopilot response I knew would keep the peace between us for now.

When I hung up, my gaze drifted to the dresser, packed with framed photos of my mother and me. There I was, petting a goat on Grandpa's farm. In another, five-year-old me licked a triple-scoop ice cream cone, chocolate smeared across my chin. I lingered over a casual shot in an ornate silver frame, my mother and I in matching swimsuits at some long-forgotten water park. No pictures of my father, of course. She'd carefully curated this gallery, making sure she'd purged him from our life.

I stopped short at a photograph of my mother, resplendent in a black, low-cut evening gown, a stunning diamond necklace at her throat, standing beside an unfamiliar middle-aged man in a tuxedo with a cheesy grin plastered across his face. His arm curled around her waist, and he looked uncomfortable, as though he had gas. But it was the other man in the picture, the one whispering in my mother's ear, who caught my attention. Because no one could mistake who that was.

What in the world was my suburban housewife mother doing schmoozing with the Vice-President of the United States?

———————————•———————————

They say when your life falls apart, stick with your routine. So I woke up at dawn and sprinted out the door for my morning run. This time it wasn't the congested streets of Brooklyn but the cozy neighborhood of my childhood, with its well-manicured lawns, pristine sidewalks, and cookie-cutter houses. As I jogged, I wrestled with why I'd fled back here to Chicago and realized it had nothing to do with my mother and everything to do with Becca. Life had dealt me a double whammy in the space of one day, and my major lifeline lived hundreds of miles away. I needed my best friend.

When I'd called and told her I was back in town, she hadn't blinked, and readjusted her schedule so we could meet today for lunch. That decisiveness was one reason I loved her. Envied her sometimes, too. Like in biology class, when we cut open the frog and she decided on the spot to become a nurse. Like when she came back from her first date with Sam and said he was the guy she was going to marry. Like senior year when she gave up carbs for six months and lost thirty pounds.

I watched for her through the picture window, and when she turned into the driveway, I bolted out the door. I hadn't seen her since Christmas, but she hadn't changed— golden-brown skin, curly black hair, dimples in both cheeks that flashed when she grinned. Still driving Chariot, the banged-up but reliable Honda we'd cruised around in all through college. She enveloped me in a giant hug, and it felt as though I was finally home.

The first words out of her mouth were, "Since when are you a blonde?"

I fluffed my curls. "I switched it up last month. Mousy brown wasn't a fit for me anymore. What's the verdict?"

She grinned. "It's totally you. So, are you moving back to Chicago? And in with your mother?"

"I've changed. Maybe she has too."

It didn't take a college degree to read Becca's expression. *Good luck with that.*

"Listen, I'd let you stay with us, but Sam and I only have

the one bedroom, and we're still getting used to this whole living together thing, so . . ."

"No worries. Crashing at Mom's is temporary. Besides, it's extra incentive to find a job." Not that I needed a reason. I couldn't wait to get back to work.

We drove away from the house, and before we'd even made it out of the neighborhood, Becca reached over and squeezed my hand. "Okay. Talk to me."

When I didn't answer, she pushed. "Seriously, where's that adventurous girl I know and love? Did something happen with your job? With that guy?"

I'd spent most of last night staring at the ceiling when I wasn't punching the pillow or clutching Jocko and crying. "The short version is I caught him cheating. I'll save the long version for when we've had a few glasses of wine. If I talk about it now, I won't make it through lunch."

She nodded. "Fair enough. I'm here when you're ready."

"So what have *you* been up to? How was that getaway trip up north you told me about?"

Becca flipped on the radio, and soft jazz filled the air. "It was nice. I got caught up on reading and spent a lot of time hiking in the woods."

"Sam must have missed you like crazy."

She didn't respond but hummed along with the music. "You said on the phone you're going to reboot your life. What's the plan?"

"Obviously the first step is finding a way to support myself. Can we run by Northwestern before we eat so I can scope out the employment listings? I tried the website last night but couldn't get in. So far all I've turned up online are a few unpaid internships and freelance gigs, and I can't afford to work for free."

Being thrown back into the job market felt like standing at ground zero. The good news was I'd amassed a stack of clippings at my last two positions, so I had a decent portfolio. The bad news was I hadn't been let go from *The Brooklyn Herald* because of downsizing like I planned to tell my mother.

I'd been fired.

TWO

We arrived at the Northwestern campus, but a mass of barricades blocked our way to the administration building. "Must be an event going on," Becca said. "Doesn't look as though we'll get any closer. Let's park here and walk."

Up and down Sheridan Road, we saw notices tacked up on poles announcing a rally against sexual violence scheduled for noon. "It's good people are finally waking up," I commented, scanning the crowd.

An older woman walking by spoke up. "Oh, the turnout's not all for the cause. Jocelyn Jones is going to speak. Folks always turn out for celebrities."

Jocelyn Jones? What a piece of luck. If someone made a list of the top female icons in journalism, she'd be right up there with Diane Sawyer, Christiane Amanpour, and Lesley Stahl. She must know everyone in the media world in Chicago. What if I could somehow meet her, explain my situation, and ask for a contact at a downtown newspaper?

I brought myself back to reality. Who was I kidding? Why should she help a stranger find a job? But I'd still love to hear her speak. "Let's go." I nodded in the direction of the crowd.

Becca's eyes widened. "This from the woman who says we should stop listening to old white boomers and come up with fresh ideas on our own?"

"Jones is different. She's been an advocate for women's rights for decades. You've got to admire that. Come on, we can spare a half hour."

We linked arms and marched to a nearby booth where we donned T-shirts with "Am I Next?" emblazoned across the front in stark red letters. The only size left was medium, which swamped Becca, but with my five-foot-eight frame, it barely covered my midsection. A volunteer handed each of us a sign demanding *Stop Violence Against Women Now*. Dozens of people milled around, waiting for the event to begin, and within minutes, the crowd had swelled to hundreds. The air was electric.

Jones stood on one side of the speaker's platform, surrounded by reporters as well as students, all jockeying for her attention. And here I'd fantasized I could casually bump into her. I scanned the crowd, looking for any former classmates who might have showed up. That's when I saw a cluster of guys standing toward the back, dressed entirely in black, heads shaved, Confederate flags on their armbands. One held a sign that read *You dress like a whore, we'll treat you like one.* They jostled and punched each other as they cat-called to the women around them. As I watched, the taste of

burnt coffee flooded my mouth. They reminded me of neo-
Nazis I'd seen on television: traveling in packs, intimidating
people around them, all swagger and no brains.

"Campus security should make them leave," I said to a
man nearby, nodding toward the skinheads.

He shrugged. "That's free speech for you. Unless they
break the law, they can stay. Ignore them. They're hoping
to stir up enough trouble to get their faces on the evening
news. If they don't attract attention, they'll get bored and
move on."

Was he joking? Guys like that didn't go away on their
own. They pushed the limits until someone confronted them.

A woman climbed onto the makeshift platform, grabbed
the microphone, and silenced the crowd. She thanked
everyone for showing up and reiterated the reason for
today's event. Two students spoke next, a male and a female,
each a victim of sexual assault. Becca and I stood side by
side near the podium and clapped after each testimonial. I
had to give these people credit. It took guts to speak out in
front of a bunch of strangers. I wasn't sure I could do it.

I recognized the woman who spoke next. Becca and I
had both taken American Lit from her our junior year.

"I'm Professor Stein from the English Department, and
today it's my great pleasure to introduce Jocelyn Jones, a
beloved journalist and later television anchorwoman. Her
career began—"

"Who cares?" one of the skinheads yelled. I spun around
and glared as his friends slapped him on the back and he
wedged himself in front of a news camera.

Stein ignored the comment. "Jocelyn worked at *Ms.* magazine in the early seventies, then wrote for various newspapers on the east coast until 1990 when she joined *The New York Times* as an overseas correspondent."

More shouts from the guys on the sidelines. People around them backed away, giving them a wide berth, which no doubt played right into their agenda. Editors loved to snag shots of protestors standing out in the crowd.

Stein paused as though unsure whether to go on, but once the taunts died down, she continued. "Jocelyn covered both the Iraq and Afghan wars, then returned stateside in 2001. She segued into broadcast journalism, first as a White House correspondent, and later as a news anchor at ABC."

I glanced at Jones, who stood behind Stein. She wore loose-fitting camel slacks, an off-white silk blouse, and simple gold jewelry. Her steel-gray hair swept off her angular face in waves, and her eyes, alert as a hawk, blazed beneath dark sculpted brows. She held her shoulders back and her chin high, a modern-day Valkyrie leading troops into battle. What I wouldn't give to accomplish half of what she had in my own career.

Stein ended with, "Please join me in welcoming my dear friend, Jocelyn Jones."

I hadn't realized Professor Stein even knew Jones, let alone considered her a friend. The crowd surged forward, chanting and cheering. Two young girls crowded me from behind. I found it hard to breathe and sidestepped to get more space so that when Jones strode to the microphone, she was close enough I could have touched her. I turned to make a comment to Becca, but realized we'd gotten separated.

"The number of women assaulted every year on our campuses is staggering," Jones's voice rang out. "There's something wrong when a culture turns the other way while—"

A skinhead in a black leather jacket shoved past me, screamed, "Bitch!" and threw a water balloon directly at Jones.

The liquid soaked her blouse, and the outline of her lace bra showed through the sheer fabric. When the guy thrust his fist in the air, a loud chorus of boos erupted from the crowd.

I stiffened, my hands curling into fists.

Unbelievable. How dare these scumbags attack a journalist who'd achieved more in a day than they had in their lifetimes? Why wasn't someone shutting this guy down? I was fed up with men who thought they could do whatever they wanted to women and get away with it.

I flinched at his stench, a mix of acrid sweat and stale smoke. Whistles sounded, but the security guards had lined up around the perimeter and the mass of people gathered around the podium blocked their way. No one nearby made a move to pull the guy back. When he fumbled in his pocket and hauled out a second balloon, I grabbed his wrist and twisted it sideways. The bright yellow balloon splashed on the ground, soaking my shoes.

He whirled and faced me—crooked nose, rank garbage breath, a jagged scar near his left eyebrow. "Cunt." He pulled back his fist.

You picked the wrong woman this time, buddy. I snapped the heel of my hand into his nose, landing a solid blow.

He hadn't seen it coming, and the surprise on his face made me smile. He staggered backwards, tripped over his own feet, and fell onto the pavement, blood gushing from both nostrils. I glanced at the podium. Jones hadn't been hurt, but she'd turned pale and Stein steered her away.

"Behind you!" someone shouted.

My pulse spiked as I swung around and caught another skinhead rushing toward me. His face morphed into the visage of the scowling gargoyles above the campus chapel. "Slut!" he yelled.

Several people held their phones aloft, recording the fight. *Shit.* I reported the news. I didn't want to *be* the news.

Time to shut this down. I raised my fists. "Back off, asshole."

The second guy crouched down to help his buddy, who lay moaning at my feet. I bent at the waist to catch my breath, hands trembling as sweat slithered down my chest. Becca waved at me from across the way, her eyes round as plates, and I gave her a thumbs-up.

That's when the guy on the ground sprang up and slapped me. My eyes filled with tears and I felt a sharp sting as blood trickled down my cheek where his skull ring must have cut me. Finally, three security guards burst through and hauled the two guys away. By then, their friends on the sidelines had disappeared like smoke.

———•———

It took a few minutes to settle the crowd, but finally, Jones layered a dry T-shirt over her blouse and resumed her speech. Becca shoved her way through the mass of onlookers to my side, and she and an event staffer steered me toward a tent where an EMT cleaned and bandaged my cut. A campus police officer took my statement, ignoring my tirade against goddamn skinheads and how they should be banned from campus rallies, instructing me to please stick to the facts.

Eventually, Becca helped me to a nearby curb where I eased myself down. My insides felt scraped out, my legs wobbly from the adrenaline rush.

"Where in the world did you learn to do that?" she asked.

I grinned, even though it hurt. "Krav Maga. I covered the political beat in the Bronx, remember? Required job training."

Becca put her arm around me. "Chicago's very own Wonder Woman."

"I agree," a voice said from behind me.

I twisted around to see Jocelyn Jones looming over me, blocking the blazing sun.

"You were quite brave back there," she said. "Are you all right?"

All I could manage was a nod. My brain hurt when I moved, and my ears wouldn't stop ringing. Was I hallucinating?

"It's been a while since I've been physically attacked. Perhaps I'm still relevant after all. Thank you for what you did, Ms. . . . ?"

This wasn't a mirage. It was actually her. I opened my mouth, but nothing came out. Somehow, I managed to stand and took another stab at answering her question. "I'm ... Megan Barnes." I stuck out my hand. "I'm sorry ... your speech." I couldn't make my mouth work right.

Jones squeezed my hand, and her skin felt cool to the touch. "Never apologize for defending yourself or other women. What you did took courage. Are you a student here at Northwestern?"

Desperate to sound halfway like myself, I stood straighter and took a deep breath. "Yes. I mean no, I graduated from here, but ... I just moved back."

"That's a coincidence. So did I. And you took time out on a Saturday to protest. Good for you."

"Not enough people bother to make their voices heard. I mean, if we don't, then before long ..." I let my rambling dribble to a halt and told myself to cool it.

She studied my face. "What do you do here in Chicago, Megan?"

Jocelyn Jones, world-famous war correspondent and award-winning journalist, was standing right in front of me, making conversation. Talk about a dream come true. I needed to get control of my emotions before I blew this chance. Finally I burst out with, "I'm an investigative reporter and I want to work at the *Chicago Tribune*."

She smiled. "Good for you. I admire people who set lofty goals. I'd like the chance to thank you properly for what you did."

"I'd like that too. I mean. Hold on." I spilled half the

contents of my purse on the ground, grabbed an old grocery store receipt, scribbled my name, cell phone number, and email address on the back, and thrust it out. "Here's how to reach me."

She let out a throaty laugh, and a warm glow spread through my body as she tucked my information in her pants pocket. This was going okay. Natural. As though we were two close friends having a casual chat.

"Listen, the march is starting, so I need to get back, but I'll be in touch. And take it easy, okay? Go home and put ice on that cheek. And again, I appreciate you coming to my defense." She turned.

I couldn't let her leave yet. "Wait!"

She spun back around. "Yes?"

"Do you have a business card? I mean, so I could contact *you*, in case . . ." In case what? She didn't call me? She threw away the slip of paper? She forgot all about me?

"I'm sorry, no." She shielded her eyes from the sun's glare. "But don't worry. I'll remember you, Megan. After all, it's not every day I meet . . . what was it your friend said? Ah, yes. Wonder Woman."

I stood motionless as she disappeared into the crowd.

The expression on Becca's face said it all. "Did that really happen?" When I didn't say anything, she felt my forehead. "Hey, you don't look so good. I'm driving you home."

"Wait. The jobs board. I need—"

"Not today, Rocky. Come on, lean on me."

"What about lunch?"

"We'll hit a drive-thru on the way."

Back at my mother's, Becca helped me crawl into bed and fetched a towel with ice. "Want me to stay? I can call a friend to cover my shift."

"Don't you dare. My face hurts like hell and I'm stiff, but otherwise, I'm fine. Mom will be home soon, and you know how she loves playing Florence Nightingale."

Becca persisted. "Where does she keep her aspirin?"

I shooed her off. "Stop already. Go to work."

"Do you think Jones will call? Promise you'll let me know right away."

Now that the excitement of the whole encounter had faded, I realized how improbable that seemed. I mean, why would Jones get in touch? She'd said she was grateful, encouraged me to keep up the good fight, and told me to support other women whenever I had the chance. What more could she say?

"My guess is she's forgotten me already."

But even if I never saw Jones again, I could always turn the incident into an article. Submit it to *Medium*. Get some exposure. People loved stories about everyday folks who bumped into celebrities. Plus, a skinhead got punched. That angle might easily go viral. I'd never written a lifestyle essay, but why not try it? They say it's not always what you know, but who you know.

And as of today, I knew Jocelyn Jones.

THREE

I napped until midafternoon and woke up chilled. When I hobbled to the hall closet for an extra blanket, I noticed a large storage box with my name on it and hauled it out. Inside were five bulging photo albums of me as a kid, stacks of old report cards, the tassel from my high school graduation. Weird. I distinctly remembered putting this box out for garbage pickup when I left for New York. Why would my mother have rescued this from the pile?

Seemed my past meant more to her than it did to me.

I carried the box to the bed and leaned back against the headboard. As I flipped through my senior yearbook, a slip of paper fell out. *What to Accomplish Before I'm Thirty.* I'd written this the day that boy in my sophomore class—Todd? Martin?—overdosed. The day I'd vowed not to waste any more time on silly things.

I scanned the list. *Have sex.* Check. *Graduate from college. Run a marathon. Try marijuana.* Check, check, check. The last item jumped out. *Write stories that matter.*

That goal hadn't changed. They say people have a calling. That was mine. My mistake back in New York had temporarily derailed that goal, but I'd find a way back. I had to.

My vision blurred. The altercation with the skinhead must have caught up to me. I closed my eyes and the next thing I knew, the smell of bacon filled the house.

She was back.

I pulled the sheet over my head, dreading the scene ahead. She'd give me the obligatory hug followed by a long stare, and then tell me she'd fix everything. It never mattered what I'd done—totaled the car, got a D in chemistry, got drunk at the school dance.

I was her sweetest girl. Her precious baby.

Growing up, it felt as though my mother would devour me if I let her. There would be nothing left of me except an odd appendage—an arm? a third leg?—sticking out of her body, impossible to separate from the whole. She called it unconditional love. I called it smothering. When I got older, I realized why she'd done it. If I needed her enough, I'd never leave.

But I had. And no way was I going back inside the cage—at least, not for long.

I examined myself in the bathroom mirror, swiped on foundation, and shuffled downstairs to the kitchen.

"Hi, Mom."

At forty-eight, she could still turn heads—slim figure, porcelain skin, deep-set blue eyes. Between Botox, Pilates, and watching what she ate, she could pass for ten years younger. But she gave off an air of *don't get too close* with her helmet of frosted blond hair that wouldn't have budged if a tornado had torn through the house. Underneath her food-spattered apron, she wore a Chanel suit, white with black piping, and a strand of perfectly matched pearls. A cordovan leather briefcase and a Gucci handbag leaned against the wall.

She took one look at me and gasped. "Oh my lord, Megan. What happened to your face?"

I knew she'd make this into a big deal. The cuts were minor, but my cheek already had a yellowish tint, despite the makeup I'd slapped on. "Becca and I attended a march at the university this morning, and someone got attacked. You know me." I gave a half laugh. "Never could resist a good brawl." I didn't go into details because first, I didn't want a lecture on staying out of fights, and second, the whole story might sound as though I'd made it up.

She flew into mother-mode. "But you're okay? Did you see a doctor? Are you nauseous? Here, follow my finger with your eyes."

For the millionth time, I wished she wouldn't treat me like a freshly hatched baby chick, but an adult who could take care of herself. Did every mother want to protect her child from harm, even if they had to stifle their independence to do it? Or was this my own particular hell?

"It's no worse than the fight I had in third grade. Remember?"

She tilted her head. "How could I forget? That black eye took forever to go away."

"Billy Sanders was a bully. Totally deserved it." I'd watched him harass my friend Herschel for three days before I'd put a stop to it.

"Who was it this time?"

"A wimpy alt-right skinhead. Big talk. No fucking balls."

"Megan, please. Language." She ran her fingers lightly over my face, and I winced when she touched my cheekbone. "Well, if you say you're okay, I'll go along, but the minute I notice you acting odd, I'm bundling you off to the clinic. And honey?" She lifted my chin. "Please be more careful. We can't let anything happen to that beautiful face."

I wasn't beautiful. My nose was too long, my eyes set too far apart. I had decent cheekbones but way too many freckles. But, in my profession, not being beautiful had its advantages. Like the time I'd scored an interview with the mother of a kid accused of carjacking. She picked me out of a pack of reporters clamoring on her doorstep because she said I had an honest face. I knew damn well she wouldn't have trusted me if I looked like Margot Robbie.

I glanced at the clock above the stove. "It's six at night. Why does it smell like breakfast?"

"I fixed your favorite: bacon and banana waffles, coming right up." She raised the spatula in a salute and her face softened. "It's nice to have you home."

"No bacon for me. I'm a vegetarian now."

"You never told me that."

The list of things I hadn't told her would stretch around the block. But she'd made an effort. Plus, suddenly I was starving. "I'll take the waffles. They smell delicious."

She looked me up and down, and a frown flickered across her face. "Shouldn't you shower first?"

Her judgment sent ants crawling under my skin. Granted, the ratty sweats I'd thrown on didn't smell all that fresh, but still. I put a kitchen towel on the chair cushion to appease her, and her shoulders relaxed.

"I'm glad I caught you. We need to talk."

"Okay. Go ahead." Going for nonchalant, I grabbed a glass from the cabinet and poured myself some orange juice. Then I sat and lit into the waffles, knowing her rule was never to talk with my mouth full.

Her gaze darted around the room and finally settled on my arm. "What's that?"

I swallowed. "I told you I got a tattoo."

"You never said it was so big. Do you think employers will see that as a negative?"

I couldn't help smiling. The tat was a gorgeous butterfly, only two inches long, wings spread wide. And I was a reporter. Editors could care less about your appearance as long as you got the story. When I didn't take the bait, she tried again.

"Does it mean something?"

It means I'm free. But it was an old wound, scabbed over and better left alone. I took another sip of juice and set down the glass. Might as well get it over with. "What did you want to talk about?"

"Well, for one thing, I'm not sure why you're here. Last time we talked, you sounded set—living with your boyfriend, challenging job, and you said you loved New York. What happened?"

I'd known this was coming and prepared ahead of time. "The paper ran low on funding and a bunch of us got laid off." Newspapers everywhere were struggling, so it sounded plausible.

"And Luke? Couldn't he support you until you found another job?"

Trust her to find the weak link in my story. "We had a falling out."

"I knew he wasn't right for you from the beginning."

Where did that come from? I hadn't gone into details about the relationship, hoping I could dodge her inevitable lecture on older men, divorced men, successful men. How they took advantage of younger women. How they couldn't be trusted.

I hated to admit it, but this time, she'd been right.

"So are you going to stick with this reporting thing?"

I winced. Why did she have to say it like that, as though it was a passing whim instead of my chosen career?

"The country needs journalists who aren't afraid to tell the truth more than ever, so yes, I'm"—and here I made air quotes—"*sticking with the reporting thing*." I laid down my fork. "What else?"

"What do you mean?" She fiddled with her pearls.

"Earlier you said, '*For one thing.*' What else did you want to talk about?"

Her face moved a fraction. "Nothing's decided yet."

She was hiding something. Something I now realized she'd wanted to tell me ever since I'd come into the room. "What's up?"

Glancing to one side, she blurted, "There's a chance I may run for the open House seat for the ninth district in the midterm election."

She might as well have announced she'd become a ballerina. My mother, a politician? And not running for county treasurer, but the United States Congress? Who'd talked her into this harebrained idea? "But you've never held elected office in your life."

A cross between a smile and a smirk played across her face. "Nowadays, that's not necessarily a negative."

I couldn't believe what I was hearing. "Please don't do this. The world isn't the same as when you were young. There's this little thing called the Internet. Everyone knows everything about everybody. You'll be probed. Dissected. You won't have a shred of privacy left. Is that what you want?"

"Pumpkin, you talk as if I've been living in Siberia for the last twenty years. I've got a Twitter account, a Facebook page, and my own website."

I'd wandered into a *Black Mirror* episode.

To buy time, I took another mouthful of waffle. When had all this happened? Who was this person, and what had she done with my mother? Helen Watkins, U.S. Congresswoman? I repeated the words to myself but still couldn't wrap my head around it. "What does Dad say?"

"When was the last time you spoke with your father?" Her voice had that pinched tone she got whenever his name came up.

"He called me on my birthday. Why?"

She crossed the room and hung her apron on a hook. "You mean three months ago?"

I pressed. "You haven't told him, have you?"

She whirled around, eyes ablaze. "Why should I? He's in Texas with that new family of his. What I decide to do with my life has nothing to do with him." She sounded angrier than she'd been when he left, which was saying a lot. "Besides, you know I'm using my maiden name now. No one will make the connection. And what if they do? Everyone's divorced these days. No one cares."

"Until your opponent ferrets out the details of the split and splashes it across social media, you mean." This was the national stage we were discussing. Big stakes. Powerful people. How would voters react when they found out she'd gone to Dad's office, put his brand-new Corvette into gear, and calmly watched as it rolled into a brick wall?

Not that I blamed her. If my husband of twenty-eight years packed his bag for a business trip, kissed me goodbye, and five hours later a messenger served me divorce papers, I'd spiral out of control too.

I took another bite while I digested this new information. Her decision would affect me too. Sources might shy away from talking to the daughter of a high-profile politician. I could lose out on assignments because of a conflict of interest. Fellow reporters might feel awkward around me if they wrote an article critical of her candidacy. I needed to convince her to drop this idea before it went any further. She was an intelligent woman. She'd listen to reason.

"Why put yourself through the ugliness of a political campaign when we both know you don't stand a chance of being elected?"

She eased into a chair across from me and bit into a slice of bacon. "You've got it backwards. The party leadership approached me, not the other way around. The man they were backing has health issues, and they're scrambling. Seems I've got a strong Q rating because of my visibility in the pro-life movement."

I'd forgotten about that.

I'd never understood what drove her, but for years my mother had honchoed grassroots efforts to shut down Planned Parenthood clinics across the state. At college, friends would rant at me in the cafeteria, repeating what my mother said on one radio show or another. All I could do was agree with them and make clear I had no control over what she did. Not that I hadn't tried to talk sense into her. But it was hopeless. We viewed the world so differently it was hard to believe we were even related.

"Besides, there's a push this year to get more women in the legislature," she continued. "Which means I've got the party's endorsement if I want it. As to why I'd do it, who wouldn't want the chance to affect how our country is run? It's an exciting opportunity."

This was exactly what frustrated me when it came to politics. People in power handpicked candidates who supported their agenda and poured money into their campaigns. Anyone outside the system didn't stand a chance of getting nominated, much less elected.

"It doesn't matter what I say, does it? You've already made up your mind."

"You're right, I have." Her eyes burned into mine. "I'm telling you what's happening, Meggie, not asking for your permission." She wiped her hands on a kitchen towel hanging nearby. "Frankly, I don't understand why you care one way or the other. I've spent my whole adult life being a mother to you. Now it's my turn."

My fork froze in midair, the last piece of waffle dripping sticky syrup onto the plate. If she did run for office, she'd be too preoccupied with her campaign to interfere in my life. I'd prayed for this day since I'd turned fifteen. Why was I trying to stop her?

"You're right. I say go for it." I shoveled the last bite of food into my mouth and took a swig of juice.

"So I can count on your support?"

I almost spit the mouthful across the room. "No. That is *not* what I said. We both know we're on opposite sides on every issue—climate control, abortion, guns."

The first time we'd clashed, I'd been a teenager, and even though I'd dreaded talking to people I didn't know, I'd worked on voter registration drives in south Chicago during Obama's first run for office. My mother, a precinct captain for the McCain campaign, hadn't spoken to me for a week.

"Maybe you could stand beside me on the podium a few times," she said. "Don't worry. You won't have to make a speech or anything. I know how you hate that."

My fork clattered to the floor. "Absolutely not. The fact you're running for office doesn't change where I stand one bit." I raised my voice to make sure she heard me. "I won't make any appearances with you at rallies, and you won't get my vote. Got it?"

She glared at me. Apparently, my back talk took her by surprise. "I take it that would be a *no* to working for me?"

The U-turn in the conversation made my head spin. "You lost me."

"You told me on the phone you'd need a job, so I asked Gavin, my campaign manager, if he could find something for you to do at headquarters. He's putting together a field office downtown and needs staff to answer phones and stuff envelopes. Nothing you can't handle. You could start right away."

At last, a mother I recognized. Fixing things for me. Only doing it all wrong.

"I've got a career too, remember? I need to work in my field, not take a job a high schooler could handle."

Her face relaxed as if relieved. So she didn't want me involved in her new adventure after all. "I knew you'd say no, but I wanted to make the offer." She retrieved her purse from the corner and pulled out her wallet. "Do you need cash? I'll stop by the bank tomorrow and have them issue you an ATM card so you can access my account."

"Thanks, but I've got enough in savings to tide me over." I only had sixteen hundred dollars to my name, but no way was I taking her money.

"Well, if you're sure." She peeked at her watch. "Listen, I've got to scoot to a committee meeting, but let's plan on dinner together tomorrow."

She kissed the top of my head as though I was a toddler who'd fallen on the playground, and my leg bounced under the table. "And go to bed at a reasonable hour tonight, sweet pea. You look tired."

She retrieved her briefcase and bag, and at the doorway turned back to me. "Honey, I'm sorry your life didn't work out the way you planned. But remember, you can't see around the next corner when your eyes are shut. Chicago could be exactly where you're supposed to be right now."

No. Right now I should be grilling a landlord who'd bribed a building inspector or digging through the tax returns of a corrupt business owner or interviewing a whistleblower who had evidence of stock manipulation. And tonight I should be opening a bottle of wine and lighting candles and cooking risotto with Luke, the man I love. *Loved.* Instead I was listening to my mother spout New Age gibberish on how to make lemonade out of lemons.

"And by the way, I love the new hair. But you might try going shorter. Play up your cheekbones."

I bit the inside of my cheek to choke back the snarky retort that bubbled up. After she'd left the kitchen, I rinsed off my plate and put it in the dishwasher. As I headed upstairs to my bedroom, I overheard her talking on her cell.

"We're not using that. Ed Underhill and I agreed we'd focus on the issues and leave rumors alone. Are we clear?"

It seemed my mother had committed to running a clean campaign. I'd been knee-deep in reporting politics for three years now.

She didn't stand a chance.

FOUR

The next morning, my body ached like I'd spent the night folded inside a suitcase, so I skipped my run. I listened for sounds in the house, but my mother must have already left for the day. I perched on the edge of the couch, booted up my laptop, and resumed my job search.

After a few hours, I stumbled across a new posting on LinkedIn at *The Morning Register*, a decent-sized newspaper located in the northern suburbs. They needed a reporter who'd cover both city hall and local arts events. Not the investigative reporting I specialized in, but hey, I wasn't in a position to get choosy. I submitted my application online and within an hour had snagged a meeting with the managing editor.

When the day of the job interview rolled around, I layered on extra makeup to cover my still-bruised face, borrowed my mother's car, and headed to Highland Park. It was nine in the morning, but a sign at the nearby bank showed the temperature had already skyrocketed to ninety-five degrees. Even running the air conditioner full blast hadn't helped. By the time I climbed out of the car, my hair hung in wilted strands and my blouse had sweat stains under the arms.

Tucking the folder with my clippings into my tote, I yanked open the heavy glass doors and rode the elevator to the fourth floor. Even though my interview wasn't for another fifteen minutes, showing up early sent the right message: I was ready to hit the ground running.

I took a seat in reception and tuned into the familiar sounds—grainy voices chattering over a police scanner, phones ringing, file cabinets sliding open and closed. Eventually, a middle-aged man with a receding hairline and a wire-brush mustache approached me. He had a nice face, serious but friendly. His gray short-sleeved shirt matched his bushy eyebrows, and his red-striped tie hung loose around his neck, drawing attention to his prominent double chin. Out of nowhere, a mental picture of him in a rowboat fishing for bluegills popped into my head.

"Megan, right? I'm Alex Diaz." His handshake was firm, no nonsense. Thank goodness. I hated people whose palms felt like a mass of slimy worms. "This way."

Newsrooms have their own unique atmosphere—the clack of keyboards, the cramped quarters, the harsh overhead lights turning everyone's face a sickly shade of yellow. In one corner, I spotted a guy my age scribbling furiously on a notepad. An older woman, long dark hair escaping from a back bun, tucked a phone between her cheek and shoulder while sneaking gulps of coffee. Another man, halfway through a donut, peered at his computer screen and adjusted his glasses. Stacks of folders littered the work surfaces, along with personal photos and one sad Mylar birthday balloon floating listlessly over an empty desk in the corner. I could have been back at the *Herald*. It even smelled the same, a mix of musty newsprint, burned microwave popcorn, and sweat.

God, I missed this.

Diaz lifted a stack of books from a beat-up chair and gestured for me to sit. A quick glance around the office signaled the man had been at this for a while—faded photos of him with a slew of politicians and celebrities, award plaques, newspaper articles with his byline. The accolades were balanced by a mug beside his computer proclaiming him *World's Best Grandpa* and a framed picture of an attractive woman with olive skin cuddling a small boy.

"Says here you graduated from Northwestern's Medill program. I've lectured there a few times. Ever run into Todd Hopkins?"

"He taught my professional ethics course. Tough, but fair. I was sorry to hear he'd passed away."

"Damn cancer. Todd was my mentor at my first newspaper job. He took me under his wing and introduced me to his sources. I was starstruck at first, but we became fast friends. We even shared season tickets to the Bears one year. He'll be missed."

I'd never met a journalist as dedicated to the profession as Todd Hopkins. If this man had been friends with him, he was someone I wanted to work for. "He challenged me to question my assumptions. For example, how can you report on hate speech without condoning it?" I flashed back to the rally and the skinheads.

"That was Todd. Journalism as a sacred trust. He'd blow a gasket if a news anchor spouted personal opinions on the air. And this whole hoopla over alternative facts? Don't get me started." He rustled through the papers on his desk and found my application. "But we're getting off topic. Tell me what you've done since college."

I'd gone over my pitch until I could recite it in my sleep. "After graduation, I worked at a small weekly in the Bronx, covering public hearings, police reports, city council meetings, that sort of thing. Shortly after I got hired, there was an influx of young professionals with families who moved into the neighborhood and pushed up housing costs."

I dug through my folder and handed over a clipping. "I profiled ten residents, older people on fixed incomes, who were forced out when their rents tripled. It got traction. Various wire services picked it up, and it went viral." I'd worked night and day on that story, researching zoning laws, buttonholing community leaders, recording in-depth interviews. It was the best piece of journalism I'd ever written.

"Let me guess. Nothing changed."

"My first reality check as a reporter. But I'd helped put a human face on gentrification. And it convinced me that's the type of reporting I wanted to do."

"We don't break a lot of major stories here in the suburbs, although I keep hoping. Let's switch gears a bit. How savvy are you with social media?"

I laughed before I could stop myself. "I'm twenty-five. What do you think?"

"We need to beef up our online presence to reach a younger audience. If you know your way around Twitter and Instagram, that's a big plus."

We chatted for a few more minutes, and finally he asked why I'd left my last job. On the drive over, I'd considered how to answer that question. I could always pretend I'd been laid off like I'd told my mother. I could downplay what happened and say the job wasn't what I'd expected. I could say a family emergency brought me back home. I could sell any of those reasons if he didn't check.

But if he did, he'd know I lied.

Who was I kidding? I had to come clean. Being honest had gotten me into more scrapes than I could count, but regardless, telling the truth was part of my DNA.

"I messed up."

He leaned back in his chair and steepled his fingers. "Tell me about it."

Inside my chest, a sparrow frantically beat its wings, desperate to escape. "My editor had me profile a new bistro in the Red Hook area. I interviewed staff, customers, sampled the food. One of the perks of being a restaurant reviewer."

I gave a small laugh, but when he didn't respond, I plowed on. "Anyway, the last day I was there, the sous chef cornered me. He told me he'd found rat droppings in the storeroom. He'd reported it, but the owner had paid off the health inspector and got his occupancy permit anyway.

Two waiters backed up his story. I couldn't believe my luck, stumbling across a classic case of corruption at the local level, so I hammered away at my editor for days, begging him to make it the lead article that weekend."

Diaz leaned forward. "Is this going where I think it is?"

I'd hooked him. I had a talent for weaving a story.

"Luckily, my editor had enough sense to send another reporter to research further. It turned out the accusation was a total fabrication. The owner was having an affair with the sous chef's wife, and this was payback. I made a rookie mistake. I should have dug deeper and realized there might be more going on."

"Rough. So your editor killed the article?"

"And fired me the next day. He said I was a good reporter, but it was out of his hands. The publisher of the paper sat on a charity board with the restaurant owner's father. There was talk of a libel suit, but since we never published the piece, they agreed to drop it."

"But they still threw you under the bus." He clicked the end of his ballpoint pen and kept his face steady. I couldn't tell what he was thinking.

I wanted him to understand I'd learned my lesson. "It wasn't fair, but I *had* violated the first rule of reporting. I'd latched on to a sexy story without examining all the details. I hated losing my job, but I realized I'd brought it on myself."

I'd made a mistake, pure and simple, and now I needed a second chance. If Diaz gave me one, I wouldn't waste it.

He locked eyes with me as though trying to figure me out. Had I made a rookie mistake, or was I a slipshod journalist? I steeled my nerves and forced myself not to look away, even though his silence unnerved me.

Finally, he nodded. "I admire your honesty. I would have found out anyway when I did a background check, but I'm glad you told me up front. It's the level of integrity I expect from my staff."

I made a last-ditch appeal. "I'm good at what I do, Mr. Diaz. If you hire me, you won't be sorry."

He stroked his mustache. "Yes, well." He stood, signaling our time was up. "I've got a couple more people to interview, but you're a strong candidate, Ms. Barnes. I can see you fitting in here. Thanks for coming by, and we'll talk again soon."

I'd driven away confident I'd aced the interview. But when a day went by with no word, I became an anxious mess, pacing back and forth, rebooting my emails every half hour, jogging around the neighborhood to work off my excess energy. When my phone rang two days later, I waited a few seconds before I answered. No need to look too desperate.

But it wasn't Diaz on the line. It was Jocelyn Jones.

FIVE

I headed to the address Jones gave me. Her house sat on several acres in Wilmette, encircled by a black iron fence with a single initial "S" carved into the pattern every hundred feet. The kind of place I'd expect to see a guard asking for my credentials before he buzzed me through.

When I punched the button at the gate, her voice boomed through the intercom. "The security code is 79031. Park in front and I'll meet you at the door."

As I drove up the long, curved driveway, I marveled at the sheer size of the place. I mean, this three-story mansion with its red brick façade was large enough for several families. Or an entire fraternity. Or a few Kardashians. But Jocelyn had called this her childhood home when she phoned.

Thick ivy covered the south wall and two eight-foot marble columns flanked the walk. I parked in front of the garage, smoothed my hair, and reapplied my lip gloss before getting out of the car. Left of the entrance, a ceramic fountain with a carved lion's head spewed water into a crescent-shaped pool. If Jones hadn't been framed in the doorway, I might have searched my purse for a penny.

She extended her hand. "How lovely to see you again, Megan."

When she'd invited me to lunch, of course I'd said yes. But I hadn't come for the food or the company. No, I was here to convince her to use her influence to snag me an interview with a major downtown newspaper. Even if she didn't know anyone personally, a recommendation from her would still carry clout.

She moved inside, and I followed her into a two-story entryway. Even though the outside of the house was impressive, it didn't compare to the inside. A multi-tiered chandelier glistened above my head in the atrium. Rich cherry paneling and heavy crown moldings covered the walls, and a staircase spiraled to a second floor. The Persian rug on the parquet floor recalled those old kings in medieval paintings. Older, but still elegant. Like Jones herself.

It was obvious she came from money, though that hadn't been mentioned in her online biography. In fact, my peripheral research hadn't yielded much information on her personal life other than her parents were both deceased and she'd never married or had children. My reporter's mind had conjured intriguing backstories. Perhaps she'd chosen career over family. Or had a passionate love affair with a man who broke her heart. Or—

"Megan?" Jones's voice brought me back to the present. "This way."

She led me to a spacious formal living room with floor-to-ceiling windows, heavy damask drapes, and a gold brocade couch with matching wingback chairs. The massive marble fireplace in the center only needed a coat of arms above it to complete the picture. The wide-screen TV mounted there instead was jarring.

"I'm glad you could make it. My housekeeper is fixing us lunch, but why don't we have refreshments while we're waiting. Soda, iced tea?"

I stumbled through "Tea would be nice" and prayed I wouldn't spill any on the carpet.

"Make yourself at home. I'll be right back." When she left, I wandered the room, eventually drawn to a sketch on the far wall. It was a portrait of a young girl, blond hair cut in a bob, sitting ramrod straight with her hands clasped in her lap. She wore a pink dress with a fancy lace collar and cuffs and appeared prim, proper, and terribly well-behaved.

But there was a lot going on behind that stare. This was a girl who wouldn't tolerate being told what to do. This was a girl who'd go far in the world. This was a girl who had a lot to say, if only someone would give her a microphone.

Jones had materialized and stood only a few feet away. "Is this you?" I tilted my head toward the portrait.

"Yes." She set a silver serving tray on the coffee table in front of the sofa, then stood beside me and stared at the picture. "My mother was an artist, pastels mostly, some oils. I posed for that when I was eight years old. Frankly, I was amazed to find it still hanging here when I moved in. There are a lot of words I'd use to describe my father, but sentimental isn't one of them."

Her statement was followed by a long silence. One thing I'd learned on the beat was how to get strangers to open up. It was a matter of discovering what the two of you had in common. It could be trivial—*gosh, we both wear the same brand of boots*—or deeper—*my mother made me feel small, too*—but whatever it was, it formed a bond. And once I did that, I could probe deeper.

Jocelyn moved to the couch and motioned for me to join her.

"My mother was an artist as well," I said. "A photographer. I went on shoots with her when I was young. But she dropped that around the time I started school. I don't think she's picked up a camera in years."

I fingered the gold chain around my neck, a graduation gift from her.

"What does she do instead?"

Leads pro-life protests. I bit my tongue. My mother and I had different last names, so I doubted Jocelyn would make the connection. But what if she did? Jocelyn's politics skewed to the left like mine. Another thing we had in common. She might not give a rat's ass who my mother was, but since I'd come here to ask for a favor, why take the chance?

I folded my hands in my lap and paused, hoping my voice wouldn't betray me. "Oh, community activities, church, stuff like that." I shrugged. "We're not that close."

"And your father?"

"He lives in Dallas. My parents divorced after I graduated from high school." It was only later I made the connection—they'd only stayed together because of me.

Which left me feeling even more guilty for not telling my mother what I'd seen.

I wanted the focus off me. "Can I ask you a question?"

She smiled. "Of course."

"Well, this place. I mean, was your family so big you needed a ..."

"Castle?" Jocelyn threw back her head and laughed. "No, there were only the five of us. My father and mother, of course, and my two younger sisters. We had a maid and a cook who lived with us as well. But you're right, lots of room to rattle around in with nine bedrooms. We even had a small bowling alley in the basement at one time. Three lanes." She laughed again. "Can you imagine?"

"Why the huge house then?"

"My father's way of letting everyone know how successful he'd become. He pretended to be sophisticated, but he still had more than a touch of the village burgomaster in him. He took architecture classes, designed this house, and had it custom-built." She pointed. "He picked out that marble on the fireplace himself at a foundry in Italy."

I frowned. "I assumed someone else owned it before. The letter 'S' on the fence."

"Oh, that." She wagged her finger at me. "Excellent detective work on your part, uncovering my little secret. I was born Eleanor—as in Roosevelt—Schiller. My father was Harold Schiller, a well-known lawyer and philanthropist here in Chicago."

My reporter's antennae quivered. None of this had shown up in my research. If I ever wrote an article in the future about meeting Jones, this would be fascinating background information.

"But if you were born Eleanor Schiller, how . . ."

"Did I become Jocelyn Jones? Simple. I changed my name when I turned eighteen."

"Why?"

"My father and I had a falling out, and I refused to carry his name anymore. Plus, a lot of bigwigs in journalism at the time served in World War II. Since I'd already decided to become a reporter, I knew having a German surname wouldn't win me any friends."

"So you just changed it?"

"Actually, it's surprisingly easy. You file a petition with the court, pay a few hundred dollars, give them a valid reason, and voilà." She snapped her fingers. "You're Betty Sue Phillips or Andrew Zanzibar or Willow Martin."

"Or Jocelyn Jones," I said. Was it that simple? Try on different names as though they were dresses, then pick one out? Jocelyn had been one gutsy eighteen-year-old.

"Yes, exactly. I discovered early on if you want something badly enough, if you're willing to do whatever it takes, you can become anyone you want to be. A whole new identity. One you invented for yourself instead of the one your parents foisted on you at birth. You wouldn't believe how many people hate their own name but don't do anything about it. How about you? What would you pick out for yourself?"

I considered for a minute. "Hmm. I never thought about it."

"Valentina? It means brave." Jocelyn raised her voice as though addressing an audience. "Valentina Barnes," she announced, flinging her arms wide. "It's got a nice ring, don't you think? You could be Tina for short."

"I'll stick with plain old Megan for now." I wasn't sure why she was telling me all this, but since she didn't have a problem opening up, I probed again. The curse of an investigative reporter. We always dig deeper. "After you changed your name, then what?"

"I took up swimming and lost twenty pounds, hired an acting coach and got rid of my Chicago accent." She eased back against the throw pillows. "Created the person I wanted to be, and when I was ready, stepped into the role."

Jocelyn had reinvented herself from top to bottom. Becca would die when I told her what I'd learned.

"From the time I was quite young, I dreamed of being a writer. I'm guessing you were the same?" Jocelyn asked. When I nodded, she went on. "My father and I used to play games together, mostly strategy ones like chess and Go. There was this one where we quizzed each other on obscure words. He kept this massive volume of the Oxford English Dictionary on a table in his library, and I'd spend all week scouring it, searching for ways to stump him. That's when I fell in love with words and all the meanings behind them. Excellent training for a journalist."

"So when you were younger, the two of you *were* close?"

A look crossed Jocelyn's face before she spoke, a look I couldn't interpret. "Heavens, you must be bored to tears hearing my whole life story. Let's talk about you! Tell me, did your parents encourage your love of writing when you were growing up?"

"Yes. Until I decided on it as my career. Then my mother changed her mind." I sipped my tea. "She told me to major in something that offered more 'financial stability,' as she put it."

"That's an odd reaction. Reporters make a decent living."

I choked back a laugh. Jocelyn lived in a bubble. The average reporter made nowhere near enough to live on, particularly in cities like New York or San Francisco. Most of my colleagues depended on other sources of income or a working spouse or help from their parents. Money wasn't what drove us.

"I'm glad to see young people enter the profession, in spite of all the fake news accusations and vilifications of the press everywhere you look."

A lightness spread through my body. Jocelyn understood what drove me. She'd been on the front lines, chased down sources, burrowed until she found out the truth. "My mother thinks it's a phase I'm going through."

Jocelyn stood and wandered over to her portrait again. "It's funny, isn't it? The hold our parents have on us, no matter how much we rebel against it."

I didn't say anything, hoping she'd say more. Minutes ticked by. When I realized she hadn't moved, I asked, "Are you all right?"

She startled. "What? Oh, yes, my apologies. Got lost in the past there for a minute."

Her housekeeper entered to tell us lunch was ready, and

we moved to the dining room, which was flooded with light from an east window. Dappled patterns played over the white linen tablecloth. A giant sideboard stood on one side, overflowing with a collection of exquisite glass paperweights.

Afraid I might inadvertently mention my mother, I steered away from local politics during the meal. But we still found plenty to discuss, from the deadlock in Washington to school violence, and, of course, the #MeToo movement. Even though forty years separated us, our opinions dovetailed on every important issue.

"At the rally, I noticed Dr. Stein introduced you as an old friend. How do the two of you know each other?"

"Ah, Rhoda. Yes, we go way back. We met when we were both at Columbia together in the late sixties. God, that was a lifetime ago."

Jocelyn launched into a story of how the two of them had spent a night in jail after being arrested at a Vietnam protest march. "We linked arms and sang 'We Shall Overcome' at the top of our lungs, and then we got the other women in the cells to join in—caused quite a ruckus." Then she brought the conversation back to the present, asking my opinion on the Cambridge Analytica scandal which had been all over the news.

After we finished dessert—a to-die-for strawberry tart—Jocelyn folded her napkin, placed it on the table, and cleared her throat. "I have to say today has been marvelous. It's been a long time since I've met such an eager reporter with so much to say. You know, I see a lot of myself in you, Megan. It's almost like looking in a mirror"—she paused, squinting her eyes—"only your hair isn't gray, and you're much, much younger." She grinned. "And to think we owe a noxious skinhead for bringing us together. Now, what can I do to show my gratitude for saving me from that scumbag?"

It was a long shot, but if I didn't take it, I'd regret it. My mouth was so parched, my tongue felt like sandpaper. "Any chance you have contacts at the *Chicago Tribune* or the *Chicago Sun-Times*? I'd love a referral."

Jocelyn placed her fork and knife slowly and methodically across her plate, and I knew I'd blown it.

"I'll be frank. I was thinking more along the lines of a gift certificate from Nordstrom."

I tucked my balled fists out of sight. In my imagination, she would say, "*Of course, where's a piece of paper?*" or better yet, "*Let me make a call.*" Well, no regrets. I'd taken a chance and asked for what I wanted, even though she'd turned me down.

"Sorry. I didn't mean to be flippant. I like you, Megan. Bright. Ambitious." She cocked her head. "But you can't expect I'd ask my contacts to give you a job at a major newspaper. I just met you."

She was right. Why risk her reputation for me? All my wild fantasies of riding the coattails of this famous journalist to a top job vanished, and I dropped back to earth with a thud. I'd met Jocelyn Jones and shared a nice lunch with her. End of story.

I sipped my water. "I'm sorry I put you on the spot. I'm anxious to get back to work and it's making me a little crazy."

Jocelyn shifted in her chair. "No need to apologize. That type of initiative is exactly what you'll need if you want a successful career in our business." She stayed quiet for a few moments, then leaned toward me as though sharing a secret. "Listen, I've got an idea. I've finished a memoir which releases next year, and I've signed with a PR agency here in town, Arrow Communications. They assigned a staff guy, Zachary something or other, as my point person. The trouble is, I can't stand him." She flicked her wrist as though swatting away a fly. "Why don't I tell the head of the company I want *you* as my liaison? I'd rather work with a bright young woman like yourself than some pimply-faced kid who vetoes every suggestion I make."

"I'm a reporter, not a marketing assistant," I blurted out, then realized how ungrateful that sounded.

Jocelyn flinched as though she hadn't expected that honest an answer. But frankly, the job description didn't match either my background or my skill set. In fact, I'd rejected a similar suggestion from my mother only a few days before. The collar of my blouse chafed against my skin.

"Okay, what if I sweeten the offer? Take the job, and we'll work together for six months. That'll be enough time for me to gauge your work ethic, your talents, and see how you function on a team. If you do well, I'll introduce you to an editor at the *Tribune* who owes me a favor. I guarantee he'll find you a spot if I ask him." Her eyes shone as she leaned back in her chair.

Okay, she'd gotten my attention with that last carrot, but still, her offer made no sense. I frowned. From what little I knew, public relations was all hype and spin and catchphrases. Truth was a commodity you either ignored or embraced, depending on the impression you wanted to create. I was a journalist. I lived and died by the truth. Could I stomach working in PR, even for a few months?

A reassuring smile lit up Jocelyn's face as she waited for my answer. She obviously expected me to jump at the chance to work with her.

"I'm waiting to hear back on a reporting position at a local newspaper," I replied.

A storm cloud distorted Jocelyn's features, and her lips drew together in a thin line. Her manicured nails drummed against the tabletop. Like a lot of wealthy baby boomers, she was used to getting her way. Still, she didn't argue, but kept her voice steady as though it was all the same to her whether I accepted her offer or not. "Well, consider my proposal as a backup if that job doesn't come through. Remember, it's a short-term commitment."

"Why would you even consider me for the job? I don't have any experience—"

She put her hand up. "You think when I first parachuted into a war zone, I felt qualified? I did not. I felt terrified and inadequate, a complete imposter. None of that mattered. I completed the assignment. I stayed on and I learned and I succeeded. Nobody gets anywhere in life doing what they already know how to do. We grow by challenging ourselves, trying out new ideas, taking risks."

When I didn't say anything, she went on. "I'm disappointed in you, Megan. Where's that fearless girl from the rally? You're smart. You could easily figure out this PR job. It's nothing more than contacting sources and writing articles. That's what you do, isn't it?" Her eyes fairly gleamed.

I sat a little straighter. She'd cooked up this idea a minute ago, but now that she'd embraced it, she was pulling out all the stops to get me to change my mind. "You're quite the spinmeister."

"I make quick decisions, that's all. I know right away when I can get along with someone and when I can't, and I need a different liaison at Arrow. I seriously hope you reconsider."

Work side by side with an icon in my field and then slide into a position with a top newspaper in town after my time was up? Why was I even hesitating?

"It's a generous offer, and I'm sure I could learn a lot from you." But a little voice inside me kept whispering, *Take your time, don't leap yet.* "I'll definitely think it over."

Sure enough, before I'd even gotten clear of the driveway, I'd come up with a dozen reasons why this was a bad idea, the main one being my gut instinct told me *The Morning Register* job was mine. But when five days elapsed and I hadn't heard from Diaz, I finally broke down and called their offices.

They'd hired someone else.

SIX

I stewed for two straight days. Why had Diaz passed me over? He'd said my recent history wasn't a dealbreaker, but somewhere along the way, he'd changed his mind. Of course, there could have been other candidates as qualified. But what if there was another reason, something I didn't realize? I needed to know so I wouldn't repeat the same mistake at my next interview.

I drove to the *Register's* offices midday, hoping I'd catch Diaz on his lunch break. I timed it right because as I entered the parking lot, he was exiting the building. But before I could catch up to him, he got in his car and pulled away. I didn't think of it as stalking so much as chasing down a source as I followed him to a barbeque joint two miles away.

The minute I stepped inside, the smell of seared meat gagged me. I swallowed twice, then headed to the back where Diaz sat alone at a booth, checking his cell. He did a double take when he saw me but invited me to sit.

I didn't waste any time. "Why didn't I get the job?"

A waitress appeared out of nowhere. She plunked two glasses of water in front of us, handed us menus encased in plastic, and swiped the scarred oak tabletop with a wet cloth. "Special today is smoked chicken. I'll be back for your order in a sec. Sorry we're so swamped."

"Not a problem." Diaz turned his phone facedown but didn't answer me.

When she was out of earshot, I tried again. "You pretty much told me I was your first choice. What changed your mind?"

He shook his head, chuckling. "You've got balls on you, kid. I'll give you that."

"My colleagues back in the Bronx called me Bull Dog Barnes. Once I get my teeth into a story, I don't give up. Look, I'm sorry for the unorthodox approach, but I need you to level with me."

"I told you there were other candidates. You were a strong runner-up, but I only had the one opening."

"And something tipped the scales against me. Tell me what it was."

He tented his fingers and rested his chin on them. "I did take into consideration your poor judgment at your last position."

"You told me in the interview you admired my honesty."

"I did. I do. Okay, that wasn't the deciding factor. We cover the northern suburbs—the arts, sports, politics—and when I researched further and found out. . . ." He gazed off to his right.

"What? I didn't hide anything from you."

He turned back and made eye contact, a hardness to his features. "Yes, you did. Your mother's Helen Watkins. You didn't mention that."

I reared back. "You researched my parents? Isn't that a bit much?"

"I admit I dug deeper than usual because of what happened at your last job. I had to be sure you'd told me the whole story."

"Okay, yes, my mother is Helen Watkins. What's that got to do with anything?"

"Don't play dumb. Your mother is running in a hotly contested election in our district. We bend over backwards to cover each candidate fairly and equally, but if a watchdog group got wind of the fact Helen Watkins' daughter was on our staff, they'd monitor our every move, which would be a serious pain in the ass. I interviewed another woman with newspaper experience and no baggage. So I offered the position to her."

I collapsed against the red leather booth. I saw his point, even though his reasoning was one of my nightmares coming true. Mother's run for office had cost me the only news job I'd turned up. Now what?

"Kid, I can tell from your portfolio you're a good reporter. But for the time being, you'll have to work outside greater Chicago or figure out another way to support yourself until after the election because no paper around here will hire you."

"I have zero connection to my mother's campaign."

"And that alone sends a message. Her opponent has four strapping sons and a pretty spouse, and they stand beside him at every rally. Once the public gets wind you're around but not supporting her, *that* will turn into a story."

"So even though I'm opposed to everything she stands for, I'm shut out simply because we're related."

"Look at it this way. The election's around the corner. Come back and see me when the race is over, and we'll talk."

"Until then, I'm a reporter no one will hire," I whispered, more to myself than to him.

"I'm afraid so. Unless you turn up a scoop which has nothing to do with politics and submit it as a freelancer. In that case, my door's open."

I needed a regular paycheck, not a vague possibility to work on spec. I called Jones as soon as I got back to the car and accepted her offer.

———◆———

A gas-guzzling, pseudo-military Hummer was parked in my mother's driveway when I got there. Whoever drove it either needed a hell of a lot of protection or they were compensating for something. When I entered the living room, I recognized the unknown man who'd been in that photograph with my mother, sitting close to her on the couch. Was she dating this person? She could do better, but at least she was putting herself out there after being single so long.

"Gavin, this is my daughter. Megan, my campaign manager, Gavin Copeland." He hauled himself up and lumbered over. His rumpled suit stretched across a bulging middle, his gray hair was thinning, and his eyes were watery and bloodshot. He still looked as though he had gas.

"Ah, yes. The liberal daughter. I hear you don't intend to support your mother. What's up with that?" Can you dislike someone at first sight? He was treating me like the enemy before I'd even opened my mouth. His handshake was like a vise, and I winced. "You do realize your absence will seriously hurt her in the polls, don't you?"

"It's nice to meet you, Mr. Copeland."

Mother stepped in as referee. "Gavin, I need a few minutes alone with my daughter. I think we've covered everything, haven't we?"

He checked his watch. "We're due at the Muldoon's at five."

"You go on. I'll meet you there." Her voice was polite but firm.

"But—"

"I should freshen up anyway." My mother strode past him to the front door and held it open. After a few seconds, Gavin picked up his briefcase.

"Okay, but don't be late. A few of the guests tonight are big donors who—"

"I'm aware." She lightly touched his arm. "Don't worry. I'll be on my best behavior. They'll be writing checks before the second round of drinks."

He hesitated as though prepared to argue, but then

backed down. The way he looked at her made me wonder if there was more between them than a professional connection, at least on his part. "Whatever you say." He didn't quite slam the door when he left, but close.

Once he'd gone, the no-nonsense candidate morphed into my doting mother again. "Have time for a glass of wine?" Her demeanor had changed as easily as if she'd shucked off a coat. An excellent talent for a politician.

She left but was back in minutes with two glasses and an open bottle of pinot grigio. "Still your favorite?"

"Thanks." I took a sip. "Okay, I have to ask. Why did you hire that horrible man?"

"Gavin? He's not so bad. In fact, he came highly recommended by the RNC. The last three candidates he worked for won by several percentage points. He's very knowledgeable."

"He may know politics, but he could use a serious personality transplant. I mean, he treated me like a wad of gum stuck to the bottom of his shoe." Although I understood why. I wasn't supporting my mother publicly, that rankled him, and he didn't care if I knew it. "So are you tired of shaking hands and kissing babies yet?"

She shook her head. "Obviously, there's more to it than that. But I will say, if I could change one thing, I'd cancel all the speeches and meet with people one on one. That's what I enjoy the most. Listening to what's important to the voters I'd be representing."

"You already know what's important to them. Making money."

"And here I thought you reporters prided yourself on your objectivity." She took a sip of wine, then went on. "My backers care about fairness, loyalty, tradition, and the sanctity of life. All principles our country was founded on."

"But it isn't 1776 anymore. Our country's facing problems Washington and Jefferson never anticipated. From where I sit, your party wants to take us back, not move us forward."

"Some values are worth preserving."

"Not if it means shredding basic human rights, poisoning the air we breathe, and widening the gap between the haves and the have-nots so no one can get a fair shake."

She held up her hand. "Can we give it a rest? I spend all day long listening to people arguing over this stuff. I don't need to hear it from my own daughter. Let's change the subject."

Maybe she was right. Why bother rehashing our positions? I sipped my wine, waited a minute, then shared my news. "I found a job."

"Congratulations. What paper are you working for?"

None, thanks to you and this crazy run for office. "I'll be working at a PR firm for a few months."

"What? When you first got back, I offered you a job working for my campaign and you turned me down flat, said you needed a job in your field. Now you're working in public relations? How is that any different?"

"Well, for one thing, I'll be working for . . . Go ahead, take a wild guess," I said, imagining how impressed she'd be.

"I have no idea."

Should I rap the table three times for effect? "Jocelyn Jones! You know, she's that famous journalist who—"

"Will you please stop acting like I live in a cave? I know who Jocelyn Jones is. What I don't understand is how you met her and why in the world you're working for her."

If I told her the real story, including what happened at the rally, she'd make a big deal of the fact I lied to her. So I lied again.

"A journalism professor of mine from Northwestern introduced us. Turns out Jones has written a book, and she's hired a marketing firm called Arrow here in town to help publicize it. I'll be the liaison between the two of them. We finalized the contract over lunch at her house. You should see it. It's out of *Masterpiece Theatre*."

"Back up a minute. Why exactly aren't you looking for a job at a newspaper?"

I deflected. "This thing with Jocelyn is temporary. A few months tops. She's a well-connected journalist. She knows everybody worth knowing in the industry, and she's pretty much promised to get me a job at the *Chicago Tribune* once I'm done with the assignment."

"So now she's Jocelyn? Does she know you're only using her for her contacts?"

"You make it sound as though I tricked her into hiring me. She's the one who pressured me to take the job."

"Well, if you're both clear on the arrangement, I guess there's no harm in it. But it does sound like you're putting your career on hold for this woman." She sat back and searched my face. "So, what's this famous person really like? As a human being, I mean."

Cultured, smart, charming. She's traveled all over the world and reported on major world events. But why paint myself as a gushing groupie? "So far, she seems nice. I've only met with her twice."

"Can your interfering mom give you a piece of advice without you overreacting?"

Great. First, her political ambitions sabotage my job prospects. Now she wants to trash the job I've accepted by cutting down Jocelyn. "What?"

"Watch your back."

I bristled. "What does that mean?"

"Celebrities sometimes step over ordinary folks who get in their way. I don't want that to be you."

"So do some politicians. Besides, Jocelyn's not like that."

"I thought you just met her? Listen, it's easy to get starstruck when you're around larger-than-life people. I know. I've met the President a few times, shaken hands with the governor. It can be heady."

My left foot bounced against the coffee table and I switched positions, folding it beneath me. How could she equate Jocelyn Jones, who stood for integrity and journalistic excellence, with politicians who twisted facts to further their own agendas and then accused reporters of printing fake news?

"All I'm saying is watch your step, honey. My guess is this woman isn't perfect. Don't be disappointed when you realize that."

My hand trembled as I reached for my wine. "She may have her faults, but she and I agree on fundamental issues." I didn't say *Like a woman's right to choose,* but I knew we were both thinking it.

I took a good long look at my mother and was caught short by how far apart we'd grown. I had no idea who she was anymore. When I was younger, she'd been a funny, carefree photographer, but then for no apparent reason, she'd morphed into a helicopter parent. Now, in this latest incarnation, she'd become an assertive, determined politician. Which was the true woman and which was the mask?

It had been a long day. I longed to slip into my sweats, curl up in my room with my e-reader, and get lost in someone else's life for a while. Expecting my mother's support was like arriving at the airport hoping to catch a train.

"You know what? I've found a job working for an important journalist who I can learn from. She'll pave the way for me to get a job at a top newspaper, and in the meantime, I'll make enough to support myself without your help. All in all, I'd call today a win."

I stood and headed to my room, but paused at the foot of the stairs. "Just this once, try being proud of me, okay?"

SEVEN

Monday morning when I headed out for my interview at Arrow, I found a Post-it note stuck on the inside of the front door. *May rain today. Might need an umbrella. There's a spare one in the closet.* I wadded up the piece of paper and threw it in the trash.

I caught the Purple Line express in Evanston and squeezed between an older man bent over his book and a young mother shushing her very talkative child. Clutching the overhead strap, I planted my feet eight inches apart for balance as the train jangled and lurched until we reached Armitage station. I clattered down the metal stairs and squeezed onto a city bus, which deposited me in front of the building.

Arrow Communications was housed in a former industrial warehouse, now subdivided into shared workspaces. The ground floor featured white brick walls and cobblestone flooring. I scanned the directory and found Arrow occupied the entire fifth floor. The other tenants ranged from tech start-ups to firms in the advertising or design fields. Dozens of people my age filled the lobby, tapping their phones, sipping cappuccinos, and chatting one-on-one.

I had a meeting today with Simon Young, Arrow's president, and I wanted to make a good impression. Even though Jocelyn had pretty much ordered him to hire me, he still insisted on talking with me before signing off, and I can't say I blamed him. What if I was a total flake?

This job might be temporary, but I still intended to listen and learn and contribute wherever I could, if for no other reason than to impress Jocelyn and earn the referral she'd promised. Plus, I'd never taken on an assignment and not given it my best. Scrounging the bottom of my purse, I found an old Tic Tac covered in lint and popped it in my mouth to mask any lingering odor from the onion bagel I'd wolfed down for breakfast.

I wedged myself onto the packed elevator and punched five. When the doors pinged open, a guy in a purple hoodie pushed past me from behind, buds in his ears, and I half stumbled into the reception area. The space sported bleached oak floors, a high ceiling with exposed ducts and pipes, and dropped halogen lights. Massive wall panels with blowups of book covers from big-time authors floated throughout the lobby. No doubt Jocelyn's banner would soon join them. I hummed to the piped-in music, bopping my head to the beat, until I saw a couple of guys in one corner smirking.

The atmosphere pulsed with energy, from the *zip-zip* of printers to the ringing of cell phones to the back-and-forth chatter of staff as they hustled by. After working for years in cluttered, dirty newsrooms, I'd landed in Xanadu.

Reporters aren't known for being fashion plates. We toss on clothes we can wear a few times before throwing them in the wash, which means a mix of grays, browns, and blacks. But I'd done my homework. Arrow's vibe was trendy West Coast, so I'd purchased a red plaid shirt, khaki capris, and zebra-striped ballet flats for my interview, and, sure enough, I fit right in.

I approached a white marble reception desk shaped like the prow of a ship where an attractive brunette with deep brown eyes greeted me. "I hope you're having a wonderful day. I'm Indigo. How can I help?"

"I'm here for an interview. My name's Megan Barnes."

"Oh, yes. Mr. Young's been expecting you. I'll call through." The girl spoke into her headset, then handed me a clipboard. "You'll need to sign this agreement. Don't worry. It's a formality. We can't have anyone stealing the recipe for our secret sauce, can we?"

I flipped through the pages. It seemed pretty boilerplate. Even if it wasn't, why raise a stink over a standard confidentiality document? I scribbled my signature at the bottom.

Within minutes, a dignified man in his late fifties with close-cropped white hair and rimless eyeglasses approached. "Simon Young." His handshake was firm, his voice strong. "Walk with me."

I fell into step beside him as he strode down the corridor, greeting workers who passed with a wave, a friendly word, or in one case, a pat on the back. I glanced at him from the corner of my eye. He was around six feet tall and built like a fellow runner, with a Fitbit on his wrist which matched mine. His face was a blank screen. Try as I might, I couldn't get a bead on his reaction to my being here.

After we'd covered what seemed like the length of a football field, he opened a door and we entered a beehive space filled with cubicles. "Here's your desk. Our IT guy will come by this morning and set you up with a password and email." He turned away.

"Excuse me." He faced back around. "I'm sorry," I said, "but don't you want to interview me?"

"That'd be a waste of both our time, wouldn't it? Jocelyn's an important client. She wants you as her liaison, so here you are. You get a half hour for lunch."

The signs weren't hard to read. He was upset and didn't care if I knew it. First Gavin, now this guy. My people skills must be slipping. I hated starting out on the wrong foot, so I offered an olive branch. "Mr. Young, I know my getting a job this way is unorthodox, but trust me, I'm a trained writer, I've got a strong work ethic, and you can depend on me."

He scrutinized my face. "Good to know. You're on Jocelyn's account team, which includes our senior marketing guy Frank and Tamara from the art department. And me."

"Zachary's not staying on?"

"No, but he'll bring you up to speed. Right, Zachary?"

A head popped over the partition separating our two desks, and I came face-to-face with a guy my own age with acne and pale gray eyes. A cowlick sent his hair shooting straight up on one side, reminding me of a lopsided rooster.

"So you're my replacement," Zachary said.

Simon frowned. "Let's all get back to work."

"You want me to start right now?" I said.

He pulled me aside and whispered, "No vacation time yet, princess. Walk back to reception and Indigo will direct you to HR."

"I'm sorry, but no one's even told me how much I'll be paid."

"Terrell in personnel will go over your salary package. If you're dissatisfied, take it up with Jocelyn. Now get busy doing your job. Or in your case, *learning* your job." He turned his smile on full beam. "And don't think for one minute you're home free, Ms. Barnes. If I sense you're not pulling your weight, Jocelyn or no Jocelyn, I'll terminate you." He headed down the hall in the opposite direction.

Before I'd even stored my purse in a drawer, Zachary piped up. "I don't know where you came from, but thank God you're taking Jones off my hands."

"What does that mean?"

"She shot down every suggestion I made." He shrugged. "But who knows? She may be happier with a female assistant."

"I'm nobody's assistant."

"Whatever. She's a piece of work. Have fun."

I met his stare. Where did this guy get off? "Jocelyn Jones is a well-respected, highly renowned journalist."

"All I'm saying is there's something off with her story.

Why'd she move back to Chicago? I mean, she hasn't lived here in fifty years."

"None of my business. Or yours." Guys like Zachary hated taking directions from an intelligent, forceful woman. Whatever his problem was with Jocelyn, I wanted no part of it. I retraced my steps down the long hallway and once again approached reception.

"Which way to the HR department?"

"So you and Simon got along well. I thought you might." Indigo stood and pointed. "That way, second door on your left. Welcome to Arrow. We're so glad you're here."

———— • ————

Borrowing my mother's car every day wasn't a sustainable plan, and I dreaded riding the train or the bus to work once winter hit, so I plunked down half of what I still had from savings, took the rest out in a car loan, and bought a used Ford Fiesta. It had a hundred and twenty thousand miles on it, rust had eaten away most of the underside, and the air-conditioning had a mind of its own, but it would do for now.

The next week, I spent time soaking up information, and it didn't take long before I realized how little I knew about what went into a comprehensive marketing campaign. What in the world was a bookstagrammer? What was a sell sheet and what should I include on one? How could I edit the massive author bio I'd written for Jocelyn down to a mere three hundred words?

Zachary was no help. He gave me his notes the first day, but after that, he pretty much ignored me. Instead I leaned on Tamara, who tolerated my inane questions and referred me to websites that helped. But segueing from hard-hitting journalism to the soft, conversational tone of publicity releases wasn't going to be easy. Could I fake it long enough to get up to speed before Simon and, more importantly, Jocelyn caught on I was in way over my head?

On Thursday, I'd scheduled a one-on-one with Frank to review the broad publicity approach for the memoir, and I'd stayed up late working on it. Midmorning, I caught myself nodding, so I popped down to the lobby for a shot of caffeine. The line snaked back and forth, and I tapped my foot, worried this might take longer than my allotted five-minute break.

"Great shoes." The voice came from behind me.

I swung around to find a guy staring at my flats. He straightened up, and I noticed his hair—it was the first thing I noticed about anybody. His was dark as coal, floppy, and curling around his ears. He towered a good seven inches over me, with that I-can't-be-bothered-to-shave-every-day look that never failed to turn me on.

"I missed what you said." I hadn't, but I wanted to hear him say it again.

His eyes—gas-flame blue with flecks of gray—caught me up short as his mouth curved into an impish grin. "I said, 'Great shoes.' Your outfit's standard fare, but those funky shoes? They tell a different story." His low-pitched voice had the deep, rich tones of a cello.

God, did I still remember how to flirt? "And what story might that be?" I countered in what I hoped was a sexy tone.

"That there's more going on behind that pretty face than meets the eye."

After the beating my ego had taken from Luke, I lapped this guy's words up like a kitten with a bowl of cream. I racked my brain, searching for a witty response.

"What can I get you, miss?" the barista shouted at me.

I studied the menu hanging behind the counter as people milled around me, impatient to place their orders. "I'll have..."

Shoe guy had rattled me. My signature drink, the one I'd ordered a hundred times before, had flown right out of my head.

"Yes, miss?" The clerk's hand hovered at the rim of the cup, pen poised.

Stop acting like a silly schoolgirl. A stranger gave you a compliment. Get over yourself. I took a deep, cleansing breath and exhaled. As I did, the words tumbled out. "Iced vente quad breve no-whip white chocolate latte, please. And the name's Megan. Without the H."

I moved to one side, then snuck a peek back at Shoe Guy. Another man had ducked in line beside him and the two of them were chatting, so I shuffled to the end of the pickup line. When they called out *"Megan no H,"* I grabbed my drink, crossed to the elevator, and punched the up button.

Right before the doors closed, I looked back.

Shoe Guy stared straight at me, a goofy grin on his face.

EIGHT

Jocelyn had asked me to stop by for a few hours the next afternoon. When I arrived, she pointed at a sealed box on a table in the foyer.

"That's a final galley of the book. Kate and I will do one last pass, but it's pretty much set. Check with Simon, but I think the plan is for you to plow through the pages as soon as possible and write a summary for the team."

We reviewed several new branding ideas, and two hours sped by. Finally, Jocelyn stood and stretched. "Enough work for today. Sitting this long makes my back stiff. Why don't we take a walk in the garden?"

I followed her through a screened-in porch which ran the length of the house and onto a flagstone patio. It didn't surprise me when the backyard was every bit as grand as the rest of the estate. On one side, six padded casual chairs covered in a wild jungle print surrounded a massive firepit; on the other, a large brick grill stood near a pebbled-glass table with seating for eight. A gray-haired man in faded jeans was bent over a flower bed and tipped his hat as we strolled by.

"That's Hank. He's phenomenal. I'm convinced this place would revert to wilderness in one season without him," Jocelyn said.

The spacious garden buzzed with activity. Hummingbirds flitted from blossom to blossom, tiny wings a blur. Bees swarmed the thistle plants. A squirrel scurried up the huge maple in the center of the yard, did an aerial leap, and chattered away at us from an upper branch. The afternoon was hot, even for mid-August, and sweat trickled down and soaked my bra.

Jocelyn had such a long stride, I had to struggle to keep up. A meandering path took us through beds of hostas as lush as any botanical garden. We paused at a bird feeder, and Jocelyn grabbed a fistful of sunflower seeds from the pocket of her slacks and poured them into the tray.

I couldn't stop watching her. It wasn't only how she walked but the way she held her head, the square of her shoulders, her graceful hand gestures. She was a flesh-and-blood example of what a woman could be, what *I* could be if I wanted success badly enough and was willing to work my tail off to get it.

We made our way around the entire garden, and eventually settled on the screened-in porch. Jocelyn lowered herself onto the love seat, and I took the white wicker rocker.

"Let's get to know each other better, Megan. Tell me about your friends, your hobbies. Where do you see yourself in ten years?"

What would Jocelyn find interesting about me? But since she'd asked, I started with my friendship with Becca, described a few of our outlandish escapades in college. Jocelyn leaned forward as though eager to know more. Inevitably, she inquired about why I'd moved back from New York, and I told her the truth—that I hadn't vetted my last article and lost my job over it. And then, even though I hadn't told anyone else except Becca, I shared the details of what happened with Luke.

"I left the newspaper office, devastated I'd lost my job, and took the subway home. It was the middle of the day, so obviously I didn't expect Luke would be there. But I sensed something the minute I came inside—a sound, a scent, I'm not sure." I shook my head. "Anyway, I found my boyfriend of eight months in bed with the painter who lived next door."

Jocelyn reached over and squeezed my hand. "The bastard."

"The woman got dressed and left in a flash, and he blabbed some excuse, I don't even remember what. Obviously, I wasn't thinking straight. I ran away from the whole mess, called my mother, and booked a flight to Chicago that same day."

"I know how this story goes. He asked for forgiveness. Begged you to come back. Wanted a second chance."

"He's sent messages and left voice mails, but I've never returned any of them."

"And why should you? You don't need toxic people in your life. At least you found out now rather than after you'd been together for years." She surveyed the garden, arms tight against her chest. "Someone I loved deceived me once too. It was ages before I trusted anyone again. Now, if someone betrays me, I cut them out of my life and never look back."

She fluffed up the throw pillows and leaned back. "Enough about men. Tell me about your childhood. Your high school years. No, let me guess. Straight-A student, teacher's pet, honor roll. Am I right?"

My cheeks felt warm. "Boring, huh?"

"Not at all. It's what society drills into us. Study hard, get good grades, and life will work out for you. It's a lie, of course. A lot of people do everything right and still don't get a fair shake. Hopefully, that's changing."

Her housekeeper came onto the porch and set down a pitcher of lemonade and two glasses. Jocelyn poured one for herself and handed me the other.

"Okay now, Miss Perfect. Ever rebel? Do something you weren't supposed to? Something even this best friend of yours doesn't know?" Her eyes fairly twinkled.

She'd caught whiff of a good story, like good journalists do. And she was right. I *had* done something. It wasn't all that bad, a little thing, but it was the one time I'd stepped off the straight and narrow and had a run-in with the authorities. It didn't paint me in the best light, but I'd moved past the point where I wanted Jocelyn to *like* me. No, I wanted her to *know* me. And telling her this secret would forge a bond between us.

"I shoplifted when I was a teenager, the summer between sophomore and junior year. Makeup, a necklace, a couple of CDs."

"Ah. And how did that make you feel?"

It was so long ago, but the memory was still fresh. "The first time, it was at Target. A tube of lipstick. They had a whole mess of them sitting out in a basket, as though the store was purposely trying to tempt me. I made a big show of pulling one out, then another, holding them next to my face in the mirror. I kept watch, made sure no one could see me. My heart beat so fast, I thought I'd pass out. When I put them back, I palmed one and stuck it in my purse."

I rubbed the back of my neck and stayed quiet, but then decided to go on. "After that first time, it got easier. In fact, it got so I craved the rush. I knew I ought to feel guilty, but I didn't. What I felt was I was cool and clever, smarter than everyone else because I could get away with taking what I wanted without getting caught."

"But you *did* get caught, I take it?"

"Yes. Magenta nail polish. I still remember the name—*Fearless*. My mother raised holy hell and stormed full throttle into the mall's security office, insisting they'd made a mistake. Did they have a witness? Video footage? She spun an alternative version of the facts—I'd always intended to pay for the polish, I'd put it in my pocket because my hands were full. She was a mother tiger defending her cub. After ten minutes of her diatribe, they let me go with a warning."

On the car ride home, my mother had said how much I'd let her down. That had been the real punishment. And it worked. That, and the stern warning from the store manager. I never stole again.

Jocelyn winked at me. "Don't worry, I promise not to tell. Actually, I'm glad you shared that with me. I'm suspicious of people who seem too perfect. I always think they're hiding the worst secrets, just doing it very, very well."

I risked a question. "Did *you* ever get away with something you shouldn't have?"

Jocelyn's cell rang. She glanced at the caller's name and took the call. "Hi, Kate. What do you need?" She listened for a few seconds, then held the phone away from her ear. "Sorry, Megan. Some issues have come up with the cover art. This may take a while. I'll touch base with you later."

I showed myself out and was halfway home before I realized Jocelyn hadn't answered my last question.

NINE

The next Tuesday when I left for lunch, I bumped into Simon. "Megan, I'm glad I spotted you. Jocelyn's throwing a last-minute cocktail party this Friday night. Seems her publisher's in town, and they're hosting the glitterati of Chicago. I left you a note with the details."

"Who else will be there?"

"The team on her account here at Arrow, of course. And she's inviting tons of media people. It'll be a great networking opportunity. See if you can interest an editor in a front-page feature on the memoir."

That's not all I'd be doing. Jocelyn's contact at the *Tribune* could very well be there. Time for some networking of my own.

———— • ————

The next day, Jocelyn and I had planned an afternoon meeting at the mansion, but at ten that morning, she emailed me at work.

Change of plans. Meeting with my publisher today.
Let's do dinner instead. Brindille's on Clark, seven o'clock.

That was a problem. Mom was at a fundraiser until late tonight, so I'd invited Becca over for pizza after her shift ended. I called and explained the last-minute change of plans and asked when we could reschedule.

"I've been trying to get together with you for a week now, and you're always busy."

My stomach twisted. "I know. I'm sorry. Look, I'll make it up to you. Dinner Thursday night. We'll go to that new place over on Main Street. My treat. Come on. I know you love Italian."

"Thursday's too late. It needs to be tonight. Please, Megan. It's important." A bead of worry lodged behind my right eye. Becca was upset with me, but I sensed another emotion underneath.

"I've got a few minutes now."

"I can't go into it on the phone."

Something was definitely wrong. "Okay. Why don't I call you as soon as I finish with Jocelyn? No later than eight thirty, I promise."

"I'll come by the house at nine. Hopefully, our friendship is important enough you'll be there."

"If I can't make it by then, I'll ..." I began, but Becca had already hung up.

I spent the rest of the day running through what-ifs. Had Becca lost her job? Had she split with Sam? Or worse, what if she was ill, had caught a staph infection from a patient? I couldn't concentrate. The whole way to the restaurant, all I could think of was getting in and out as quickly as possible.

"May I help you?" the hostess asked.

"I'm meeting a client for dinner. The reservation's for seven o'clock under Jones."

"Are you Megan?"

When I said I was, she continued. "Ms. Jones left a message for you. Her meeting is running long. She'll catch up with you tomorrow."

I gritted my teeth. Jocelyn was so cavalier. Why hadn't she texted me earlier? I'd driven all the way home, changed into nicer clothes, headed back downtown, and overpaid for valet parking for no reason. I pasted on a smile. "That's too bad. I've read glowing reviews of your restaurant. Maybe next time."

I considered calling Becca, but decided that would be an even bigger diss. *I got stood up, so now I've got time for you.* No, I'd wait until nine as we planned. I ducked into a nearby bar and wolfed down a Caesar salad and a glass of white wine. When I got to Mom's house at eight thirty, Becca was already squatting on the stoop, her head buried in her lap.

"Finally," she said when I approached, her voice hoarse. When I saw her face, it was obvious she'd been crying. I let her in, flipped on the lights in the living room, and we curled up together on the couch.

Before I could say anything, she blurted, "I ran a test today at the hospital, and it confirmed what I pretty much already knew." The catch in her throat reinforced my worst fear. A test. What was it, breast cancer? A virus?

She fingered the sleeve of her shirt and shot me a nervous look. "I'm pregnant."

Thank God. She wasn't seriously ill. But wait, what? "That can't be right. You've been on the pill as long as I have. Even if you forgot one time and Sam didn't use protection—"

Her voice was low and steady. "One woman in a hundred who's on the pill still gets pregnant. I won the lottery, only in reverse."

I put my arm around her shoulders and squeezed. "Okay, the timing sucks. But hey, you've always wanted a big family, and with Sam's parents nearby and your brothers and sisters, you've got support. And I promise I'll babysit whenever you need me. Trust me, everything will work out."

She didn't answer but picked at her cuticles.

"Is there more?" Another long wait as my head throbbed. "Bec, what is it?"

"Promise you'll be quiet and listen?" When I nodded, she went on. "This spring, I got worried. I mean, what if Sam and I got married? He'd be the only guy I ever slept with. I mean, in my whole life. Don't you think that would be weird?"

She'd picked the wrong person to ask. I'd had sex with four—no, five—guys, none of whom I cared to see again, including that scumbag Luke. I was no expert on relationships. "Not necessarily. It sounds kinda sweet."

She ignored me. "I kept thinking, what if I missed out? I mean, what if someone else could turn me on more? Or, I don't know, do things differently? You know, in bed." She hesitated, looking down at her hands. "Maybe better?"

I weighed my words. "It's less about sexy moves and more about having an emotional connection, isn't it?" I sounded like my mother, but it was actually how I felt.

"I know that now, but . . . let me get this out before you launch into a lecture, okay?" She scratched at her neck. "Sam was pushing me to get engaged, but I wasn't ready. I mean, we'd just moved in together. I felt trapped. I told him I needed time to myself before I could make that kind of commitment, and we had a big fight. He accused me of not loving him, and I said he was being controlling. Long story short, he stormed out in a huff and went to stay with another guy on the force."

"When was all this?"

"A month before you moved back. I didn't tell you about it because I was still working things out in my head." She fidgeted. "Anyway, a friend from work offered to loan me her family's cabin in upstate Wisconsin, and I took ten days off. Remember, I told you about going? I downloaded a half-dozen books, strapped my bike on top of the car, and drove up."

Becca glanced away, then back at me. "I'd only been there a day when I met a guy at a country-western bar, of all places." She shrugged, as though whatever happened had been no big deal. "He was a dead ringer for Chadwick Boseman. You know, magnetic smile, great body. Anyway, he bought me a drink, and one thing led to another."

My heart rate soared. Becca cheated on Sam after all these years together? I tried to sound supportive. "You had a one-night stand. It happens."

She dipped her eyes. "Make that a five-night stand. This Jimmy guy and I did things I'd never done with Sam. Things I'd only read about in *Cosmo*." Her voice was so low I had to struggle to hear her. "It was pretty damn amazing."

"And then?"

"One day, I hiked into these thick woods behind the cabin, and I tripped over a loose branch. I came down hard on my right hand and it hurt like shit. And there I was, spitting dirt, pulling twigs out of my hair, my wrist throbbing, and I started bawling. Because I missed Sam. I missed how he tosses his head back when he laughs. I missed the funny way his ears wiggle when he gets upset. I missed the way he buries his face in my neck when we're sleeping."

Luke rubbed my feet when we watched TV and gave me daisies every Sunday.

Becca's voice brought me back. "I knew if Sam was there, he'd carry me to the cabin, bandage my wrist, and rush me to a hospital for X-rays. He'd take care of me like he always has. And I'd betrayed him with this hot sex machine who didn't care one hoot about me. And vice versa."

"And?"

"I wrapped my wrist, packed my suitcase with my one good hand, and drove to a walk-in clinic one town over. I didn't even leave Jimmy a note. Luckily, I hadn't broken anything. It was only a bad sprain. When I got back, I stayed inside the rest of my vacation, had food delivered, and thought long and hard about my life and what I wanted."

"And you decided you wanted Sam. And asked him

to move back in." I cleared my throat. "And now you've convinced yourself the baby is Jimmy's. Are you sure?"

"I can count. I got pregnant when Sam and I were apart."

I didn't argue. Becca was a nurse. "I can't believe you've been going through all this and I've been oblivious. I'm a shitty friend."

"You had your own stuff to worry about. But now I need your help."

"Whatever you need, you know that. What are you thinking?"

"I can't raise a baby with Sam and pretend it's his. I won't do that to him. So I called around and found a clinic in Rockford that had a last-minute cancellation for this Saturday, and I grabbed it. Sam never needs to know."

As an ER nurse, Becca routinely made split-second decisions. But had she thought this one through? "I had a friend in New York who was at the same stage you're at. They give you a pill when you're at the clinic and another for later once you're home. It can be a rough time. Sam would catch on. And if you disappear for days, he'll be suspicious."

"That's where you come in."

I paced the room. "Shouldn't you take more time? Is there a chance this baby is Sam's?"

Becca shook her head. "It's not."

"What if this Jimmy comes looking for you?"

"He doesn't even know my last name. Please, Megan. I get that you don't agree with what I did, but that's beside the point now."

She was so calm when I was a jangle of nerves. "This is a lot to take in. I could use a glass of wine. Do you want some apple juice?"

The corners of her mouth tilted up. "I'm not going through with the pregnancy. I'll have a glass of wine too."

I fled to the kitchen, hands tingling, and processed what Becca said. After a minute, I took a deep breath, came back into the living room with two glasses, and sat beside her.

"Okay. Tell me what you need me to do."

She ticked the points off on her fingers. "First, Rockford's an hour away, so there's zero chance of running into someone from the hospital or one of Sam's friends. Second, I'll tell Sam you and I are treating ourselves to a spa weekend in Lake Geneva. He's working a lot of nights this month, so I barely see him anyway, and he's always after me to pamper myself."

"What if he notices there's no charge for the hotel on your credit card?"

"I thought of that. After it's done, we *do* drive to the resort and don't come back until early Monday morning. By then I'll be past the worst of it, and I'll work my regular shift as though nothing happened." Trust Becca to have it all planned, down to the smallest detail. She locked eyes with me. "Will you do it? There's no one else I trust."

Becca had nursed me through mono our sophomore year, held my hair back whenever I got roaring drunk, and introduced me to the editor of the campus newspaper, which led to my first reporting gig. Even if I didn't agree with what she'd done, she was my best friend.

"Of course I will."

"Thank you." She hugged me so tight I could barely breathe.

That's when I heard the sound of the garage door opening. "I didn't expect her back this early."

Becca wiped under her eyes. "Do I look okay?"

Her face was puffy, but otherwise, no one would suspect anything was wrong. "You're fine," I whispered a second before my mother entered the room.

"Becca. Megan told me you were coming over, but I didn't realize you'd still be here."

We both bounced up. "Nice to see you again, Mrs. Watkins. How's the election going?"

"You'll have to ask my campaign manager. I just go where he tells me and give speeches."

An awkward silence followed. Finally Becca hoisted her bag over her shoulder. "Well, I've got an early day tomorrow. I need to get home."

I followed her to the door. We both knew Mom could hear every word we said.

"So we're set for the weekend?" she asked, her tone light and casual.

I gave her a long hug and whispered in her ear, "Don't worry. We'll get through this." Out loud, I chimed in with, "I'm looking forward to it."

After Becca left, I gathered the wine glasses and carried them into the kitchen.

Mom hovered in the doorway. "What's all this about the weekend?"

I loaded the glasses in the dishwasher. "No biggie. Becca got a gift certificate for a spa. She invited me along."

"A girls' getaway. I could use one of those once the election's over. Should be fun."

The farthest thing from fun. I retreated upstairs, praying all the details in Becca's plan would click together and Sam would never find out about Jimmy.

Or the pregnancy.

TEN

Jocelyn's party didn't start until six, but I arrived early that afternoon so she and I could review the media kit going out the following week. Once the caterers appeared, I retrieved the garment bag from my car, and Jocelyn showed me to a spare bedroom and bath on the second floor. I reapplied my makeup, changed into my simple black dress and patent leather heels, and had just smoothed down my hair when I heard a knock on the door. Before I could answer, Jocelyn burst in, still in her robe.

"You look lovely." She formed her hands into a square as though capturing me inside a picture frame. "A perfect choice. Understated but classic. But there's one thing missing." She pulled out a maroon velvet box from her pocket and placed it in my hands.

"What's this?"

She smiled. "Open it and see."

Inside was an intricately carved black and silver pendant hung on a thin chain. When I examined it more closely,

I saw the pattern formed the ancient symbols of yin and yang. A single diamond chip was set in the center of each curved segment.

Jocelyn beamed. "Try it on."

"I couldn't. I mean it's stunning, but..."

"Nonsense. Your simple outfit will set it off perfectly. Here, let me."

She stood behind me. "We should take off this gold chain. It clashes." She undid the necklace my mother gave me and slipped hers around my neck in its place.

"I'll wear it tonight, but—"

"No, it's yours to keep. I picked it out especially for you. It represents a lesson it took me years to learn. Life has two equal but opposing sides—light and dark, feminine and masculine, negative and positive. If you embrace one and ignore the other, you become unbalanced. Instead, you must train yourself to examine a situation from all angles and realize your way may not be the only path to the truth."

"Jocelyn, this is too much. I can't accept it."

"Nonsense. Can't friends give each other gifts? Please don't hurt my feelings by refusing." She moved to the door. "See you at the party."

I gazed at myself in the mirror. As I lifted the pendant, it caught the light and shone through my fingers like a star. It wasn't my imagination.

Jocelyn Jones thought I was special.

The workers had cleared the living room, setting up a long buffet table at one end and an open bar at the other. Three young women stood at attention in starched black-and-white uniforms like a trio of penguins, balancing trays of crème fraîche tartlets, caramelized figs, and lobster avocado toasts.

An hour later, the room teemed with people—agents, editors, reporters, owners of small presses, and authors, many of whom I recognized from my research at Arrow. New arrivals were greeted with shrieks of recognition, hearty handshakes, and air kisses. Frank chatted with another Arrow client in the far corner, and Simon stood in the drinks line with an editor from Random House. Strangely, Zachary and Indigo were also there, laughing together like besties, clinking champagne glasses and gobbling up shrimp. Kate Spaulding, Jocelyn's editor, moved between groups, schmoozing, radiating poise and a casual elegance. Eventually, she found her way over to me.

"You must be Megan, Jocelyn's new protégé."

I fingered the necklace. "I'm part of the PR team handling her account."

Kate narrowed her eyes. "She sees something in you. She told me as much."

"I'm grateful for the chance she's given me."

"Spoken like a true diplomat. But there's no need to be coy. I've known Jocelyn a long time. She enjoys mentoring young women like you, launching them into the world. She always says other people helped her get ahead; it's her way of repaying the debt. You can learn a lot from her. But fair warning: don't get on her bad side."

Kate made it sound as though Jocelyn saw my potential and would use her clout to make me a success. Which was fine with me. Now that I'd won her over, all I needed was to keep her happy. As for Kate's warning, I discounted it. Jocelyn and I got along fine.

One of the wait staff stuck an array of stuffed mushrooms in front of us, and instead of taking one, Kate moved on. I scarfed two of the hors d'oeuvres and balanced a third on my napkin, so hungry I could have eaten the entire tray.

A male voice bellowed from a few yards away. "Abner Lynch, you old devil. What are you doing here in Chicago?" Two middle-aged men in navy blue suits clapped each other on the back like long-lost fraternity brothers.

"The DNC's recruited me. I'm taking over Underhill's campaign."

My ears pricked up. Edward Underhill was my mother's political opponent. I studied the carpet and pretended to stifle a yawn, but little by little, I edged closer until I'd positioned myself right behind the two men. Lynch's face reminded me of a toad, given his creepy habit of flicking his tongue in and out as he talked. Still, there was a keen intelligence behind his dark sunken eyes.

"The polls don't look too good. That Watkins dame's gonna be tough to beat. Intelligent, personable, morally beyond reproach. I'm not sure a middle-of-the-road white progressive like your guy stands a chance. All the pundits say this is the Year of the Woman."

Lynch snorted and waved the comment aside. "I was one of those pundits until last month, remember? Trust me, the talking heads don't know squat. All they do is regurgitate sound bites and think up catchphrases. After twenty years in this business, the only absolute I know is when voters get inside that booth, they do whatever they damn well please. And any pundit who says different isn't worth shit." He took a sip of what resembled bourbon. "The party brought me in because I don't play by the rules. Not like that pansy Underhill put in charge before."

I hadn't paid much attention to the election other than seeing my mother's face plastered on billboards throughout the county, so I wasn't sure how this man coming on board would affect her. But I'd definitely make a point to tell her what I'd overheard.

Lynch's eyes stayed in constant motion, scanning the room, and when they landed on me, his nostrils flared. Goosebumps traveled up my arms. Was there a chance he'd recognized me? I edged my way to the buffet table out of his line of sight and grabbed two more mushrooms.

I'd begun to mingle when Jocelyn materialized on the second-floor landing, and the room quieted. She paused, then glided down the stairs like a queen at her coronation dressed in a fire-engine red jersey dress with a cinched waist and a cowl neck adorned with a brooch shaped like a panther. She's styled her hair in loose waves, and diamonds sparkled in her ears—full-on party mode. And why not? This was an important night for her. The publication of this memoir signaled the final chapter of a long and illustrious career.

She approached a group of guests, greeting each in turn, oozing charm. Where did she learn to do that? I got along fine at parties if I focused on one person at a time, but being the center of attention in a crowd like this? I'd rather put my hand in a bear trap. No, I'd stick with my trusty fly-on-the-wall technique: blend in, watch, listen. Over the years, I'd heard snippets of conversations at gatherings like this that led me to stories no one else had gotten wind of yet.

My gaze drifted back to Jocelyn. She'd launched into an anecdote, gesturing as she spoke. Half a dozen people stood hypnotized in a circle around her. Her hands flew into the air, and the pitch of her voice rose. It must have been the punch line because most of the people in the group grinned or laughed. One man even clapped his hands together and shouted, "*Bravo!*"

But an older gentleman, his posture signaling ex-military, scowled. Jocelyn took hold of his arm, separated him from the herd, and steered him into a corner. She spoke a few words, then tilted her head as though listening intently to his responses. Her eyes never left his face as her lips curved into a half smile. It wasn't long before the two of them were laughing together like old friends.

It was a unique gift, one Jocelyn knew how to use to her full advantage. She could make anyone feel as though all she wanted to do was listen to whatever they had to tell her. I'd noticed it in our private meetings, particularly the afternoon we'd strolled through the garden. Luke had a talent for making me feel that way, too. And I'd fallen for it.

Still hungry, I inhaled an asparagus spear. I gazed around the room and caught Kate out of the corner of my

eye. She'd answered her cell phone and turned away from
the crowd, covering up her other ear to cut out the noise.
She nodded a couple of times, said something to the caller,
and when she hung up, made a beeline for Jocelyn. They
whispered back and forth for a few seconds, and Jocelyn's
eyes narrowed. Her wine glass shook, and she placed
it down on a nearby tray. Then the two of them left the
party and headed in the direction of the library. I raced
after them but stopped halfway down the hall. If this was a
family emergency, I should back off. But then Jocelyn didn't
have any family, did she?

That's when I spotted Jocelyn behind her desk, her head
in her hands, massaging her temples. Kate came out of the
library, closed the door behind her, and approached me.
"Have you seen Simon?"

"He was over by the fireplace a minute ago."

"Please find him. Tell him Jocelyn needs to speak with
him."

What had happened? Who was on the phone? When
I hesitated, Kate spoke again, this time more forcefully.
"Megan? Now, please."

I retraced my steps and scanned the crowd. No one else
had reacted to Jocelyn's abrupt departure. The drinks still
flowed. The appetizers still circulated. In fact, the chatter
had swelled to a loud crescendo as people's tongues loosened
from the booze. Simon and Frank stood in one corner and,
not wanting to arouse anyone's attention, I sauntered over
to them as though I had nothing more on my mind than a
little cocktail banter.

I took hold of Simon's arm, my voice a harsh whisper. "Kate sent me. Something's wrong. Jocelyn needs to see you in the library. It's out the door on the left."

His brows furrowed, and he excused himself. A long five minutes ticked by before he reappeared and pulled Frank and me into a huddle. "I'm calling an emergency meeting for tomorrow at noon. We've got ourselves a situation."

I lowered my voice. "What's going on?"

"A Twitter post that Jocelyn thinks is directed at her. Look, we can't talk here. We'll go over everything tomorrow."

I shook my head. "I can't be there. I've got plans for the weekend."

Simon's jaw clenched. "I don't think you understood me, Megan. Our high-profile client, the woman who pretty much ordered me to hire you, is in the middle of a crisis which could damage her reputation. Everyone on our team needs to show up, including you." The look he gave me was clear. *Cancel your plans.*

Becca had taken off work, and Sam had bought the story of our spa weekend. The clinic might not have another opening for weeks. It would send the wrong message, but no way would I let Becca down. "It's personal. When I'm in on Monday, I can . . ." But Simon wasn't listening. He'd turned his back on me and gone over to Zachary.

"Word to the wise," Frank whispered. "Simon doesn't like being told no."

ELEVEN

By seven thirty Saturday morning, we were on the road to Rockford. Today was all about Becca, but a part of me couldn't help worrying about Jocelyn as well. What had the tweet said that was so upsetting? By the time I got to work on Monday, the entire team would be three steps ahead of me and I'd be *persona non grata*, not only with Simon but with Jocelyn as well. Had I blown it?

Becca pulled a tissue from her purse and dabbed at the corner of her eye.

I patted her knee. "Doing okay?"

"You mean other than feeling like a complete shit for lying to him?"

"It won't do any good to beat yourself up." Though I agreed with her. Sam deserved better. It was another ten miles before she spoke again.

"Are you still planning on three kids? What was it, two boys and a girl?" she asked.

I'd forgotten that long-ago conversation. "Sure, I guess. Someday."

Becca let out a long sigh. "I've always wanted an armload of babies."

"You've got plenty of time."

"And anyway, what do I know about raising kids, right? I'd probably mess it up big-time."

"Now you're being silly. Remember when we volunteered as camp counselors and you helped Carol what's-her-name get over her fear of water? And that sixth grader you tutored all sophomore year? Trust me. Any baby would be lucky to have you as their mother."

She leaned her head on her hand and rested it against the window. "I know it's the right decision."

"Only a little while longer. You can do this." I waited, but Becca didn't say anything else. Eventually, we reached the turnoff, exited the freeway, and followed the GPS to the outskirts of town.

The clinic occupied one corner of a small strip center. Dozens of protesters paraded out front, waving hand-lettered posters with angry slogans—*Unborn Lives Matter, Abortion Stops a Beating Heart, Life Trumps Death*. Others had formed a line, their arms linked, so they effectively blocked the entrance. I tried to steer the car around them, but they held their ground, so we gave up, parked in a nearby garage, and walked back.

"You're not doing anything wrong," I said. "Ignore them." I sounded braver than I felt. Becca's palms were sweaty and shaking. I draped my arm over her shoulder, and she leaned against me as we made our way. She didn't make eye contact but focused her eyes on the sidewalk.

The minute we stepped onto the lot, four women surrounded us and shouted, screaming that we were murderers. Several others stood back from the crowd, their heads bowed seemingly in prayer. We sidestepped around them and kept walking.

Within seconds, a white-haired woman with a wrinkled but kind face approached me. "What you're doing is wrong, sweetheart. Even if you have to give up your baby, he deserves the chance to live." She thrust a pamphlet into my hand.

I almost said it wasn't me, I was only here helping a friend, but that was irrelevant. The woman had no business spewing her moral judgment. Becca was a grown woman, free to make her own decisions. I caught her eye and made sure she saw me drop the pamphlet in a nearby trash bin. Once again, I took hold of Becca's elbow, and the two of us weaved first one way, then another as we headed across the parking lot.

That's when I saw her: Nancy Peabody, an old friend of my mother. The two of them sang together in the church choir, served on the same PTA board, and raised money every year for cancer research. Nancy stood on the curb behind a line of cars, surrounded by a crowd of protesters whose signs showed gruesome pictures. There were throngs of people between us, and as far as I could tell, Nancy hadn't seen me. She lived in Evanston. What was she doing all the way up here?

Even if she glanced this way, I hadn't seen the woman

in years, so I doubted she'd recognize me. But what if she did? What if she called my mother tonight and said she'd spotted me entering an abortion clinic? Mother would assume I was pregnant and hadn't told her. Or worse, her political opponent would learn of it. That guy at the party wouldn't hesitate to blast that tidbit across the internet.

I lowered my head, covered my face with my bag, and picked up the pace, and finally we reached the buffer zone near the entrance where an escort greeted us. The crowd chanted and screamed and gave a final rallying cry of *"Don't kill your baby!"* as we escaped through the opaque glass doors.

After the pandemonium outside, the clinic felt as still as a dense forest after a snowfall. Three women sat in the waiting room, each staring blankly at the magazine resting in their lap. I eased myself into a molded plastic chair beside Becca, who wrapped her arms across her body and shrank away from me. Light from an upper window threw black bars of shadow across her face. The giant clock on the opposite wall read ten thirteen.

A heavyset woman with tortoiseshell glasses approached us. "Becca Whitaker?" she whispered. When Becca nodded, the woman handed her a clipboard with a form to complete and an information pamphlet. "You'll need to initial each page at the bottom confirming you're aware of the risks. Once you're done, bring it back up to me. We're running behind schedule, but it shouldn't be much longer." She turned to me. "Are you her ride home?"

"Yes. And I'm staying with her for the next two days."

"Good." The woman inclined her head toward the front. "I hope they didn't upset you." She returned to the front desk.

Becca still hadn't said a word. She crossed and uncrossed her legs and tore her used Kleenex into tiny pieces.

"Bec? One step at a time, remember?"

She rolled the pen back and forth between her fingers. Slowly, she made it through the disclaimers and initials, walked up to reception, and placed seven one-hundred-dollar bills, one by one, on the counter.

<hr>

We settled into our hotel suite, ordered salads from room service, and sat on the couch waiting for the food. "How are you feeling?" I asked.

"I'm okay." Her voice wavered a little—obviously, she wasn't. "There's some cramping, but it's tolerable. The doctor told me not to take the second pill until after five tonight. A few hours after that is when it might get bad." She rubbed her nose with her sleeve. "I think I'll take a nap. I didn't sleep much last night." Her voice was weak and halting, and I didn't want to push her. She needed time to be alone.

"Why don't I give you some privacy? I've got my cell with me if you need anything."

She crawled under the covers, and I pulled the curtains shut to darken the room. Then, laptop under one arm and Jocelyn's galley under the other, I retreated to the lobby, found a corner away from the traffic, and switched focus. The team meeting had begun an hour ago. What was happening? The image from last night resurfaced: Jocelyn slumped at her desk, rubbing her temples, so different from the vivacious woman she'd been only minutes before.

I opened the memoir, but my mind wandered and I found myself searching Twitter for any mention of Jocelyn. Finally, I turned up a post from nine fifteen that morning.

C'mon, nitwits. It's definitely Jocelyn Jones. What has she been up to?

I scrolled down and eventually found the original tweet from the night before, the one Jocelyn must have seen.

What media personality violated their code of ethics and got away with it? Justice won't be denied. Tell the truth, JJ.

The handle was @freethetruth.

I dug deeper. The tweet had whipped through the internet with the force of a tsunami. People began posting wild guesses as to the identity of the mysterious JJ. Jesse Jackson. January Jones. Janet Jackson. Jimmy Jones. Okay, some of them could loosely be called "media personalities," but Jocelyn was right to worry, since she was the obvious choice. But what kind of ethics violation? My mind flipped back and forth. Paying a source? Fabricating a story? Plagiarism? A sexual incident? All possible. All bad.

I brought up @freethetruth's profile, but there was only the single post. I hated to add one more count to the ticker, but I needed to read the next tweet the minute it hit.

My finger hovered over the keyboard. Finally, I hit follow, then the alarm icon to alert me to future tweets.

And waited.

———————●———————

I stayed downstairs until five, alternating between reading Jocelyn's galley and scanning Twitter. Eventually, my back stiff from sitting in one position, I came upstairs. Becca said she'd already taken the second pill a few minutes before. We ordered dinner from room service and played a round of gin rummy. After that, we sat on the couch, Becca's head in my lap, and watched hour after hour of *Law & Order* reruns.

"This reminds me of Saturday nights at our place on Colfax," I said. "Remember that fireplace with its fake logs? And those matching ratty afghans with the brown and orange zigzags? We must have watched *The Notebook* a good fifteen times that year."

"*You are, and always have been, my dream,*" Becca parroted. "God, who could resist? I still drag Sam to every Ryan Gosling movie out there. Even *La La Land.*"

"And poor Mr. Whiskers. You never did let him nap, always tickling his belly and kissing his nose."

"You forgot about the wine. All it takes is one swallow of Yellow Tail Shiraz and I'm right back there."

I stroked her hair. "You were brave today."

She reached for my hand. "I couldn't have done it without you."

Life might have taken us in different directions these last few years, but we still had each other. Always would.

———————•◦•———————

I woke at midnight and saw Becca wasn't in her bed. I heard sobbing, followed by the flush of a toilet. I waited a few minutes, but when I didn't hear anything else, I got out of bed and stood outside the bathroom.

"You okay in there?" When she didn't answer, I eased open the door and saw her stripped down to her underwear, sitting on the edge of the white porcelain bathtub, her head in her hands. A pad with streaks of blood was in the trash can beside the sink, and her pajama pants, which lay in a heap on the floor, were spotted as well. For a brief moment, a sensation of déjà vu engulfed me, as though I'd experienced this same scene before. The feeling was ephemeral, almost like a dream, and within seconds, it vanished.

"Come on, let's get you in bed." I took hold of her hand and helped her stand.

"I want . . . the shower. I need to wash."

"Okay." I eased back the curtain and turned on the water. Once it heated up, I helped her step in and went to get her fresh clothes.

When I returned, she'd already shut off the water and toweled herself dry. She didn't speak, but let out a long, shuddering sigh, wrung out her wet hair, and slipped into the set of pajamas I handed her. We crawled back into our separate beds, and I flipped off the lights.

Minutes ticked by. Becca had faced the opposite wall, but even so, I heard her crying. Not loudly, but I was attuned to the slightest sound from her corner.

"How about a hug?" I asked.

She rolled over, and in the light from the moon shining through the curtains, I saw tears pooled under her lids. "I'd like that."

I crawled in beside her. Her hair was still damp from the shower, and I rubbed her back until she fell asleep. As I too drifted off, I flashed back on that brief moment in the bathroom, the strange sensation of reliving an experience I'd had before. It must have been a scene from a movie I'd forgotten. It's funny how the mind works sometimes.

TWELVE

Becca and I drove back from the resort Monday morning. I pulled up to the front entrance of the hospital and double-parked so she could make it to her shift on time.

But she didn't get out. Instead, she stared down at her hands, folded in her lap. "I don't want to lie to Sam, but I know I have to."

It was an opening. "Do you? I mean, he'd be hurt and upset, but this is the man you love, Bec. The two of you could get past this."

She looked straight at me. "You don't know him like I do. This would break his heart, and nothing would ever be the same between us." She took a deep breath, then nodded as though coming to a final decision. "No, I have to put this whole incident out of my mind and go on as though nothing's happened." She grabbed her purse from the back seat, leaned over, and gave me a long hug. "Thank you for going with me. Truly."

"I'll call you later. And think about what I said. Sam loves you. Trust that."

If only she could see this secret could seriously damage her relationship. Becca was my friend and I'd never betray her, but I also felt Sam deserved to know what had happened. I hated to think of him being blindsided if he ever found out. I knew what that felt like. It hurt like hell.

———— • ————

I hadn't even typed in my password when Zachary poked his head over the partition. He didn't bother with hello.

"Simon's not happy. He had me attend the meeting on Saturday in your place. Want my advice? Never saw off the branch you're sitting on."

When would he stop treating me like an itch he couldn't scratch? I'd had enough. I spit out my words. "You've had it in for me since day one. What is your problem?" Rhianna, sitting in the cubicle across from us, glanced up, then refocused on her computer screen. But I knew she was listening in.

Zachary shot back. "My problem? You're the one with the problem. You waltz in here without so much as an interview, no PR background, and suddenly you're the point person on our top client's campaign. And then you turn around and skip a crucial meeting because you have—what was it again?—oh, yes. *Other plans.*"

Hey, buddy, you don't know anything about me. I punched a fucking skinhead to get this job, okay? Not to mention I've been blacklisted from working as a reporter for now. And as for my other plans, I helped my best friend through a crisis instead of dropping everything and attending a last-minute confab. A choice I'd make again in a heartbeat.

But I didn't say any of that. It was obvious Zachary saw me as a flaky dilettante who'd taken this job as a lark. I got it. I was white, educated, and came from a well-to-do family. And he was right on one score. In today's world, that *did* give me a leg up. But he was wrong if he thought I took my privilege, or this job, for granted.

I lowered my voice. "Why are you so upset? You hated working with Jocelyn."

"In case you haven't noticed, there are other people on the payroll. Simon could have assigned one of them."

I hadn't considered that. "Okay, fair enough. But I'm the one here now. Can't we call a truce?"

His answer was a half-hearted shrug.

"Tell me what happened at the meeting."

"Jocelyn was furious you weren't there."

"Okay, I'll deal with her. Does she know what the tweet refers to?"

His voice was calmer as he launched into information mode. "She says no. But I overheard her and Kate talking afterwards, something to do with hate mail she got last spring and whether this might be related."

My journalist's antennae perked up. "What exactly did you hear?"

"Kate mentioned the Ku Klux Klan, and Jocelyn agreed

there might be a connection. But that's bizarre. Why would the Klan target her?"

It might not make sense to Zachary, but it did to me because I'd done my research. Jocelyn's last news special at the network before she retired had focused on white supremacist groups. She'd profiled wives trapped and intimidated by their Klan husbands. This @freethetruth could be linked to that far-right group, which actually would tie in with the protestors at the rally. Had someone from that exposé discovered an event in Jocelyn's past to threaten her with?

It was Journalism 101. Follow every lead, no matter how small.

"Anyway, Simon says sit tight, there's nothing we can do at the moment. If I were you, I'd call Jocelyn. Before she boots you out, too, like she did to me." And with that, he disappeared behind his cubicle wall.

He seemed more upset over Jocelyn replacing him than he'd let on. Well, I couldn't worry about that now. From what Zachary had shared, the plan was to wait, which meant we'd given all the power to the troll for now. That was so not the right move, but I wasn't the person in charge. I dug out the galley from my backpack and flipped to the back section. Simon had asked me to present a synopsis of Jocelyn's memoir at the next team meeting, and I needed to get busy on that.

But the pages blurred together. If I believed there was a better solution to this problem, then as Jocelyn's liaison at Arrow, I should speak up. Which meant a face-to-face with Simon.

I marched into his office and found him talking on the phone. The receiver rested between his chin and his shoulder as he used his free hand to jot notes on a yellow pad. He motioned me in. "That's great. Call and tell me what he says."

He hung up, but before I could say anything, he jumped in. "We missed you at the meeting."

"I told you I wouldn't be there." I slid into the chair opposite him and braced myself.

"I hoped you'd change your mind. What can I do for you, Megan?" His face and voice remained calm.

I scooted forward in my chair and clasped my hands together. "Zachary told me what happened Saturday, and here's my thought. What if I spent this week at Jocelyn's house instead of here in the office? I could dig deeper, see if I can get a sense of what the troll's referring to. She and I have a rapport. She might share ideas with me she didn't want everyone else at the meeting to hear."

"You think so?" he replied in an oh-so-reasonable tone.

"At the party, Kate told me Jocelyn views me as her protégé. I know she's upset I didn't show up Saturday, but I think—"

"You're full of ideas this morning, aren't you?"

"Well, I had time these last two days to examine what—"

"I didn't mean it as a compliment." Simon's face morphed into Uranus, Greek god of lightning, set to hurl a crackling bolt straight at my head.

"You don't want me to spend time with Jocelyn?"

He scowled. "I want you to complete the assignment I gave you. Flesh out the schedule for the PR campaign, write an outline, summarize the memoir, and present all that to the team next week as planned. Can you do that, Megan? Or should I reassign the task to Zachary?"

Blood rushed to my ears. *Do not go ballistic.* Obviously, he was livid I'd missed the meeting. Maybe I'd feel the same way in his place. "I'll concentrate on the presentation then."

"Good." He picked up the phone again, but stopped when I didn't move. "Was there something else?"

This wasn't the ideal time, but I didn't have much choice. "I wanted to let you know I won't be in the office on Wednesday. Jocelyn asked me last week to join her at a conference downtown. She's giving the keynote, and there are people there she wants me to meet."

"Then I can't very well say no, can I? But if I were you, I'd make sure she hasn't changed her mind, given your little disappearing act over the weekend."

———•———

I swung by Starbucks after work and then headed to the hospital. I glimpsed Becca through the plate-glass doors as she wheeled a woman strapped to a stretcher back to the triage area. She was the model of efficiency and calm. No one would ever guess what she'd gone through two days before.

I approached the nurses' station. "Hey there."

She startled, obviously surprised to see me again so soon, and a grin spread across her face. "Hey yourself. What are you doing here?"

"Reinforcements to get you through your last couple of hours." I handed her an iced white chocolate mocha.

"You're a lifesaver."

"I'm not your best friend for nothing."

Becca grabbed a coworker. "Ling, can you cover for me? I'm going outside for a few minutes."

We sat on a cement ledge near the ER entrance. "The coffee was an excuse. I wanted to see how you were doing."

Becca lowered her eyes. "Surprisingly okay. It's been busy today, which helped." She put her hand on my arm. "So does having someone who worries about me."

We swung our legs back and forth and sipped our drinks. "Have you seen Sam yet?" I asked.

"No. I went home at lunchtime, but he wasn't there."

"I still think you should—"

"Mind if we change the subject?" She tucked one leg underneath her body. "What's the latest on Jocelyn and the tweet?"

Over the weekend, I'd filled her in, although I left out the part about missing the emergency meeting. Now I told her of the exchange between Kate and Jocelyn that Zachary had overheard.

"Is it too far-fetched to think the KKK might be involved?" I asked.

She thought for a minute. "I suppose anything's possible. I mean, the woman's been a major newscaster for years. She's bound to have rubbed a lot of people the wrong way. But if this *is* someone carrying a grudge, won't that be a long list?"

"It's not fair for her reputation to be trashed like this in the media."

"Since when does the internet play fair? All that counts is the next scandal, the next rumor, the next big thing. But this person hasn't posted anything since Friday night. Maybe it's a one-off."

But she didn't think so, and neither did I. No, the troll would be back. The only question was when they'd post again.

And what they'd say.

My phone chirped. I glanced at the caller ID and raised my index finger. "It's my mother. Give me a minute."

Before I got a word out, her voice blasted in my ear. "We need to talk right now. Come by campaign headquarters in an hour."

"What's going on?"

"I'll explain when I see you." She hung up.

I'd seen her briefly Saturday morning when I'd headed out for the weekend, and everything had been fine between us. What had happened since then? I wracked my brain for what could be wrong and came up with nothing. But regardless, this wasn't a request. More like an order.

"You look as though someone hit you between the eyes with a two-by-four. What did she say?"

"She pretty much commanded me to meet her."

"What's going on?"

"I have no idea. But whatever it is, she is seriously pissed."

———— • ————

I turned into the shopping mall off Evanston's main drag. The storefront was small, tucked between a Payless shoe store and a Thai food restaurant. Posters of my mother's smiling face against a background of red, white, and blue stars and her *Vote for a Change* slogan covered one long wall. On the adjacent wall hung a gigantic American flag along with a bulletin board showing a map of the district with a flood of Post-it notes attached. Folding tables and metal chairs lined the far end of the room, arranged in a horseshoe pattern, and five worker bees of various ages, each equipped with a headset, a laptop, and a phone, were dialing one voter after another.

A middle-aged woman dressed in an ill-fitting beige pantsuit rushed up as soon as I entered. "Welcome. Can I give you some literature on the candidate?"

"I'm her daughter. She asked me to stop by."

She did a double take. "Of course you are. Gosh, Megan. I didn't recognize you. The last time I saw you must have been high school graduation. I'm Sybil Jenkins. My daughter Rebecca was in your class."

Like I could forget Becky with her frizzy red hair and coke-bottle glasses, clutching the spelling bee trophy she'd snatched from my hands in fifth grade. I did a quick reconnaissance of the room. "Is my mother here?"

"Her office is around the corner at the end of the hall. I hear you're—"

"Sorry, Mrs. Jenkins, but I'm pressed for time." I headed down the corridor and knocked.

Gavin swung the door open. "Well, this is unexpected. Nice to see you again." His words said one thing, his clenched fists and aggressive stance another. Was he the one behind this 180-degree pivot in my mother's attitude?

She rounded her desk and laid her hand on his shoulder. "We'll catch up tomorrow."

He left, but not without a parting grunt. As soon as he was out of earshot, she glared at me as though she wanted to spit in my face. "Are you purposely trying to lose this election for me?"

My mouth turned to sawdust. "I told you up front I wouldn't campaign for you."

There were dark smudges under her eyes. She paced back and forth, her right hand trembling. "That's not what I'm talking about, and you know it." She spun around, the set of her jaw telegraphing anger. "Is this the real reason you came back here?"

What the hell? I took three steps back. "I'm lost. What are we arguing about?"

"Did you think nobody would find out? I'm in the public eye now. Everything I do is scrutinized, including my daughter's behavior."

"It's obvious you're angry over something I've done, but I don't have a clue what. Does this have to do with my working with Jocelyn?" Maybe Gavin had given Mom flak over my affiliation with a liberal journalist.

"You can work for whoever you want."

Okay, enough with the guessing. "Then what's wrong?"

"You told me you were on the pill."

The puzzle pieces—the worried set of her mouth, her strident tone, the wan skin—snapped into place. Mom's friend *had* seen me at the clinic and shared her juicy innuendo the minute she got back.

When I didn't respond right away, she jabbed again. "Nancy Peabody saw you."

Two choices: betray Becca's confidence—not going there—or pretend I'd gotten an abortion, which was way too big a lie for me to stomach.

I bought myself some time. "Saw me where?"

"At Planned Parenthood on Saturday. Obviously, the only reason you'd be there was—"

"Hold on." My mind shifted into overdrive, and then it came to me. "Becca and I were in Lake Geneva all weekend at a spa. I told you about it." I rummaged in my purse and produced the credit card receipt for my Sunday afternoon massage. "I couldn't be in two places at once, right? Nancy must have spotted someone who resembled me. I mean, it's been years since she saw me."

Mother's gaze didn't leave my face. "She said you had blond hair. How would she know that?"

That added an extra wrinkle. But I stuck to my original story. "No idea, but obviously, she made a mistake. You've got yourself all worked up over nothing."

"Are you lying, Meggie?" she snapped. "Because if you *were* there, I mean, if you were carrying my grandchild and you decided, well, I'd deserve to know."

The hair on my arms stood up. "No, you wouldn't. Not unless I chose to tell you."

"You're saying if you were pregnant, you'd keep it from me?"

Pick your battles. This was quickly escalating into a major confrontation when it didn't need to. I took hold of her shoulders. "Mother. Look me in the eyes and listen." When I had her attention, I went on. "I swear on Grandma's grave, I did *not* have an abortion last weekend." Which was true. Hopefully, I'd put an end to this. She'd believe her own daughter over a woman everyone knew was a notorious gossip.

She stared at me for a good twenty seconds without saying a word, and finally her breathing slowed, as though someone had pricked her with a pin and let the air out. "Thank God. I'll call Nancy tomorrow and tell her she made a mistake." She leaned back, rested her hands against her desk, and gave a slight laugh. "Which will be an interesting conversation because trust me, that woman does *not* like being wrong."

My jaw tightened. "Then she needs to keep her nose out of other people's business. I don't know who she saw at the clinic, but whoever it was deserves privacy."

She straightened up. Crap. I'd been out of the woods and now I'd set her off again. "You have to understand. A lot of people feel strongly that aborting a child goes against the sanctity of everything this country—"

I cut her off. "Save it for your stump speech, Mother."

"I can't help it." She recoiled. "My gut says it's wrong."

"And my gut tells me women should be in charge of their own bodies, not some government agency run mostly by men." With that, I left and slammed the door behind me, a frisson of anger eating away at my insides.

THIRTEEN

Wednesday morning, a black town car stopped in front of the house promptly at seven. I'd been waiting outside on the porch, afraid my mother would scoot out and introduce herself before I could stop her. Jocelyn might recognize her, and I couldn't afford that, today of all days, when I was already in her crosshairs for missing the meeting.

The rear window powered down, and Jocelyn waved for me to join her in the back. When I'd called and given her the address, I'd tried to apologize about Saturday, but she'd shut me down, said we'd discuss it when we were face-to-face.

I slid in beside her and launched into the speech I'd prepared. "I understand why you're angry but—"

"Did I say I was angry?" Jocelyn's face hardened. She hit a switch, and a tinted privacy divider slid into place, separating us from the driver. She clasped her hands in her lap, knuckles bone-white against her paper-thin skin. I wasn't sure how, or even if, to respond, so I kept quiet.

After a long minute, she added, "I wasn't angry so much as disappointed." She faced me, her lips stretched taut. "I couldn't understand why you would disappear at such a crucial time."

Why couldn't she rant and rave? That I could have handled. "I'd made a commitment I couldn't break." When she didn't say anything, I added, "Zachary told me what went on, and honestly, I'm not sure what more I could have added."

She flinched. "We could have used your creative thinking. Plus, you'd have been another familiar face in the room. Half the people there were strangers, and here I was, entrusting them with my most treasured possession—my reputation. Everyone told me to calm down, ignore the tweet, it was obviously a prank, some troll trying to make a name for himself by being provocative. Which is total bullshit."

She wasn't in the mood for a rational analysis right now. What she wanted was my reassurance that I was in her corner and I'd pounce on anyone who attacked her, like I'd done that day at the rally. The trouble was, I'd thought over the situation these last few days and decided Simon was right. Staying quiet *was* our best option. We needed to wait for more information and not give the fringe media any more ammunition.

"We need to make this stop," she said. "You understand what's at stake. Talk sense into the rest of the team. By doing nothing, we're giving this sniveling coward all the power."

"I hear what you're saying, but for now, please don't provoke the troll. If someone mentions the post at the conference today, downplay it. Whoever this is, they're after publicity. Don't give them any." Today's event would have several hundred powerful women in attendance, and Jocelyn was the keynote speaker. If she issued a rebuttal in this public forum, we'd have a PR debacle on our hands.

She considered this for a minute. "Fine, I won't. For now. But Megan? Make this go away. Don't let me down again."

In other words, pull a rabbit out of a hat. And soon.

We pulled up in front of the Drake Hotel. As soon as we got out, an older, well-dressed woman introduced herself as Penny Powell, organizer of the event, and whisked Jocelyn away, leaving me adrift. I followed the signs and retrieved my information packet from the registration desk on the second floor. When I read my name badge, I was caught off guard. *Megan Barnes, Ass't to Jocelyn Jones*.

Did someone assume I was her employee, or did Jocelyn describe me that way when they asked? I had a title—publicist. It might not be as prestigious as the other women attending, but I wanted it reflected on my name tag.

I flagged down a volunteer and showed her my lanyard. "My badge is wrong. Can you print me a new one?"

"Let me ask." She approached another woman standing in the corner who stopped shuffling paperwork long enough to shake her head. When the volunteer came back, she had a sheepish look.

"I'm sorry, but we don't have a printer here. Could you correct it with this?" She held out a red Sharpie.

"Thanks, but no." I wasn't going to scribble over my badge like a preschooler. I pulled out my business card from

Arrow, placed it in front of the printed tag, and slipped the lanyard over my head.

Jocelyn materialized at my shoulder. "There you are. There's some women I want you to meet." We entered the VIP room where she shepherded me around, praising the work I'd done for her, and occasionally plugging Arrow as well.

I'd landed in the middle of boss lady heaven. A former U.S. Commerce Secretary, the head litigator at a top law firm, the CEO of a major plastics manufacturer. These were invaluable contacts, women I could call on once I got that job at the *Trib*. I felt like Cinderella at the ball, gliding alongside my fairy godmother.

The morning sped by. I attended two workshops, sitting at the back, quietly observing how high-powered women executives networked. When lunchtime rolled around, I joined a table of eight near the front of the grand ballroom. To my left sat the COO of a social media giant, and on my right, a singer/songwriter from Queens. Initially, I didn't say much, but as I got more comfortable, I told them I worked as a publicist for Jocelyn and shared the story of how we'd met, which earned me a round of applause. Even though these women intimidated me, I held my own. After all, wasn't that the first lesson Jocelyn taught me? We grow by challenging ourselves.

The Chancellor of the University of Chicago introduced Jocelyn to thunderous applause, and I settled back, praying she'd stay on script.

"Let me tell you a story," she began. Then, instead of

launching into a rah-rah motivational speech, she shared an anecdote from her early years as a reporter. She framed it as though we were all sitting around a campfire, listening to her tale. She barely glanced at the notes in front of her. I considered myself a good storyteller, but she was a master. The audience broke into applause several times, and when I sensed Jocelyn was winding down, my shoulders relaxed. She hadn't mentioned the tweet.

"And now let's shift gears and focus on the future. I know many of you brought a younger woman in your company with you today. Someone you believe has leadership potential. Someone you're mentoring. My next words are directed to those women."

Was it my imagination or did Jocelyn stare straight at me as she said this?

"I believe girls with dreams become women with vision. But the path is not easy. There are roadblocks along the way, and one such roadblock is the alarming loss of privacy. I say this as someone who has dedicated her life to uncovering the truth behind the hype, to exposing the corruption and lies governments and corporations try to hide. But whether we like it or not, we now live in a 24/7 news cycle, with instantaneous communication around the globe and unlimited platforms for fake news. Which makes it even more urgent for us to vet our media sources, use our common sense, examine every angle of a story, and not listen to innuendos and gossip."

My knee bounced, hit the table, and jiggled the water glasses. I shrugged to the woman beside me to smooth over the faux pas. Not that I didn't believe in what Jocelyn was saying, but her words were veering into dangerous territory.

"I know the appeal of the easy answer, the quick fix, the natural tendency to think everything we hear or read is true. But we must fight that urge. We can't sit in front of a screen or tether ourselves to our phones and absorb history. Instead we need to harness the technology. Reach people around the world in real time, not as an instrument to spread hate or create divisions between us, but as a means to embrace our shared humanity. Shape a world where every person alive can find meaning in their life. Where everyone can be the best version of themselves."

The crowd leapt to its feet as Jocelyn held fast to the podium, acknowledging the applause with a smile. This admiration, this near hero-worship, was what she was terrified of losing. This was what was at stake.

I let out the breath I'd been holding. Jocelyn had warned the crowd of the danger of fake news without mentioning her own situation. I knew inside she was seething and would love to lash out. But she was a consummate professional. She'd given the audience the message they expected instead.

I might have had doubts prior to today, but now they vanished. The tweet had nothing to do with Jocelyn. She was a charismatic leader and a concerned advocate for women, as well as a journalist who stood up for truth and the value of a free press. I vowed to stand by her and do whatever I could to help her out of this mess.

At the end of the day, everyone reconvened in the
ballroom, which had been rearranged with rows of chairs and
a temporary stage at one end. The last presentation of the day
focused on the evolving nature of both print and broadcast
journalism in the age of the internet, and the panel consisted
of a political reporter from *The Washington Post*, a news anchor
from the local NBC affiliate, and Jocelyn. I hovered near the
front in case she needed anything. Once the discussion ended,
a conference worker roamed the audience with a microphone,
soliciting questions. The third one came from a young woman
in the back, who wore aviator glasses and a severe black
pantsuit, her red hair pulled back from her face in a twist.

"Dr. Jones, you've been silent about the recent tweet
accusing you of unethical behavior. Given your remarks at
lunch urging us not to believe everything we see posted on
social media, would you care to comment?"

My chest tightened. Jocelyn took a sip of water, but her
expression gave nothing away. The woman had put her on
the spot and there was no way to avoid answering, although
from the puzzled looks on people's faces, most of the crowd
didn't understand what the question meant.

"First off, let me share a bit of context as to what this
young lady is alluding to. Late Friday night, someone posted
a tweet accusing a media personality with the initials JJ of
unethical behavior. I learned of it over the weekend from
my publisher, but since I knew it didn't refer to me, I haven't
given it much thought."

I gave Jocelyn credit. No one would ever suspect she'd
had little else on her mind for the past five days.

"I will say, however, this is a perfect example of how, given the ubiquitous nature of the internet, an unsubstantiated accusation can gain traction with nothing more behind it than a single individual with a Twitter handle writing a buzzy post."

Unfortunately, the questioner didn't relinquish the microphone. "A follow-up, please. You don't agree people should be held accountable for their actions?"

Jocelyn shot back. "Please don't twist my words. What I'm saying is if the person who posted this tweet has hard evidence of wrongdoing, they should bring it out in the open so this JJ, whoever they are, can respond. But I suspect that won't happen—that this is nothing more than a fleeting attempt by a malicious troll to ruin a person's reputation in exchange for their own personal fifteen minutes of fame." She paused, glancing toward the back of the room. "And now I see one of our organizers is signaling for us to wrap this up so everyone can attend the cocktail reception on the ground floor. Thanks to all of you for coming."

Most of the audience had focused on Jocelyn during this last exchange, but I'd kept my eyes on the woman at the back. She'd held her phone in front of her during Jocelyn's answers. Which meant she'd taped the response. Which meant it would hit the internet within the hour. Which wasn't good. Because Jocelyn had pretty much dared @freethetruth to post again.

FOURTEEN

It was the end of my third week at Arrow, and even though Zachary still kept his distance, several other staff members had made a point of welcoming me. I'd gotten into the rhythm of the workplace and grown more comfortable with my duties. Jocelyn had given me a list of contacts—read: personal friends—at major publications including *Marie Claire, Elle,* and *Entertainment Weekly*, and I'd scheduled book reviews with most of them. I'd written a boilerplate press release, sent it to the culture desks at newspapers in all the major cities, and compiled a list of top reviewers on Instagram and Goodreads who should receive advanced reader copies. When I went over my notes with Frank, he seemed pleased with what I'd accomplished so far.

In the restroom, I overheard two girls chatting at the sinks about a party that night.

"I know you're tired, but it's the last one this year. Even if you pass on the free food and beer, at least come listen to The Half-Smoked Cigarettes."

"Okay, I'll drop by before I head out. Catch you there."

The first girl left, and the other turned to me. "You're new, right? I'm Lakshmi Dara. Ad buys."

"Megan Barnes. I work on the Jocelyn Jones account."

"Ah, yes. Zachary filled me in." I started to protest, but she waved me off. "No worries. Obviously, he's upset he got taken off the big account, but he'll get over it. You can learn a lot from him. There's not a better social media whiz out there."

So his attitude wasn't only over my waltzing into a cushy job. It *was* personal. Working on Jocelyn's team had apparently been a coup for him professionally, maybe even a pay bump. No wonder he didn't welcome me with open arms.

"What's this about a party?" I asked.

She clued me in. Four times a summer, the building managers cleared the parking lot, brought in seating and food, and hired a band. "You get a chance to unwind after the work week, plus meet people from the other floors. Everyone's invited. You should come."

"Thanks. I think I will." I headed back to my cubicle, then remembered what Lakshmi had said and detoured to the first floor. "One of those muffins, please," I said to the barista.

I bypassed my own desk and stood behind Zachary, who had his head buried in a folder. "Any chance you could look over my plan for Jocelyn's author Facebook page?" I placed a napkin and one of the muffins in front of him. "It's gluten-free."

"How did you—"

I chuckled. "You eat hamburgers wrapped in lettuce."

"Is this a bribe?"

"Let's call it a peace offering. Seriously, I could use your help."

He looked at me and back at the muffin. He took a bite, then another, and his lips curled into a half grin. "Okay. Show me what you've got."

———◆———

By five o'clock, the parking lot teemed with people. Most had grabbed folding chairs and sat chatting and laughing with friends. Feeling like the new kid at school, I headed to the food tent where long buffet tables were stacked with cookie trays, chips and dips, and containers of mac and cheese. Men in red-checked aprons and white chef's hats were manning three barbeque grills, flipping burgers and brats. I filled a plate with potato salad, raw vegetables, and baked beans, grabbed an ear of corn from the grill, then glanced around, desperate to spot a familiar face.

"I can't see anything I don't like about you," a voice whispered in my ear.

My mouth was uncomfortably full. I quickly swallowed, turned, and found Shoe Guy once again standing behind me, precariously balancing two brats slathered in sauerkraut and a slice of chocolate cake.

"But you will!" I parroted the next line from *Eternal Sunshine of the Spotless Mind* back at him. One of my all-time favorite movies. Luke hated it, called it too clever by half. If only there really was a Lacuna machine which could wipe out my memories of that asshole.

Shoe Guy narrowed his eyes, his gaze sweeping over my face. "Actually, you remind me of Clementine. Without the orange hair, of course."

"Tangerine."

"I stand corrected."

"*Spotless* is great, but if you want your mind blown, you have to watch *Adaptation*. It's pure meta."

He broke eye contact. "Ah, sorry. No idea what that means."

The conversation had come to a dead stop, and I scrambled. "No, I'm the one who should be sorry. I was trying to look cool and instead I came off as a pretentious jerk."

He met my eyes and flashed a smile. "But now that you've admitted you were showing off, you *do* look cool. So no harm done." He gave a slight bow. "You know, if we're going to keep running into each other, we should probably introduce ourselves. You're Megan something or other, right? I'm Nick Russo."

He scored points for remembering my name from our one encounter in the coffee line. I noticed a small scab to the left of his bottom lip—he must have cut himself shaving that morning. One of his earlobes held a diamond stud, and he smelled of peppermint. I wiped my fingers on a napkin and stuck out my hand.

"Megan Barnes. I work at Arrow on the fifth floor. What do you do?"

"I'm a cyber investigator. My firm's on three."

"Very double-o-seven." As soon as the words left my mouth, I realized how dopey I sounded. James Bond was a spy, not a computer guy.

But Nick didn't seem to notice. He produced a half bottle of chardonnay from his jacket pocket, a thin film of moisture coating the outside. "Can I tempt you?"

I glanced at the crowd but still didn't see anyone I recognized. "I guess. I mean, sure."

"This way." We found two empty chairs, and after we settled, he studied me. "So, what's up with you, Megan Barnes?"

"You mean, what do I do?"

"If that's where you want to start."

I described my job but left out the part where Simon hired me based on Jocelyn's say-so. I wasn't sure why it still bothered me. After all, lots of my friends used contacts, particularly friends of their parents, to land jobs.

While I talked, he opened the bottle and poured each of us some wine into a paper cup. I sipped mine and lobbed the conversation back to him. "You know, I actually have some idea of what a cyber investigator does. It's a web sleuth, right? You search for missing documents, locate people who don't want to be found, piece together links which seem unrelated but aren't." I'd paired up with a similar PI once for an article back in New York.

"Think of me as a techie Sherlock Holmes."

Actually, he *did* remind me of Benedict Cumberbatch. Same hair, same piercing blue eyes, same tall rangy build.

"Have you lived in Chicago long?" he asked.

"Pretty much my whole life, until three years ago when I moved to New York. You?"

"It's a small world. I was raised in Manhattan, but I like Chicago better. Friendlier." He grinned. "People here don't get bent out of shape if a stranger strikes up a conversation with them."

He clinked his glass with mine, took a bite of his brat, and a massive dollop of mustard plopped in the center of his denim shirt. We both laughed as he wiped most of it away with a napkin, but it left a stain. "And here I wanted you to think I'm perfect. Truth is, I'm a klutz."

I pointed at a similar spot on my own blouse where I'd dribbled artichoke dip at lunch. "Takes one to know one."

"Hey there, handsome." A striking brunette with fierce dark eyes materialized behind Nick and put her hand on his shoulder. She didn't even acknowledge my presence but jabbered at him instead. "Am I going to see you at the run? They're expecting an even bigger turnout than last year. Plus, it's for a new charity—a literacy program for Chicago public schools."

"I signed up, but I haven't trained much, what with work and all." Nick made a slight move away from the woman, dislodging her grasp on him. "Megan, this is Claire Somers. She works at Epic Design on two. Megan's a new friend. She's at Arrow."

Without missing a beat, Claire hauled a chair over from another table and sat down with us. She narrowed her eyes and examined me up and down. "I haven't seen you around before. But then it's hard keeping track of Nick's friends. He's quite the social butterfly."

I ignored her remark. "What's this about a run?" I'd been in plenty of races and always enjoyed the competition. Plus, it would be a way to meet new people and raise money for a good cause at the same time.

Claire and Nick took turns filling me in. The half-marathon, which circled through downtown Chicago and ended at Grant Park, drew thousands of runners. They even closed off Lake Shore Drive to traffic that day.

"Nick, why don't the two of us get together for lunch afterwards?" Claire said.

He stared past the food tables at the vacant lot across the street, then swiveled back. "Actually, I may not be able to join in this year. I'm playing it by ear."

His tone was dismissive, bordering on rude, and within a few minutes Claire excused herself and moved away.

I leaned toward him. "What did I miss?"

"It's nothing." He swallowed the last of his wine. "Listen, if I do run, I have to train. If you want to team up, I'm free Tuesdays and Thursdays after work. There's a track a few blocks from here we could use."

So why had he told Claire a different story? This was worse than awkward. I didn't want any part in what was going on between the two of them. "I'm more of a morning person."

A microphone squealed from a makeshift stage at one end of the parking lot. Three men with guitars and a woman with a tambourine clambered onto the platform where drums and an electronic keyboard had already been set up.

Nick stood. "Sorry. Duty calls. I'll get you information on the run." He touched my arm. "Seriously, I'd like it if you'd buddy with me." Before I could say anything, he jogged across the lot, cut behind the guitar players, and grabbed the drumsticks.

A voice came over the loudspeaker. "Attention, everyone. Put your hands together for The Half-Smoked Cigarettes, with our very own Nick Russo on percussion." People cheered, clapped, and a few wolf-whistled as the band launched into their tribute version of "Play That Funky Music."

Claire stared straight at Nick. She seemed hurt, maybe even a little heartbroken. That's how I must have looked the day I discovered what Luke had been doing behind my back for months.

What do people say about guys in a band? Rebels. Notorious flirts. Good for a weekend fling but not someone to get involved with. Not someone to lose your heart to.

Not someone to trust.

FIFTEEN

The noise inside Duncan's Irish Pub hit me like a jackhammer. The line at the bar to order drinks was two deep, Beyoncé's voice blasted through the speakers, and three jumbo TVs blared from the walls, each broadcasting the same baseball game. Becca and Sam waved from a small table in one corner. I wove around bodies and made my way back to them, shoes sticking to a floor where dozens of drinks had spilled over the years.

Sam moved to the opposite side of the table so Becca and I could sit side by side. He'd put on weight since I'd seen him last and his strawberry-blond hairline had receded, but otherwise, he was the same old Sam who'd been my best friend's boyfriend since the Ice Age. But now, knowing what he and Becca had been through these last few months, I couldn't help feeling badly for him. Did he suspect anything about our weekend in Lake Geneva?

Becca slid a lemon drop in front of me. "Ladies' night, five-dollar martinis. My treat."

Sam leaned over the table. "Nice to get time with you, kiddo. Still liking the new job?"

Becca saved lives in the ER and Sam patrolled the streets, keeping all of us safe. And what was I doing with my time? Spending my days writing puff pieces for a woman so famous she was a household word and pitching a book already destined for the best seller list. And, if I was being honest, enjoying every minute of it. It was a head rush calling *Vogue* editors, *Tonight Show* booking agents, and top Instagram influencers. If I didn't get back to hard-hitting news pretty soon, I'd lose my edge.

"There's a lot of hype, but I'm grateful for the paycheck." I licked the sugar rim of my martini. "Anyway, now that I'm employed, I need to move before Mom and I come to blows."

"I hadn't realized it was that bad. Does this have something to do with the other night when she practically ordered you to meet her?" Becca asked.

I deflected. "That was a misunderstanding."

"Then what's the problem?" Sam asked.

"When I leave the house, she asks where I'm going and when I'll be back. She buys me food she thinks I'll like and does my laundry without asking. It's high school all over again. I need my own place."

"It's not going to be easy to find something affordable," Sam said. "In fact, it's one of the big advantages of having a partner, right, hon?" He shot Becca a nervous look across the table. Becca didn't answer, just studied the menu.

Oblivious to Becca's body language, Sam kept talking.

"And speaking of partners, what's with your love life? When are you jumping back into the dating pool?"

"Hey, I'd love someone special in my life, but it's hard." I pictured Nick from last night. "Everyone seems to know the key to relationships except me."

"If you ask me, the most important thing's honesty. If Becca and I have a problem, we discuss it. Right, babe?"

Becca squeezed my leg under the table. I didn't move a muscle, just pretended to listen as Sam launched into a story concerning a friend on the force who'd cheated on his wife, had his partner cover for him, then their captain found out, *yadda, yadda, yadda.* When I glanced at Becca, the secret we shared was written all over her face. How was it possible Sam didn't sense it?

A roar erupted from the crowd. The Cubs must have scored. I seized the opportunity and changed the subject. "Well, I don't know anyone in town well enough to room with them, so unfortunately, that leaves *moi.*"

Sam's face lit up. "Hey, maybe we could find you a place tonight if we think outside the box. What do you say?"

He was being cryptic, but what did I have to lose? He stood and dinged his fork against his glass. "Attention, everyone. May I have your attention?" He waited, but nobody stopped talking. As a last resort, he let out an ear-piercing whistle through his teeth, and within seconds, the place quieted down.

He pulled out his best farm-boy-from-Iowa twang. "My name's Sam, and I've got a little problem. I'll pay the bar tab of anyone who can help me solve it." People cheered and raised their glasses. "My friend here needs a rental." He shot the question my way. "Near north side?"

I nodded. Where was this going? Next time Sam had an idea, I'd ask for more information before I signed on.

"Got that? Between here and Wrigley Field. Somewhere clean and safe. And cheap. No matter what, it's gotta be cheap. So, if you want to take advantage of this one-time offer, step right up." He paused, but nobody moved. "Ah, come on, folks. Someone must know of a place. She's a nice girl. Well-behaved."

Sam must have blocked out the march against police brutality I'd organized, and the two-day sit-in on the library steps. I hadn't exactly been the poster child for well-behaved in college.

Several guys near the front whooped and hollered. *How would you know? She'd have better luck if she misbehaved. How nice is nice?* Gross stuff like that.

Most people ignored us, still hypnotized by the game. But an older gentleman with flyaway white hair and a florid complexion slid off his barstool and lumbered over. Reaching into the pocket of his tweed jacket, he plunked a dog-eared business card down on the table.

"Hell of an approach, son. But effective, I'll give you that. I've got a deadbeat tenant who skipped out on his rent last week, so his apartment's unexpectedly available. Duplex near Wicker Park. The flat upstairs is a mother and her kid. Decent people."

I picked up his card. "How much, Mr. Wies ..."

"Wiesnewski. Aleksander Wiesnewski at your service."

He bowed at the waist. "For you, my dear, eight fifty a month. All it needs is a good cleaning and a coat of fresh paint."

I did the math in my head. I could swing it. "And for everyone else?"

"Eight fifty a month."

A landlord with a sense of humor. I could do worse. "When can I take a look?"

Wiesnewski pushed back the frayed sleeve of his shirt and glanced at a watch which still had hands. "Twenty minutes from now. Or next Wednesday when I'm back in town."

"Let's go," Becca said.

"You mean right now?" I replied.

Sam added his two cents. "Why not?"

Wiesnewski told us the address and said he'd meet us there. After Sam paid both the man's bill and our own, the three of us piled into Becca's car, and twenty minutes later, we pulled up in front of the house. No garage, not even a driveway, but that wasn't a deal breaker. I'd park on the street. Wiesnewski waited for us on the front stoop.

We huddled in a shared entry with stairs on the right leading to a second floor as Wiesnewski fit a key in the door on the left and pushed. Nothing. He tried again. This time the door creaked open a scant three inches. Sam moved in front of the landlord, rammed the door with his shoulder, and after two more hard shoves, opened a space wide enough to duck inside. Five bulging trash bags sat wedged against the frame.

Sam wrinkled his nose. "Mother Mary on a moped. What's that smell?"

Wiesnewski retreated back into the entryway. "I'll wait out here. You three go ahead and take the tour."

Cobwebs hung from the ceiling, and the threadbare carpet in the front room had a stain in one corner which could be blood, but there were massive built-in bookshelves on either side of a full-size gas fireplace. The off-white sofa had wide rips in both seat cushions, and the battered wooden desk in the corner was held together by duct tape. But there was a sweeping picture window facing west, perfect for catching the sunset.

Becca had sped ahead, and now she yelled. "Megan. You won't believe this kitchen."

She'd turned on all four of the stove's burners, but only one worked, and the handle on the avocado refrigerator had split in two. "When I flipped on the lights, you should have seen the cockroaches scatter. But it does have a walk-in pantry, so there's that."

We wandered through a hallway with peeling wallpaper and found a tiny bathroom. Both the shower and the linoleum floor were caked with dirt—apparently the last tenant had never met a mop—and the mirror above the sink had a gigantic crack across the front.

The hardwood floor in the bedroom needed a new wax and stain, but it had a decent oak grain. I scrawled my initials in the dirty windowpanes, then spotted a magnificent old oak tree and a trio of well-trimmed shrubs right outside.

"What a pit," Becca said from behind me.

"Well, it was always a long shot," Sam added. "Don't worry. I'll ask around the station. We'll find you something."

It was obvious the place needed work—a top-to-bottom scrubbing, a fresh coat of paint, and a host of minor repairs. But I could bike to work on nice days, this was a safe neighborhood, and the rent was within my budget. And best of all, it came with no parents attached.

This apartment meant freedom. I'd finally be living on my own. No roommates. No boyfriend. Just me.

I'd stand my ground with Wiesnewski—instead of a security deposit, I'd fumigate and repaint the place. As for repairs, I'd hire help, provide the receipts, and subtract the expense off my first month's payment. If I left, he could rent the place out in a nanosecond at twice the price.

I whirled around and faced my friends. "What are you two jabbering about? Haul that guy in here so I can sign the lease before someone else snaps this place up."

———————————— • ————————————

A few nights later, as I put the finishing touches on the baseboards in the front room, a short dark-haired boy dressed in khaki cut-offs and a Harry Potter T-shirt poked his head around the corner.

"Are you my new neighbors?" he asked.

"Well, it's just me." I balanced my brush on the edge of the paint can and stuck out my hand. "I'm Megan. And you are?"

"I live upstairs with my mom." He kept his hands behind his back.

"I mean, what's your name?" This must be the boy Wiesnewski had mentioned. At a guess, I'd say eleven years old. The age I'd been when I went through my Goth phase.

"Mateo. Mateo Rodríguez. My mom's Vinita."

"I don't think I've ever met a Mateo before. It's nice."

"It means 'God's gift.' Mom says that's what I am. She told me she prayed, and the next thing she knew, there I was. 'Course I'm not a kid anymore. I know all about DNA and chromosomes and stuff from the internet, so I know that's not really how it works. But it's a nice story."

"It's only the two of you?"

"My dad's in the Army." Mateo peeked behind me into my apartment. "Do you have a dog?"

I grinned. "No. Do I need one?"

"If you get one, I could walk it, is what I meant. I want my own dog, but my mom says one, we can't afford it, and two, she doesn't need anything else to take care of." His words tumbled out like a fast-moving train. "But then I tell her I'll feed him and take him for walks and play catch with him, but then she says she can't even get me to clean my room and wash the dishes, so why would she think I'd—" He stopped short and looked down at his shoes, his long hair obscuring his face like a curtain. "Sorry. I talk too much sometimes."

I crouched in front of him. "It's okay. I do, too. It means you're enthusiastic." I stood up. "I think I've got a Coke in the refrigerator. Want one?"

When he nodded, I retrieved a can and poured a glass of iced tea for myself. "Sorry there's nowhere to sit."

"You can borrow my beanbag chair."

"It's okay. I don't officially move in until next week, and by that time, my furniture will be here. But I could use your help putting it together."

"You got it." He wandered the room and stopped at the spot I'd planned for my writing desk. "Who's this?" He pointed to a photograph I'd thumbtacked to the wall.

"Her name's Gloria Steinem. She's a famous feminist."

"She's pretty. What's a feminist?"

What definition would he understand? "Have you ever heard anyone tell a friend of yours she can't do something because she's a girl?"

"Sure. Victor. He's this big kid in my class. He's always telling my friend Ellie she can't play on the basketball team even though she's the best at free throws. The coach agrees with him."

"A feminist is someone who says that's not true, girls can be anything they want to be. In fact, it's against the law to treat them differently."

"Good. Then they can arrest Victor because I hate him." Mateo moved closer to Steinem's picture and read the quote I'd attached. "*We have to behave as if everything we do matters. Because it might.*" He faced me. "Did she say that?"

When I nodded, he asked, "Are *you* a feminist?" He swayed back and forth, his gaze never leaving my face.

"Yes. I'm definitely a feminist. Listen, you tell your friend to ask the coach if he's ever heard of Title IX. And tell her to keep shooting hoops, okay? Now, I need to get back to work. We'll see each other again soon." The boy didn't say a word but scurried out the door and pounded up the stairs.

I peered back at the photo. Steinem's quote summed up why I'd gone into journalism. I wanted to write stories that mattered. Instead, I was working for a woman so famous people posted selfies with her online. At least in New York I believed what I wrote made a difference, if not in the grand scheme of things, then to the everyday people on the street whose stories I told. But I had to be realistic. Mother's run for office meant I was stuck where I was for now.

Unless. That editor Diaz was hungry for a major scoop. He'd as good as told me so. If I could catch a bank officer discriminating against loan applicants, or an entrepreneur lying about product safety, or a felon falsely imprisoned, he'd publish my story regardless of who my mother was. But what chance did I have of that?

Still, what if this tweet about Jocelyn had legs? What if she *was* the JJ who @freethetruth was targeting? A powerful and respected journalist who'd exposed dictators, fought for women's causes, held politicians accountable for their actions, toppled by a single individual with nothing more than an internet connection. That story had possibilities. That was a story that might matter.

SIXTEEN

A t dawn, I headed out for my morning run. This was the day I'd present to the team and convince them to stand by Jocelyn. I'd stayed up past midnight making sure everything was set. Even after I'd tumbled into bed, PowerPoint slides still played in a sputtering loop through my brain most of the night.

When I got in line for my caffeine fix at ten thirty, Nick waved at me from a corner table. He'd sent me several emails since the party in the parking lot, but I hadn't responded. Getting involved with a player was the last thing I needed right now. Clutching my latte, I headed back to the elevator and pressed five, but Nick rushed forward, putting his hand between the doors so they bounced back open. My shoulders tensed. I didn't have the time or the energy to deal with this today.

"What's up with you?" he asked.

I held up my hand. "No time. I'm late for a meeting."

"Okay, I'll ride with you." God, this guy could not take

a hint. The minute the doors squeezed shut, he said, "Why are you treating me like the walking dead?"

"I don't have a clue what you mean." I shrugged. "Sorry."

He studied my face. "I'd avoid lying to people if I were you because you're really bad at it. Your ears turn bright red." He shifted his weight from one leg to the other. "Does this have something to do with that conversation with Claire the other night? I searched for you after the first set, but you disappeared."

Talk about clueless. "Why were you so cool to her? She was talking and you pretty much ignored her. Is that your MO? Date a girl, throw her over, act like she's invisible when you run into her again?"

"Whoa, whoa, whoa. Back up the truck a minute. You lost me."

"It's obvious you two have a history."

Nick flinched. "You are so off base, I don't even know where to start. Let me ask you something. Ever tell a guy he wasn't your type and he didn't get the message?"

"So you admit you've got a *type*?" My instincts were right. Nick was a guy who sorted women into neat little boxes—rowdy bartender, prim librarian, best pal, driven career woman. I wondered what pigeonhole he'd stuffed me in. I punched the elevator button again, harder.

"You're not listening." Nick leaned back against the wall.

"I just got out of a seriously messed-up relationship, and I don't want to get involved with anyone new right now. As for training for a run, my job's crazy busy, so my schedule's limited."

"Message received." His voice was sharp. "Don't worry, I won't bother you again."

"Good." We reached the fifth floor, and I barreled out of the elevator, sloshing half my latte on the floor.

———————•———————

I checked my slides for grammar and spelling errors one last time and played out the presentation in my head. At one fifty, I gathered my handouts and my laptop and hurried to a small conference room at the far end of the building. When I got there, Frank and Tamara were seated around the table, but Simon hadn't arrived yet. I glanced at my watch. Three minutes to go. I attached the cord for the overhead projector and displayed my first slide on the screen—an image of Jocelyn in full camo gear in the middle of a war zone—then passed out copies of the proposal. Frank commented about what an impressive woman Jocelyn was and how he was anxious to hear my ideas for her book. Neither of them mentioned the tweet.

I paced back and forth and poured myself a glass of water. At two minutes past two, Simon entered the room and sat at the end of the long table, positioning a blank yellow pad and pen in front of him. "Okay, Megan. Let's hear what you've come up with." He stared past me at my first slide.

I cleared my throat. *Relax. You can do this.* "As you're already aware, this book is Jocelyn's memoir," I began. "And it has one major theme throughout: a free press is essential to our democracy and reporters must be vigilant in their search for the facts, even if doing so puts them at risk for criticism, censure, even physical danger." I made eye contact with Frank, who gave me a subtle thumbs-up. "This book begins when Jocelyn's a reporter in New York and takes the reader through her years as a war correspondent in various hotbeds of conflict. The last part of the book covers her time as a news anchor during the Clinton, Bush, and Obama administrations."

I leaned forward and put my hands on the table. "And through it all, Jocelyn has made it her mission to expose corruption in foreign governments, to confront lying politicians, and to draw attention to human rights violations. At a time when some people in the media often don't research the facts, but regurgitate press releases and ignore obvious lies, Jocelyn has refused. She hasn't pandered to what's fashionable, but reported the truth, no matter who pressured her not to."

I flipped to the next slide, which showed a chart of what we'd done to date. "So far, we've approached this campaign like every other book launch—press releases, blurbs, feature articles. But what if we pushed the envelope? What if we made Jocelyn's belief in the power of truth the linchpin of our focus? Position Jocelyn Jones as a symbol of how a person—a *woman*—can be successful in their chosen career without sacrificing their integrity."

No one at the table moved a muscle as seconds ticked by. At last, Simon spoke up. "In other words, Saint Jocelyn?"

What was wrong with that? A bead of sweat trickled down my temple. "People are hungry for heroes."

Simon nodded. "Agreed. And if you'd pitched this a few weeks ago, I'd have championed it. But that was before the tweet. What if Jocelyn *did* violate her code of ethics somewhere along the way? Your approach would blow up in our faces. It might be a good idea to have a fallback strategy."

"We know from her reaction to the tweet Jocelyn believes she's the JJ the post refers to. But she also insists the accusation isn't true," I argued. "Who should we believe—an online troll or our client?"

Frank spoke up. "Megan's right. If we buy into this innuendo, we're as bad as the people who believe every pundit they hear on cable news. For heaven's sake, Simon. This is Jocelyn Jones we're talking about. She's been a respected journalist for almost forty years. If she says there's nothing to this, I believe her."

"It's not a matter of who or what we believe. It's a matter of basing an entire PR campaign on a premise that may not be true." Simon crossed his arms. "Which would be devastating for Jocelyn and reflect poorly on our firm as well, as though we hadn't done our homework."

"The tweet may turn out to be nothing," I countered. "It's been over two weeks with no other posts. The whole thing may be a prank."

"And if that's the case, your idea makes sense and we'll run with it. But if there's more to come, well . . ." Simon shrugged.

"So you want me to tell Jocelyn the team's worried she might be lying and we're playing wait-and-see for now? Is that really the message you want me to deliver?" As soon as the words came out of my mouth, I saw I'd gone too far.

"That's not what I said." Simon stood. "I'm suggesting we give ourselves breathing room. If Jocelyn questions you, say we're narrowing our focus. Her book doesn't launch until this time next year, so there's still time. Meanwhile, I've put a cyber investigator on retainer. Nick Russo."

My stomach did a double backflip. The guy I'd told to get lost an hour ago? Great.

Simon went on. "If the troll has a vendetta against Jocelyn, we'll expose the slander and make it part of the story. 'Respected journalist attacked by lying troll' will dovetail with Megan's idea. But for now, I'm tabling the discussion."

Everyone filed out of the room except Simon. I gathered the five-page handouts they'd left behind on the table, unplugged the projector, and shoved my notes into my briefcase.

Simon shut the door. "You and I need to talk."

I sank into my chair, drained.

"I can see you put a lot of time and effort into your presentation."

At least he recognized that, even though he'd shot down my idea. "Jocelyn deserves our loyalty. If she's being targeted—"

"Let me finish." His tone was measured and even. "You obviously admire Jocelyn. I get it, I do. She's one terrific role model and a successful, independent woman. But I'm old enough to know anyone can have secrets they don't want exposed. All I'm saying is let's cool it until we're certain there's not an actual threat here. In the meantime, research Jocelyn's background. Watch what's being shared on social media. And talk to her. See if she can remember anything in her past which could tie into this. Sound reasonable?"

I nodded. But where should I start?

My journalism training kicked in. Start with the facts. See where they lead.

———— • ————

The rest of the day I dived deep into research. Many of Jocelyn's articles and broadcasts were available online—reports she filed from the front lines and network specials where she interviewed world leaders. After wading through hours of footage and reading dozens of articles on her career, I didn't notice anything suspicious. I quit at five, exhausted, my mind whirling from all the random information I'd taken in.

The next morning, I started up again. By eleven, I still hadn't found anything except reams of data which reinforced my initial conclusions. I stretched, took a bathroom break, then grabbed a snack bar from the vending machine. When I got back, I burrowed deeper, eventually turning up obscure sources which delved into Jocelyn's early days as a cub reporter, her time at college, and her teenage years here in Chicago when she was still Eleanor Schiller. By that afternoon, I'd even discovered a few yearbook pages from her old high school.

And stumbled on an interesting fact.

Simon and Jocelyn had attended New Trier at the same time. They were both in a photo of the debate team, her as a senior, him as a sophomore. Which meant they'd at least known each other as teenagers, even if they hadn't been close friends. It was feasible the connection was why she'd hired Arrow in the first place. I remembered Simon's remark about people having secrets they didn't want exposed. Had something happened back then which colored Simon's view of Jocelyn?

I decided to ask him.

The space outside his office had morphed into a boisterous party. Balloons and streamers hung from the ceiling, and a small group of employees, including Frank and two other account managers, stood in a circle, glasses raised in the air as though giving a toast. Simon, dressed in a fitted dark-gray suit and mauve tie, stood in the center. On his left stood a taller man with ebony skin and a bald head, wearing a tailored navy blazer and white pants. I wasn't sure what was going on, but this was clearly not the right time for a private conference. I turned to go, but Frank spotted me and yelled across the room. "Megan! Join the festivities." I gave him a half-hearted wave and took the paper cup he handed me.

Simon whispered in the tall man's ear and pulled him in my direction. "Megan, I don't think you've met Tyler Barrow. Tyler, Megan Barnes. She's the one working on Jocelyn Jones's book launch."

The man smiled. "Ah, yes. The prima donna." I wasn't

sure if he meant me or Jocelyn. "Pleasure to finally meet you, Megan."

Finally? Was Tyler a new client? Regardless, he was obviously someone important. "Nice to meet you too." I was terrible at small talk. "So what kind of work do you do, Mr. Barrow?"

"I'm a cartoonist. Mostly political satire these days. The administration makes it so easy." His booming laugh took me off guard. "But mainly I keep Simon in line. There are weeks that's a full-time job."

Several people raised their cups in a salute, and Simon chimed in. "And this morning we signed a long-term contract." And then he kissed Tyler on the mouth.

I covered my confusion and congratulated them both, realizing I'd never once thought about Simon's life away from the workplace.

"I've been asking him for a year, and last night when he agreed, I wasn't going to give him a chance to wriggle out of it so I hauled him to the courthouse two hours ago and *voilà!*" Simon whipped out a piece of paper from his suit pocket and held it up. "A license issued by an official Cook County judge."

People cheered, and Simon went on. "Listen up, everyone. I need all of you to pitch in while Tyler and I go on our honeymoon. Any major emergencies, see me in the next two hours, because after that, I'm turning off my phone and not even looking at my computer for the next seven days." He raised his glass and drank it down. "Now get back to work, you peons."

The crowd dispersed, but I stayed behind. Simon had his back to me, talking to Frank and Tyler. When I tapped him on the shoulder, he swung around, a question on his face.

"Could I grab you for a few minutes?"

"Not a problem. Take a seat in my office."

I waited there, and before long, he joined me. "Okay, you've got my undivided attention. What's up?"

"First, congratulations. Tyler seems like a great guy."

"There's no need to butter me up. What's on your mind?"

Simon and I might've butted heads, but I appreciated the fact he didn't mess around with niceties. "I researched Jocelyn yesterday and again this morning, like you asked, and discovered the two of you were in school together. I know it was a long time ago, but did something happen back then that makes you doubt what Jocelyn's telling us?"

"You *are* thorough, aren't you?" He leaned against the edge of his desk, hands resting on each side. "This isn't something I want shared with the team, but yes, Eleanor, now Jocelyn, was good friends with my older sister, and they're still in touch."

"Okay, so the two of you had a previous connection. Isn't that even more reason for you to be on her side?"

"It's the opposite." He hesitated a moment, then went on. "When she was a senior, Jocelyn got caught cheating on her SAT test. I overheard my parents and sister talking right after it happened. But Mr. Schiller, her father, was an important man. He collected on a few favors and got it buried. I didn't think much of it when she signed on as a client, but now, with this tweet thing, I'm not sure." His voice trailed off.

Simon didn't necessarily trust Jocelyn. Interesting.

"All I'm saying is she might not be as squeaky-clean in the ethics department as she appears. Leopards don't change their spots."

"High school was a long time ago."

"It was. Listen, let's not get ahead of ourselves. For whatever reason, the troll's gone quiet. It could have been a one-shot deal. Or the message could have nothing to do with Jocelyn. Once I'm back from my trip, we'll regroup. Until then, keep Jocelyn off Twitter. I don't want her engaging."

"There must be something more I can do in the meantime."

He rubbed his chin and let a moment pass. "If the troll does resurface, we need to be ready. When she pressured me to hire you, Jocelyn filled me in on your background as a reporter. Let's utilize your skills and team you up with Russo, see what the two of you can find out. Decide if we're worrying for no reason."

Great. I blow the guy off yesterday and today I'm teamed up with him. But I didn't feel I had a choice. Besides, just because I was working with Nick didn't mean I had to be friends with him. We'd be colleagues, nothing more.

"No problem," I said. "I'll drop by his office and we'll put our heads together."

————————•————————

I knew meeting Nick again would be tense, but it made sense for Simon to put him on the team. We needed someone with expertise in tracking people online, and he was only two floors away. The next morning, I put on my big girl pants and took the stairs down to Rucker and Russo Investigations. I must have set off a silent alarm when I stepped inside because a tall guy with a full beard poked his head around the corner. "Hi, there."

"Is Nick here?"

"No."

"When do you expect him back?"

"I'm his partner, Jamal Rucker. Can I help?"

"I'm Megan Barnes. I work for Arrow Communications and—"

"Ah." His eyes widened. "So you're the woman Nick said almost . . ."

"Almost what?"

"I'll take it from here, Jamal." Nick stood in the doorway. "Hello, Megan. Simon told me you'd be dropping by."

I was dying to know what Nick had told his partner about me but kept quiet. Nick led me down a hall to a glass-walled space, shut the door, and motioned to a table near the side window.

"This is awkward," I said.

"Not at all. We're adults. But before we get down to business, there's something I want to say." He pulled a chair over and sat across from me. "You jumped to the wrong conclusion about me and Claire. I tried explaining that day in the elevator, but you wouldn't listen."

I shrugged. "It's none of my business."

"You're right. It's not. But if we're going to work together, we need to trust each other, so let's clear the air. Claire's married. Not happily. When she first came on to me, I made it clear I wasn't interested. I told her what I think of people who cheat on their spouses and to take me off her list. But, like you, she didn't listen."

He rejected Claire, but not because *he* was a player. Because she was.

My cheeks turned warm. I'd judged him without having all the facts. "I didn't realize."

"It's fine. Let's get to work."

But I couldn't leave it like that. "I apologize."

"Apology accepted." His gaze was piercing. "Why don't we make a pact? If anything I do doesn't sit right with you, ask me to my face instead of spinning wild tales, okay?" The skin around his eyes crinkled into a smile, and I realized he'd given me a pass. "Now, let's compare notes."

I shared everything I'd found out in my research, as well as Zachary's information on the Ku Klux Klan. Nick agreed it was a long shot but said he'd look into it. We'd been at it for an hour when Jamal rapped on the door.

"There's been another tweet."

Nick and I exchanged glances and simultaneously grabbed our phones.

If someone stole your work,
wouldn't you be angry? Want revenge?
Time to come clean, JJ. Clock's ticking.

SEVENTEEN

I called Jocelyn all night and again the next morning, but she didn't pick up, so I drove over to check on her. I knocked three times, shouted, even honked my horn, but several minutes went by before she swung open the door.

"What're ya doing here?" Her face was blotchy and her words slurred. It was nine o'clock in the morning, but it was obvious she was well on her way to being drunk.

"I was worried. You weren't answering the phone."

Jocelyn's hand shook as she balanced against the doorframe. "I don't need . . ." She flapped her hands in the air, eventually settling on, "babysitting."

"I read the latest tweet and thought you could use some company."

Her eyes flamed. "It's a damn vendetta. Who's behind this? What do they want?"

"There's still a chance you're not the JJ."

"I am. You know I am."

I couldn't see leaving her in this state. "Mind if I come in?"

Jocelyn swayed, then steadied herself on the jamb. I held her elbow and steered her toward the sun porch, tightening my grip when she veered off course. We settled side by side on the wicker sofa. "Have you had breakfast?" I asked.

"Hannah has the day off."

"Should I fix you something to eat?"

She shrugged. "Knock yourself out." She slipped off her shoes, leaned her head back, and closed her eyes.

When I returned from the kitchen balancing a tray of scrambled eggs, a sliced banana, iced water, and two mugs of steaming black coffee, she'd fallen asleep. Her breathing was steady but shallow. I grabbed an afghan draped on a nearby chair and wrapped it around her legs. Flipping to a book I'd downloaded on my phone, I sat nearby and kept watch.

I don't know what I'd expected—that she'd be smashing plates, cursing a blue streak, railing against the stupidity of people who believed everything they read online. But no. She'd sat all alone in this house drinking until she was ready to pass out. That might be her way of dealing with stress, but even so, why was she so upset? Surely she didn't think a few anonymous tweets could wipe out the spotless reputation she'd spent four decades building. Where was the woman who defied despots, faced down critics, and stood up for those who had no voice? The internet might be pervasive, but we could use that to our advantage. Once we confronted the troll and proved they'd lied, we could stand back and let the platform spread the story. Why was Jocelyn crumbling before we'd even begun to fight?

An hour dragged by before she leapt up like a scared cat and spied me in the corner.

"How long was I out?"

"Not long. You should eat something. I'll reheat the coffee and eggs."

When I came back, Jocelyn had resumed her place on the sofa. She'd brushed back her hair, put on her shoes, and finished the banana and both glasses of water.

"I guess I should say thank you."

If Jocelyn pushed me away out of embarrassment, I'd never get to the bottom of this story. "Compared to all you've done for me, it's the least I can do." I put the tray down on the coffee table in front of her and once again plunked down on the rocker, tucking my legs beneath me. "Want to talk? It's obvious you're upset."

Her face blazed red. "Upset? I am not upset. I'm furious." With no warning, she sprang up again and paced the room. Finally, a glimpse of the real Jocelyn.

"People tell me I'm a good listener."

"You wouldn't understand. You're too young."

What did age have to do with it? "I'm the only one around. Why don't you try me?"

She kept pacing. "How old are you, Megan, twenty-five? Twenty-six? I remember what that was like. Your whole life's about wanting. You want a successful career. A nicer apartment. A new car. You want to travel, you want to afford dinners out on Friday night." Her tone grew softer. "You want to find a partner. Someone you can love and trust and build a life with. Your whole future's ahead of you, and you want to grab it with both hands, get as much as you can, experience every last bit of it. Am I right?"

"But that's human nature isn't it?"

She stopped mid-stride. "For a while. But trust me, when you turn sixty, it all changes." Her left hand twitched as she gazed off into the distance. "Your life becomes all about fear. Your children leave home, your spouse dies, and you get scared. Scared you'll lose your job. Scared you'll run out of savings. Scared you'll wind up alone. Hell, what if the worst happens and you get dementia and lose your *mind*?" She turned and stared straight at me. "The only thing that's important is to hold on to what you have. Make sure you're not left with nothing. That's why I'm so angry. That after all I've worked for, all I've sacrificed, I could lose everything."

She transferred her gaze out the patio doors to the garden, and a steely edge crept into her voice. "We have to figure out who's doing this. Drag them out of the shadows."

Good. Jocelyn the fighter was back. "I've teamed up with Nick Russo, the cyber investigator Arrow hired. He's working to locate the troll."

"I won't stand idly by and let my reputation be dragged through the mud. As soon as this Nick finds out anything, I want to know. I don't care who or where this @freethetruth is, I'm going to knock on their door and demand they produce evidence to back up these insinuations. Because trust me, they won't be able to. And then I'll call a press conference and expose their lies."

Jocelyn kept insisting she'd done nothing wrong. But I'd shuffled through scenarios in my mind all night. This woman had been a reporter for four decades, both as a foreign correspondent and a television anchor. What if somewhere along the way, a member of her team used original research they'd obtained from a fellow journalist, then submitted the story to Jocelyn without acknowledging the other person's contribution? Maybe they wanted all the credit. Maybe the research didn't seem substantial enough to mention. Maybe in the crunch to get the story out, they simply forgot. Regardless, Jocelyn trusted her colleague, filed the report, and now the troll held *her* responsible when her only crime had been putting her faith in someone she shouldn't have. I knew what that felt like.

If @freethetruth *did* have evidence of wrongdoing, then Jocelyn, my role model and mentor, was smack in the middle of a media maelstrom. Because what if she held a press conference, insisted on her innocence, and this stranger produced proof?

If that happened, nothing I could do would save her.

———————◆———————

I met Becca at the hospital cafeteria that afternoon during her shift break. I'd debated whether to let her in on the Nancy Peabody situation, but eventually decided she should know. After making our selections from the soup and salad bar, we carried our trays to a quiet table in the far corner.

"What's up?" Becca said.

I lowered my voice. "A friend of my mother spotted

us at the clinic. She asked me point-blank about it the evening after we got back. That's what that weird call was about."

"Sweet Jesus. And you're just now telling me this? What did you say?"

"That you and I were at a spa in Lake Geneva that weekend. Not the rest of it."

"Did she believe you?"

"She said yes. But it'll be a problem if word leaks out this close to the election."

It took Becca a few seconds. "You mean she thought *you* had the abortion?"

"I swore to her I'd never been pregnant. Which is true. I said this Nancy person made a mistake, that it wasn't me. Mom said she'd handle it, stop any rumors. But if she ever mentions it, we ought to have our stories straight."

Becca shook her head. "You need to tell her it was me."

"She'd think my best friend was covering for me. Don't worry. I finessed it."

"I could show her the paperwork."

"You paid in cash, remember? And you threw away the forms in the hotel room so Sam wouldn't stumble on anything." I stabbed a baby carrot and popped it in my mouth. "Speaking of Sam, how's that going?"

Becca toyed with her salad, pushing around a stray crouton. "He and I have been together so long, gone through so much, I was sure the minute he saw me, he'd know. But he didn't. He asked a few questions about the spa, grabbed a beer from the fridge, and made dinner like normal." She played with her knife. "Be honest. Do you think I sensed Sam and I weren't working out, that we're not the perfect couple everyone thinks we are, and that's why I went off with Jimmy?"

"I've never heard you talk like this. You're not seriously considering breaking up with Sam, are you?"

"If I tell him, it could break us apart. But what if I don't?"

I squeezed her hand. "I get it. You want the person you love to know the real you." I wiped my mouth with my napkin. "Why don't you suggest counseling?"

"And how exactly would I explain that to him? No, I'll give it time. See how I feel in a few weeks."

Becca was hurting, but I didn't think pushing her was the right move at the moment. She'd talk to me before she did anything rash.

"Let's change the subject, okay?" She took a sip of water, then dug back into her salad. "I noticed Jocelyn trending again. Any idea how you're going to find this person who's harassing her?"

"Do you remember me telling you about Nick?"

"Shoe Guy?"

"Yep. Simon hired him. He's a cyber investigator—sexy job title, huh?"

"And is he?" Becca motioned for me to go on.

"Is he what?"

"Sexy?" She wiggled her eyebrows.

"We're colleagues. That's all."

"Isn't this the same man you said was a player?"

"I was wrong. Turns out he's a good guy after all." I swiped at the tomato soup I'd dribbled on my blouse. "Can I ask your advice?"

"Yes, take it slow with this Nick. I don't want to pick up the pieces of your heart again so soon after Luke."

"No, it's concerning Jocelyn. This whole Twitter fiasco has rattled her."

"Social media's a powerful thing."

"You're right about that. I mean, any one of us could get caught in a situation like this. Once Twitter decides you're guilty, it's impossible to get anyone to believe you're innocent."

"Is she, though?"

I wasn't sure what Becca meant. "Is she what?"

"Innocent. In nursing school, the first lesson they teach us is when you hear hoofbeats, think horses, not zebras."

"Sorry. Right over my head."

"It means don't look for an exotic medical condition when a commonplace solution is a lot more likely. I get that you admire the woman, but stop and think. What's the most logical explanation? That she *did* steal a story somewhere along the way."

"You mean on purpose? But that doesn't make sense. She's a prize-winning journalist. She wouldn't need anyone's help landing a major scoop." It was frustrating how everyone was so ready to believe the worst.

"All I'm saying is keep an open mind," Becca continued. "You don't have the greatest instincts when it comes to situations like this. When you care for someone . . ."

"What?"

"It can blind you to what's going on."

But Jocelyn was different. Jocelyn wasn't Luke.

"And if I help her through this, I'll have a grateful mentor who'll praise me to every media outlet in the Chicago area. So right now, I'm focused on two things: exposing the troll's lies and making sure Jocelyn doesn't fall apart in the meantime."

"When did this become *your* responsibility? Where are her friends? Family? Why aren't they rallying around her?"

"All her family's dead. She's tight with her publisher Kate, but she's back in New York. The only other friend I know about is Dr. Stein. She and Jocelyn are old friends, and Simon told me to dig into Jocelyn's past. Do you think I'd be out of line to go see her, find out if she knows anything useful, maybe ask her to contact Jocelyn and offer support?"

"Uh, yes. Wouldn't she have contacted Jocelyn already if the two of them were close? I mean, can you imagine me being in trouble and you not rushing to my side, doing whatever it was I needed? If Stein hasn't done that, there might be something you don't know about their history together."

"Jocelyn needs someone in her corner besides me. Stein could—"

"My advice is to stay away from her personal life. This whole situation is bad enough as it is. Don't do anything to make it worse."

EIGHTEEN

All week I worked on a slew of press releases, and at night I schlepped to my new apartment, hauling paint cans, mops, and cleaning supplies up the front steps. Slowly, my new home morphed from a cesspool to a fairly livable space.

Mother and I hadn't spoken much since our confrontation at her headquarters. I had told her what I'd overheard at Jocelyn's party, that Lynch had taken over Underhill's campaign, but she shrugged it off, said Gavin had told her weeks before and they were dealing with it. Mostly we stayed out of each other's way, which wasn't difficult given she was at campaign events every night and I worked full-time during the day.

When I'd taken the job at Arrow, I'd told her I'd be finding my own place soon, but I don't think she actually believed I'd do it. So when I came downstairs Friday evening, suitcase in hand, I steeled myself.

She was sorting papers at the dining room table and glanced up. "Are you going away for the weekend again?"

"I've found my own place. I'm moving out."

She put down her pen. "When did all this happen?"

"Why are you acting like I've sprung this on you? We discussed it weeks ago."

"I assumed you'd come to your senses. Honey, you're barely squeaking by. Why would you spend money you don't have when you can stay here? There's plenty of room, and I've stayed out of your way, haven't I?" She stood and gave me a hug. "Besides, I like having you around."

Where you can keep an eye on me. "I appreciate you taking me in when I needed a place to stay, but it's time for me to move on."

She scowled. "Where are you going? Have you signed a lease?"

"A week ago."

"Why didn't you tell me?"

I set my bag on the floor. "I'm telling you now."

"Does this have to do with our argument last week? Okay, we're on opposite sides politically, but that doesn't mean we're enemies."

"I'll be more comfortable living in my own apartment. And remember, this isn't the first time I've been on my own. I survived in New York for three years."

"And look how that turned out."

I backed away. She could be mean when she wanted to. Just when it seemed she'd come to terms with my being an adult, she had to go and remind me how I'd messed up. I let it drop.

But she wasn't done. "When you moved back, I thought

we'd get the chance to reconnect. Do things together, like we used to."

"You mean grab a few minutes between campaign stops? Let's be honest. I've been home for over a month. How many times have the two of us sat down to dinner during that time?"

I could see my words stung.

"Okay, I deserve that. But the election's around the corner. Once it's over, life can go back to normal."

She couldn't be that naïve. Regardless of how the election panned out, her life would never be the same. Which was a good thing. I didn't want to see her revert to full-time mothering. Politics aside, I liked this new version of her.

"The two of us need to figure out how to relate to each other as adults, and I don't see that happening as long as I'm living here. I'll call you once I'm settled, and we'll get together. But right now, I have to get going. I'm meeting Becca."

"Okay," she said, shadowing me to the door. I was halfway down the porch steps when she called after me. "You forgot to tell me your new address."

I pretended I hadn't heard her.

———— • ————

Saturday was spent unpacking the stuff the movers brought over from Mom's and doing last-minute cleaning. When the furniture I'd ordered—maxing out my last credit card—arrived tomorrow, I'd be done. I'd have a place of my own.

I flung an old quilt across the futon in the bedroom and fluffed up a couple of pillows as a backrest. Then I lit two scented candles, poured myself a chilled glass of wine, and snuggled in for a quiet evening with the latest page-turner from Megan Miranda.

I'd been reading for half an hour when I heard two voices outside my door—Mateo, the kid from upstairs, and wait . . . Mom? How had she found this place?

I stepped into the entry and closed my apartment door behind me.

"Hello, Mother."

She spun and flashed a wide smile. "Hi, sweetheart. I've been having an enlightening conversation with Mateo here about the last election. I must say, he's got some very interesting theories about what happened."

I tucked my hands into the front pockets of my jeans. "What are you doing here?"

"Aren't you going to invite me in?"

"I'm still unpacking."

"Don't be like that. I brought peace offerings." She pointed at two presents wrapped in shiny silver paper, complete with outlandishly large bows, sitting beside her purse.

My shoulders tensed. She'd trapped me. "Okay. But no comments on the place. It's not officially open for visitors yet."

"I'm hardly a visitor." She bent down and put her hand on Mateo's shoulder. "I enjoyed meeting you, young man. Next time I'm here, we'll talk more. Wait. Would you like a present too?" She snapped open her purse and produced a red, white, and blue campaign button with her beaming face plastered on the front, along with her slogan *Vote for a Change*. She handed it to Mateo, who glanced first at her, then at the object in his hand.

"Wow, you're a real-life politician?" He looked at me. "You never said your mom was famous. What are you running for?"

"The U.S. Congress. But trust me, it's not as glamorous as it sounds."

He handed the button back. "I'm not old enough to vote."

"That doesn't matter. I want you to have it."

His face lit up. "Gee, thanks." He pinned the button to his shirt and bolted upstairs.

She'd always been good with other people's kids. I'm sure that came in handy on the campaign trail. Once inside, she stood in the middle of the room and cased the joint.

"The furniture comes tomorrow."

"Ah." She leaned against the fireplace, arms crossed in front of her. "It smells nice in here. Lavender, isn't it? I love that scent. It's so relaxing."

I'd planned on inviting her over once I'd assembled the sofa, chairs, and coffee table, hung a couple of pictures, and filled the empty corners with plants—once I had my life together. Trust her to throw me off-balance. "This is a surprise."

"You forgot to give me your new address, so I asked the movers. Anyway, I'm here now. Want to give me a tour? Then I'll treat you to dinner to celebrate your new home."

I sighed. "It's been a long day, and I was going to order pizza and turn in early. You can keep me company if you don't mind the floor." My mother liked being comfortable. There was no way she'd agree.

But she didn't even flinch. In fact, she looked positively giddy, like a kid at her first sleepover. "I haven't done that since college. What fun! Are there more pillows?"

I might as well give up. She was staying. I called up DoorDash and placed my order, then grabbed two mismatched wine glasses and a bottle of merlot from the kitchen and sat cross-legged on the carpet across from her.

"So how's the campaign going? The polls I read have you ahead of Underhill by a strong margin."

"It depends on who's doing the polling. We've got a few rallies coming up, but those mainly attract folks who've already made up their minds. The hard part is reaching the undecideds."

"I'm surprised you've positioned yourself as a moderate. I mean, your party's moved pretty far right in the last couple of years."

She sat up straighter. "When I agreed to run, I made sure the party leaders knew I wasn't going to pretend to be someone I'm not. But it's a tricky balancing act. All some voters pay attention to are sound bites. They won't listen to a nuanced discussion of the issues, and they sure don't want me saying the other party has any good ideas." She sipped her wine. "Don't get me wrong. Obviously, you have to stand up for your basic values, but the real business of politics is compromise."

"Aren't you being hypocritical? I mean, there are issues you won't budge on—abortion for one."

She fiddled with her ring and broke eye contact. "You're right. I can't see my way around that one."

I kicked myself for bringing up abortion again so soon after our last confrontation. There was a time to fight my battles and a time to shut up. I gulped my wine. She coughed a couple of times. "Anyway, bottom line is I haven't bought my ticket to DC yet."

I hadn't thought that far ahead, partly because I never believed she'd win. But now it seemed like she might, which meant she and I wouldn't be living in the same city come January. We'd had plenty of opportunities to reconnect since I'd been back, but instead, we'd spent all our time arguing. It was clear we were never going to see eye to eye when it came to politics. The question was whether we could move past those differences and ever be close.

My cell chirped, telling me the pizza had arrived. "Back in a sec." I stepped out on the stoop where a young guy in a Chicago Bears sweatshirt and Buddy Holly glasses stood balancing an insulated red bag in one hand and my receipt in another. I scribbled my signature and came back inside. Mother had disappeared. I found her rattling around in the kitchen.

"What's up?" I asked.

She turned. "I was looking for plates."

I pointed at the cabinet to the right of the sink. "Bottom shelf."

"And napkins? Forks?"

"Forks in that drawer, although I usually use my hands. As for napkins, here you go." I tossed her a roll of paper towels.

She laughed. "Okay. Not a problem."

We started in on the pizza, and at her insistence, I told her a few anecdotes about my work at Arrow. Nothing too personal and nothing proprietary. Mainly how much of a fish out of water I'd been in the beginning, but also glitzier stories, like how I'd been chatting two days before with the book editor of *The Atlantic*.

"I've read about the tweets implying Jocelyn stole a story. How's she handling that?"

"What do you think? She's livid. And I don't blame her. I'm working with a cyber guy to figure out who's behind the accusation."

"Rumors are hard to bottle up once they're out in the world."

"Obviously, she's not the JJ mentioned in the tweets. I mean, steal a story? It's impossible."

"I hope she appreciates how lucky she is having you on her side."

After we'd devoured the margherita pizza and finished the bottle of wine, Mom wiped off her hands and set the two presents in front of me.

"You know I'm terrible at buying you presents, but I thought you might like these."

Plus, you knew if you came bearing gifts, I'd have to invite you in.

I tore the wrapping off the first box and found an elegant

leather-bound notebook with a snap closure and refillable lined pages nestled inside. My name was embossed on the cover. It was exactly the right size to fit in my bag, for recording notes from interviews or scraps of information I found in researching a story. This wasn't something my mother had found at the local department store. She'd spent time picking this out and ordering the personalization, long before she knew I was moving out. I was afraid if I spoke, I'd tear up.

"Just because you're working in PR right now doesn't mean you won't find a reporting job soon. That's where you belong."

"It's lovely," I said, meaning it. I fingered the smooth calfskin.

"I wasn't sure about this second gift, but I thought it might go nicely in your new home."

The simple pewter frame held an old photo of our family sitting under a flaming-red maple tree in a park, the remains of a picnic lunch spread on a sky-blue tablecloth in front of us. I was around four years old, wedged between my mother and father.

A warm feeling flooded my body. "I haven't seen this in ages. We all look so happy."

She sighed. "We were."

I glanced back at the photo. My parents had their arms around each other, smiling. Not a hint that, years later, they'd be living separate lives, Dad married to another woman.

"We've never talked much about how you and Dad met." I hesitated. "You were what, twenty-one?"

"Twenty-two. Three years younger than you. I'd graduated college, and he was a few years older, working as an associate at a big law firm downtown. His roommate and my best friend were engaged, and they fixed us up."

My father had been movie-star handsome as a young man, with his dark hair, his strong jawline, and his cleft chin. "How did you know he was the one?"

"That's a good question." She tilted her head. "What I remember is everything was easy and natural with him." She stared off in the distance, evidently lost in the memory. "I could tell him anything, and I mean *anything*, and he never made me feel strange or weird. He said I was interesting. And I thought he was interesting too, because even though he wasn't *exactly* like me, he was a *lot* like me. Very, very close." She shrugged. "Anyway, close enough. It's hard to explain."

It wasn't though. She'd described what being in love felt like in such simple terms that I intuitively knew what she meant and also realized I'd never experienced that feeling. Certainly not with Luke.

"Wow." It was all I could manage.

"And his sense of humor, his quirky take on life? God, your father could make me laugh."

I couldn't remember the last time I'd heard her laugh. "But you two are so different. I mean, he plays golf. You play tennis. You love to curl up in front of the fireplace and read. He always wants to go out to a party or travel somewhere exotic. All the advice columnists say to find someone with common interests."

Her face softened. "Oh, honey, none of that matters in the beginning. That comes later when it's already over. When you're searching for excuses to avoid facing the real reasons you broke up." She glanced away. "Life doesn't always turn out the way you plan."

"When did it change?" I'd blamed my father for their divorce, for falling in love with his secretary, Suzanne. The year before he left, I'd been on a date and seen the two of them coming out of a restaurant, holding hands and kissing. I'd never told my mother.

She reached over and touched my hand. "What does that matter? Your father and I loved each other when we got married. That's what's important. And when we had you, it bonded us even more."

Behind her, I could see the last vestiges of the sunset through the windows, all purple and brilliant orange like a circus tent draped across the horizon. In this light, my mother appeared fragile, delicate, vulnerable.

"I miss him," I said.

My mother lowered her head. "I miss him too." As she wiped the corners of her eyes, I saw subtle age lines I'd never noticed before. She still thought about him after all this time—still loved him in a way.

Once more, I examined the photo. "I always wondered why you didn't have another child. I wished so hard for a little sister."

Her breath caught, and it was several moments before she answered. "Life's complicated. I couldn't...." She glanced at her hands, folded in her lap, a tone of regret coloring her words. I heard something else as well—something which sounded like sorrow. "Anyway, it didn't happen. And now the three of us are such different people than we were back then." Her face had a faraway look. "God, it was more than twenty years ago. Even if we had a time machine and could go back to that day in the park, I doubt we'd recognize ourselves."

Whatever it was I'd seen on her face a moment ago was gone, and her mask was back in place. "I'd better head home." She stood and smoothed out her skirt. "But first, I need to visit the restroom. Is there toilet paper?"

End of conversation. It was such a familiar pattern. My mother would start to share feelings, and when the conversation became too intimate, she'd clam up. I'd have to be patient with her, take it slow, push only so far, and then back off. At least we'd talked about something other than politics. Real stuff.

"Make a right at the kitchen. And jiggle the handle. It sticks."

When she returned, she paused and examined the wall. "I think you missed a spot." Sure enough. She pointed to a two-inch area where the paint was too thin and the primer showed through. She had a knack for spotting my mistakes. "You know what they say. Anything worth doing is worth doing twice."

I took her remark in stride. Pick your battles. "Thanks for the heads-up."

"You know, I think I've had too much wine. If I order an Uber, will my car be okay here overnight? Gavin can retrieve it in the morning."

I breathed easier. Since we'd drunk a fair amount, I'd toyed with suggesting the same thing, but I knew she'd resist the idea if it came from me. "Don't worry. The car will be fine."

Five minutes later, a honk sounded outside, and I walked her to the front door. "Honey, are you sure this is a safe neighborhood? Because I've heard some areas near downtown are—"

"Sam checked the police stats. It's a peaceful area. No gang activity."

"Still, I wish you hadn't rented on the ground floor. I've read it's the first place burglars target, particularly if they know you're single and living alone. You might want to get a gun."

I smiled and shook my head. "I am *not* getting a gun. Stop being so paranoid."

"You sound like your father. The world is a dangerous place, Meggie. There are bad people out there, and anyone who doesn't realize that and act accordingly is naïve."

I flashed to an argument I'd overheard between my parents right before my seventh birthday. "No, we are *not* buying her a new bike," my mother had shouted. "Don't you know there are perverts out there driving around the streets, eyes peeled for girls her age?" Dad had shot back, "You're being paranoid. We've got to let Meg find her own way. I'm not going to teach her to be afraid of adventure, of going out in the world. You can't keep her your little girl forever."

I took hold of Mom's arm. "I know you're concerned, but I'm careful." When the worry lines still didn't leave her face, I added, "And I've got a baseball bat under the bed, just in case."

We hugged. She hurried to the waiting car, and I watched as she disappeared down the street. The first visit to my apartment was over, and we'd both survived.

Light-headed from the wine, I undressed and crawled onto the futon, but something had lodged at the back of my brain, a detail in our conversation which failed to register earlier. It was like trying to remember the name of some old movie. The more you obsessed, the more frustrated you got for not remembering. And then it came to me. That awkward pause when I'd asked why she and Dad never had any more children.

What had my mother meant when she said it was complicated?

NINETEEN

B ecca had warned me not to contact Professor Stein, said I could make the situation worse by interfering. But I didn't agree. After all, Stein had introduced Jocelyn at the rally as "my dear friend." The two of them had marched in the streets together. Of course she'd want to help. I phoned, explained I was a member of Jocelyn's PR team, and we made a date to meet at University Hall Wednesday afternoon.

A plaque on the wall outside her door read *Dr. Rhoda Stein, Professor of English*. Two voices seeped through the walls, one low and steady, the other angry and shrill. The door sprang open and a student barreled out, almost knocking me over. The girl lowered her eyes, whispered an apology, and hurried down the stairs. When I peeked around the corner, Stein was leaning back, hands clasped behind her head, eyes fixated on the ceiling.

"Professor? I'm Megan Barnes. Is this a bad time?"

She sat up straighter. "No, just delivering unwelcome

news to a would-be author. I could use the break." She took another look at me. "Wait. You're the girl from the rally, aren't you? The one who attacked that skinhead? When you called, I didn't make the connection."

"I gave Jocelyn my contact information, and we met together for lunch, and, well, it's a long story, but I've joined the team handling the publicity for her memoir."

"That's so her. She meets you. She likes you. She folds you into her life." She motioned to a chair across from her desk. "Take a seat. But I remember you from somewhere else. Weren't you in one of my classes a few years ago?"

"A survey class on American women authors. I analyzed *Gone with the Wind* for the final. You gave me credit for calling out the racism but took off points because I labelled Scarlett anti-feminist." I smiled. "You said I'd ignored the reality of her situation, said she'd used the only avenues available to her—her beauty and her brains—to survive."

"As women have done throughout history." Stein folded her hands together. "Well, we're not here to discuss Scarlett. You wanted to talk about Jocelyn. Does this have to do with the tweets? How's she coping?"

I wasn't surprised Stein had heard the rumors, but I was surprised she hadn't contacted her friend. "The team's trying to deal with the fallout. I wondered if you could shed light on Jocelyn: her background, her history. The more I know, the better I can help her. You two have been friends a long time, right?"

"God, yes. Back at Columbia, we were inseparable. We even roomed together one year in the early seventies. Fourth-floor walk-up in Greenwich Village." Stein scrutinized my face. "You remind me of her in those days. Not your features so much as the way you present yourself. The way you gesture when you talk."

I wasn't sure how to respond, so I moved on. "It must have been a heady time. I mean, all the protests over the war, the women's movement, Watergate. You were at the forefront of real societal change."

Stein stared out the window. "It seems like yesterday—beads in our braided hair, long ponchos, bell-bottom jeans. We marched every weekend against one thing or another. You're right, first it was the war. Then civil rights. Then women's rights." She gave a low laugh and fiddled with her shirt collar. "We'd stay up half the night swigging cheap wine, arguing the social implications of communism versus socialism. God, we talked about everything—grades, Castro, how much we loathed sororities, what we planned to do with the rest of our lives. We borrowed each other's clothes. Each other's class notes."

I gave a slight laugh. "Each other's boyfriends?"

She shook her head. "No, never that. Oh, Jocelyn had close male friends, but she never dated anyone seriously. She stayed true to Robert."

I searched my memory but came up with nothing. "I'm sorry? Who's Robert?"

"Who was Robert?" Stein echoed. "I guess you'd say he was the love of her life. For Jocelyn, there was never anyone but Robert. They met at an anti-war rally right here in Chicago while she was still in high school. He was a few years older. This was during the Vietnam buildup. He was drafted, served overseas in the army during the time she and I were undergraduates."

"He was killed in the war?"

"No. He did two tours and came home. He joined Jocelyn in New York as soon as he got back."

I was stunned. I'd read everything I could get my hands on concerning Jocelyn, and of course, the memoir covered her life from her mid-twenties on, but I hadn't run across any mention of this man. How sad Jocelyn had a great love and lost him somewhere along the way. Perhaps her career had come between them.

Stein continued. "It was around that time she and I drifted apart. I studied for my PhD, and Jocelyn began work at *Ms.* magazine. Then I got married, and we moved here to Chicago. Shortly after that, Jocelyn took a position at the *Times*, she got famous, and ..." She fiddled with some papers on her desk. "Anyway, we haven't been close for years."

"You didn't try to stay in touch?"

Her laugh had a bitter edge. "Of course I did. But after a while, it got too one-sided. I stopped keeping track of the phone calls she didn't return and the letters she didn't answer. Even when I did hear from her, it wasn't personal. More a travelogue of where she'd been, where she was going next, who she'd be interviewing once she got there." Stein leaned forward in her chair. "I don't hold it against Jocelyn. It's who she is. Who *we* are. But no, we're not close anymore. We're what I'd call *surface* friends. We remember each other's birthdays, and we touch base at holidays, but honestly? Most of what I know of her life is what I read in the media."

"My best friend Becca was in your class too. Even after I moved to New York, we still talked every week. She's like family."

"That's how it was with Jocelyn and me once. But now? I have no idea whether she's happy, if she's satisfied with how her life turned out, how she's dealing with getting old. The kind of stuff I share with my close women friends. That day at the rally was the first time we'd seen each other in years. If I had to guess, I'd say Jocelyn doesn't have many friends, only followers."

"Would you be comfortable reaching out to her?"

"I don't think that's a good idea. Jocelyn's a proud woman. If she sensed I contacted her out of pity, she'd resent it."

"I hate to see her going through this alone."

"But she's got you, doesn't she?"

I was taken aback. "Me? I've only known her a few weeks."

"That's all it takes with Jocelyn. You must have noticed. She's a magnetic force. She pulls people in. Always has. It's part of what's made her successful. When we met in class that first day, I fell for her right away. I can still remember how much it hurt when she dropped me. It took a long time for me to get over it." She tapped her pen against the desk. "If I'm honest, that's another reason I'd rather not contact her."

She sounded as though she'd been in love with Jocelyn. Maybe in some ways, she had. Maybe I was a bit, too.

Should I tell Stein how Jocelyn had been so drunk Friday morning she could barely stand? I decided against it.

Jocelyn deserved her privacy. "She's having a tough time coping."

Stein leaned forward. "Underneath her bravado, Jocelyn's fragile. A lot like Scarlett now that I think about it."

It was a different take on Jocelyn than I'd heard from anyone else. I hesitated, but curiosity got the better of me. "Can I ask? I mean, you may not know, but is there a way I could reach out to Robert? Even if he and Jocelyn broke up, he might want to help."

Stein shook her head several times, and when she spoke, her tone was hesitant. "The war damaged Robert in some fundamental way. Today, we'd call it PTSD. He'd wake up in the middle of the night screaming. He had trouble holding a job. Berated his boss. Lashed out at his coworkers." She paused. "He even hit Jocelyn a couple of times when she startled him, but she stood by him and supported them both financially. She never gave up on him."

I hated to press, but this was important. "What happened to him?"

Stein shut her eyes and stayed silent for a long while before she continued. "Jocelyn found him in their garage. He'd hanged himself. Left a note asking for her forgiveness. Said he couldn't outrun the nightmares." She whispered, "She was three months pregnant. She lost the baby." Tears welled at the corners of her eyes, and she shook her head. "I'm sorry. I shouldn't have told you all that. It's just I haven't thought about it in so long."

My throat tightened, picturing Jocelyn in what must have been the lowest point in her life. She'd lost everything, but she'd found the strength to go on. Several minutes went by, neither of us saying a word.

Stein rose and stood by the window, looking out. "When she embedded herself with those combat units, I wondered if she'd purposely put herself in harm's way so she could understand what Robert had experienced." She turned. "She became a fanatic opponent of war. She'd rant over the waste of human life, the atrocities, the cruelty it normalized."

Was it possible Jocelyn's hatred of war and the heartache it had brought her caused her to set aside her ethics to expose a tyrant? To stop a genocide? Did the tweets tie back to this tragedy with Robert?

I rose and tucked my notes away in my bag. "I appreciate you sharing your insights on Jocelyn. You've helped me understand her better."

Stein followed me to the door. "You need to remember, my generation was convinced we were on the right side of history. We were going to tear down the military-industrial complex. We were going to push through equal rights for women. We were going to repair a hundred years of racial injustice." Her eyes lit up. "We were going to change the world."

Then why didn't you? Because as far as I could tell, things hadn't changed all that much.

The boomer generation. In the beginning, they'd had optimism, energy, camaraderie—all the ingredients a major movement needed to succeed. But they'd given up, settled, got comfortable.

And left my generation to clean up the mess.

TWENTY

Several pundits online had chimed in, identifying Jocelyn as the most obvious target of @freethetruth's tweets. When I called her midmorning, she sounded as though I'd woken her up. Regardless of whether she'd had a late night with the bottle or downed sleeping pills, the strain was obviously taking a toll. But she asked me to stop by.

A half-dozen reporters elbowed each other outside the mansion. They peered through the fence, their cameras held high. When I drove up, they rushed my car, knocked on the window, and shouted questions in my face.

"Are you a friend of Jones?"

"Does she know who's behind this?"

"Any chance at an interview?"

That had been *me* six months ago, desperate to land a hot story, anxious for a juicy sound bite. Now I was on the other side, purposely keeping my expression neutral so I didn't give anything away. I punched in the code, drove in, then waited until the gates closed, making sure none of them slipped in behind me.

Based on what I'd learned from Professor Stein, I wanted to probe deeper into Jocelyn's history to see if I could identify what happened in her past that might have set all this in motion.

The front door was locked, but the housekeeper let me in and asked me to wait in the library. Floor-to-ceiling bookshelves filled the cavernous room. I brushed my fingers along the spines, flipped open *The Great Gatsby*, and was stunned to discover it was a first edition. Shelved beside it was *For Whom the Bell Tolls*. Same thing. I examined book after book. *Adventures of Huckleberry Finn. The Catcher in the Rye. Fahrenheit 451*. All of them were original publications, and a few were signed.

"I see you've discovered one of my father's obsessions." Jocelyn stood in the doorway.

"I didn't mean to pry, but this is unbelievable."

"The entire collection's listed with a broker. The *Gatsby* alone should bring in $150,000."

"Your father must have been a fascinating man."

"He was a bastard." Jocelyn's voice was as pointed as an ice pick. "I won't stop until I've gotten rid of every last one of them."

Her harsh words shocked me, and I fumbled for an appropriate response. I closed the book in my hands and slowly slid it back on the shelf.

"You're shocked. Don't be. In a perfect world, fathers would always be the loyal and trustworthy men we think they are when we're children. I discovered mine wasn't when I was seventeen."

I was seventeen, too. "I remember you told me the two of you had a falling out."

"It was much more than a falling out." A shadow flickered across her face. "He killed the man I loved. Not something you ever forget. Or forgive."

She must be talking about Robert. But that didn't fit with what Stein had told me. "What do you mean?" I hoped my response was open-ended enough to keep her talking.

"Mother took his side, of course. After all, she'd spent two decades cowering under his thumb. Once I disowned him, she finally found the courage to divorce him."

I sank onto a nearby leather ottoman. "Are you okay sharing this?" I wanted to know more, but only if Jocelyn was okay with it.

"That's what friends do, isn't it? Share family history? To understand me, you have to understand my relationship with my father. It's a big part of who I am."

So that's why she moved back here—to expunge her father's memory by living in his house and selling off his prized possessions. She strode to the far end of the room and stood by a bar cart with an assortment of glasses and several decanters of liquor. "Can I offer you a drink?"

"It's barely noon."

Jocelyn laughed under her breath. "Not in London." She poured a jigger of dark liquid into a large tumbler and collapsed opposite me on the couch, its deep brown leather rubbed beige on the arms from years of use.

"This particular story starts in 1972. The boy I loved, Robert Janssen, was subject to the draft. He got a low lottery number, which in those days meant a ticket straight to Vietnam. But there was a loophole. At that time, married men got moved to the bottom of the list. It was our way out. We planned a hurried wedding, even though I was underage and needed my parents' permission. Father agreed, but when the day came, he refused to sign the papers."

"You must have been devastated."

"I'd trusted my father, and he'd betrayed me. Robert was scheduled to ship out in three days. We had no money, no one to turn to, and no time to make other arrangements."

Now Jocelyn's earlier statement made sense. Harold Schiller's actions had repercussions long into the future. "And you had to keep living here, seeing your father every day, knowing what he'd done." A sense of sadness for the girl Jocelyn had been settled in my gut. Yet that was the same year Jocelyn's father had pulled strings and covered up the cheating she'd done on the SAT. His controlling nature might have sabotaged her plans with Robert, but it had also saved her from scandal. Talk about a complicated relationship.

She sipped her liquor. "I couldn't stand the thought of turning to him for money. I had a merit scholarship to Columbia, and my mother gave me all her savings for expenses. The last day of high school, I packed my bags, called a taxi, and raced out the front door. When I looked back at the house one final time, I saw my father silhouetted at an upstairs window. Our gazes locked for an instant before he dropped the curtain. He lived to be ninety-five years old, and I never saw him again." She paused as the memory washed over her.

"And Robert?" Even though I knew the answer, I didn't want Jocelyn to know I'd talked to Stein behind her back.

"He died because of the war." She gazed into the distance. "And I pulled myself together and went on living. But that experience with my father changed me. I made damn sure no one ever had that much power over me again."

"And now it feels as though this internet troll has that power."

"Which is why we need to shut him down."

I kept my voice low and measured. This would backfire if I upset her, but I needed more information. "Think back. Could there be a story buried in your past that's at the heart of this? If we can pinpoint a particular article, it could be the lead we need."

"Don't you think I've spent every waking hour wracking my brain trying to recall something? There's nothing," Jocelyn shot back.

"I know I'm pushing you. But here's my thinking. We figure out what incident this person's upset about, then we put your version—the truth—out front. We arrange interviews with other witnesses who can support your side and publish it. Force them to retract the tweets and publicly apologize. Problem solved."

"Aargh!" Jocelyn burst off the couch and paced. Her jungle-print blouse conjured up the image of a caged leopard prowling the room. "How is this not verbal terrorism? Why can't I call the police? I can't sleep. I don't eat. I walk around like a zombie." She flung out her left arm, sending a delicate sky-blue vase on a nearby table spiraling through the air; it landed on the floor and shattered. I gingerly picked up the jagged pieces and dumped them in a nearby wastebasket.

That didn't slow her down. If anything, she gained steam the longer she ranted. "I need to stop this little shit. Every day my reputation is being doused with kerosene and set on fire in the public square, and there's nothing I can do about it." She poured herself another shot of liquor. "I've spent my whole adult life being in control of my destiny, and now a nobody with a keyboard and an internet browser has made me a victim."

But Jocelyn was no fool. She knew as well as I did that's how the world worked now. The comments we made online, the photos we shared, the rants we posted, the *thumbs-up* we casually sent—they all got absorbed into the gigantic maw of the Internet, and we were helpless to stop it.

"Let's approach this more systematically," I offered. "You've got a chronological table at the end of your book. Let's see if anything jogs your memory. Do you have a copy here? I left mine at the office."

Jocelyn strode to the large desk at the far end of the room, opened a drawer, and handed me a bound manuscript. "After two years of working on this, I'm sick of my own story." She flung it my way. "You look."

While I flipped to the back pages and scanned the index, she returned to her desk, opened her laptop, and peered at the screen. "God, they're still piling on. There's three dozen posts supporting this ass since the last time I looked." She rummaged in one of the drawers, pulled out matches and a pack of cigarettes, and lit up.

"I didn't know you smoked."

She didn't bother to answer, only continued to punch her keyboard so hard it set my teeth on edge.

"You've got to stop obsessing over this. Let's concentrate on pinpointing the story they're referring to, okay?"

She closed her computer and came back to the couch. Since I had nothing to go on, I picked a random starting point: the year she first shipped overseas. "In 1991, the *Times* had you cover Desert Storm." I shot a look her way. "With a war raging all around you, was there ever a time you didn't get a chance to double-check your copy? Sent off an article you hadn't fully vetted yet?"

"Ha. That describes every story I filed. That's why they call it *breaking* news, Megan. Never enough time. Always a deadline looming." She gazed at the back garden. "By the time I got there, Iraq had already invaded Kuwait. It was the first time I saw the effects of war up close." She shook her head. "Indescribable. A war zone is your worst nightmare times ten. But in an odd way, it energized me, like when I marched against the war back in college. I'd been given the chance to expose the atrocities going on under the guise of patriotism, to wake people up, and get them to pressure our government to change policies." Her chin dropped. "But it didn't work out that way. Protests fizzled. Viewers didn't care what happened halfway around the world." She puffed on her cigarette. "Eleanor Roosevelt got it right: '*Nobody won the last war. And nobody will win the next one.*'"

It was obvious Jocelyn had a fierce hatred of war. Maybe it had started with Robert, but it became more than that, until it colored every action she took while embedded in those combat zones.

"I remember my first month in Iraq. I'd scheduled a feature on the rapes which were a daily occurrence in the middle of the marketplace. I got so upset when I reviewed my copy, I vomited. My photographer had to loan me his bandana to clean up."

I couldn't picture it. My experience was limited to local scandals and misbehaving public officials. This was something else entirely.

Jocelyn made eye contact. "The savagery, the inhumanity, the pure . . . evil's the only word for it. I aired the report, and you know what happened? Nothing. People went on with their lives. No one cared."

She glanced away, her eyes damp. "I need a moment." Before I could say anything, she left the room.

Jocelyn was a paradox. On the one hand, a fiercely independent woman who'd succeeded in the rough-and-tumble world of high-stakes journalism at a time when men had all the power. On the other hand, a person who wore her vulnerability like a second skin. The tragedy she'd experienced with Robert, paired with those she'd witnessed early in her career, still lived inside her. When she came back, she held a glass of water and her eyes were clear.

"Are you okay to go on?" I asked.

"I'm fine." Short. Succinct. Shut down. Exactly what my mother would have done.

————•————

We spent the rest of the afternoon working our way through Jocelyn's time as a war correspondent, from the Persian Gulf to the Yugoslav Wars, Kenya, and later Tanzania.

"It's hopeless. It could be anything," she said.

"We might be looking for a local reporter who thought they were responsible for a story. Thought you didn't give them the credit they deserved. What if—"

Her laugh had an ironic twinge. "It's not that clear-cut. What you have to understand is in a foreign country, you depend on indigenous contacts. They're not only your translators and guides. They're also your eyes and ears in the community. There is simply no way to do the job otherwise. I was embedded in an active war zone. I couldn't stop and parse out who should get credit for what. I had the reach, the audience, and the responsibility to report on what was happening. My editor didn't care where the story came from as long as it was accurate and timely."

"You're saying you might have aired a story someone else wrote, like the troll's implying?"

"Of course not. What I'm telling you is sometimes the only way to ensure a story got told was for me to put my clout behind it. I worked for *The New York Times*, for Christ's sake. I controlled what got reported."

She was hedging. *Crap.* Yes, she'd signed up to go to the most violent places on earth. She'd witnessed the horrors people committed in the name of freedom. She'd put herself in harm's way time and time again. She'd done it to honor Robert's sacrifice. She'd done it because she loathed war. But she'd also done it for the byline, the recognition, the glory. Did that blind her to the people who might feel slighted when she didn't acknowledge their contributions?

The troll could very well be one of them.

TWENTY-ONE

Simon was due back from his honeymoon Monday, and we were still no closer to figuring out who @freethetruth was or what they wanted. Delving into her background information had helped me understand how Jocelyn might have inadvertently used another reporter's notes to shore up an article, but it didn't get us anywhere as far as stopping the pile-on of tweets, which multiplied daily. The postings divided down the middle—some folks sided with the troll, but others praised Jocelyn and railed against online jerks who tore down successful women without having the nerve to show their face.

I'd emailed Nick and asked for an update, and we'd agreed to meet at the end of the day and compare notes. As the two of us walked to Nick's private office, one of his coworkers handed him a slim manila folder. We situated ourselves at the small, round conference table.

"Please tell me you've found him," I said.

"Let's see what my guys came up with." Nick flipped

through the report, rhythmically tapping his pencil against his leg as he read, while I chewed on my bottom lip and tried to be patient. When he got to the last page, he put the report facedown on the table. "It's not good news."

"I thought with all your fancy programs and spyware, you'd locate them in no time."

He shook his head. "These are anonymous posts, meaning we can't track an IP address. Internet providers and social media sites keep a tight lid on that information for good reason. We could petition a judge to compel the ISP to give it up, but we'd have to argue there's a crime involved, and that isn't the case here."

"If we can't get the IP address, what can we do?"

"We start with the date someone first used that handle and examine their other postings, searching for geographical clues or patterns in the writing style, or cultural references. Unfortunately, we've only got the two tweets."

"Meaning there's no hope?"

"Don't give up so fast. We've barely scratched the surface. Most trolls have more than one online account. They usually have a range of profiles going at the same time. And to make themselves seem more legitimate, they have their various profiles interact with each other. They like and share their own postings, and this network of accounts acts like a group of hyperlinks, all pointing at one specific hub. Bad news is, as near as we can tell, @freethetruth only has the one handle."

"And tens of thousands of followers, myself included. So there's no information in their profile that helps?"

"What profile? There's no photo, no biography, no website link. They've blocked the location tracker and specified no contact through email or phone."

"What about likes? Wouldn't their friends like the post to boost its ranking? Could we cross-reference those people, figure out where they live, home in on him that way?"

"Again, we're talking huge numbers. And it's growing every day. So that approach will take way too much time unless our software identifies a pattern that isn't obvious."

"There has to be a way."

"Sometimes we get lucky by monitoring their responses to comments. Trolls can give away information without meaning to when they answer back. But whoever this is hasn't written a word beyond the initial tweets, despite tons of follow-up questions being lobbed at them."

"I keep coming back to one question: what's their end game?" I leaned forward. "I mean, are they after the notoriety, or do they want something from Jocelyn? And if so, what?"

"And I keep coming back to whether this *is* about Jocelyn. I mean, I don't mind her paying my fee, but it'll all be for nothing if the tweets are targeting Jesse Jackson. '*Stole your work*' could be anything from a song lyric to a sermon."

"What's next?"

"My guys keep searching. And we pray the troll gets overconfident, posts a third message, and provides us a clue. Although something tells me we're dealing with someone who doesn't make many mistakes."

"Our very own Moriarty."

"Let's hope not, or we might never catch them."

Jamal stuck his head around the corner. "I'm closing up shop. Want me to lock you two in?"

"No, we'll be leaving soon. Have a good weekend."

Nick and I stood at the same time. "How about catching an early dinner?" he asked.

My mind was elsewhere, still thinking about what the troll might be after. "I'm sorry, what?"

"There's this low-key place off Armitage with a fantastic chef. Care to join me?"

His crooked smile threw me further into confusion. I'd been so preoccupied with Jocelyn I hadn't spent much time thinking about my personal life. And here was Nick, sliding right into first-date territory with such ease. I balanced on the dating diving board, bounced up and down a few times, then held my breath and plunged in. Why not? It was only dinner.

"I'd like that."

"You can follow me in your car."

"I took the train in today."

"Not a problem. You can ride with me, and I'll run you home after."

Mother's voice rang in my head. *And then he'll know where you live. How well do you know this guy?*

I ignored her. I trusted Nick. Hell, he was the nicest guy I'd met in a long time.

———— • ————

Nick obviously came here a lot—the bartender and waitress both greeted him by name as soon as we came through the door. The manager led us past table after table of smartly dressed young couples gazing into each other's eyes over breadsticks before seating us at a secluded booth in the back. He lit a white votive nestled in an etched glass pillar, and the scent of sandalwood hit my nose. Andrea Bocelli's rich tenor voice played in the background.

We ordered a bottle of wine and an appetizer and fell into the comfortable ebb and flow of flirting. I usually hated this part of first encounters—tell me your entire life story in ten minutes, and I'll tell you mine—but with Nick, it felt effortless.

"What's your favorite ice cream?" he asked out of the blue.

I grinned. "Mint chocolate chip. Preferably while relaxing in a bubble bath reading a good novel."

"Favorite sound?"

"That's easy. The buzz of a busy newsroom. You?"

"My mom singing Irish folk songs while she's cooking." He grinned. "Favorite Star Wars character?"

"Rey, of course. Kick-ass fighter. Are you Team Han or Team Luke?"

"Han Solo all the way. When Kylo killed him—oh, wait. You saw that one, right?"

I laughed. "For a private investigator, you're not very good at keeping secrets."

"That's cyber detective to you."

This was my first real chance to talk to Nick, and I liked what I saw. With some guys, it's like pulling teeth to get them to open up, but not him. We argued over whether Matt

Smith was the definitive Doctor Who (him) or whether they should have hung on to David Tennant (me). We shared our dream vacations: winemaking in Tuscany (him) and photo safari in Africa (me). He'd taken improv classes so he could learn to live in the moment, and I'd taken tango lessons for exactly the same reason. Nick's laugh was loud and clear and so infectious, my cheeks ached from grinning. What was it Mom had said about Dad? *He made me laugh.*

By the time the bruschetta arrived, we'd moved on to more serious subjects. "You haven't said much about your family," I said. "Want to share?"

"My father's first-generation Italian, and my mother's people come from County Cork. Which in my family meant you either entered the seminary or became a cop. But I'm no good at public speaking, and guns scare me, so I opted for computer science at NYU."

"You're the black sheep."

"Hope that's not a problem."

My insides quivered. He was talking as though we were a couple. "Not at all. I love people who color outside the lines. I do it all the time." I steered the conversation again. "Did you come from a big family?"

"I'm smack in the middle of a pack of five kids. You?"

I swallowed. "An only child."

The waitress approached our table. "Ready to order?"

I handed over my menu. "The mushroom ravioli doesn't have any meat in it, right?" When she assured me it didn't, I ordered that and a small salad. Nick chose the garlic-herb linguine.

"You're a vegetarian, I take it?" he asked once she left.

"I haven't eaten meat for over a year now, ever since I saw that documentary *Chasing Ice*. Did you know methane gas is one of the major causes of climate change?"

"I'm trying to cut back on meat, but sometimes I slip."

"Sorry. I can get on a soapbox when it comes to causes."

"I find women who are passionate about causes very sexy."

My cheeks warmed. Unsure how to respond, I studied the flickering candle for a moment, then changed the subject.

"How did you wind up here in Chicago?"

"I need to work on what to say when people ask me that."

I sensed a story. "Pretend someone just did."

"Fasten your seat belt, because we've come to the point in the evening where we share our ex stories." He leaned back against the banquette. "Okay, full disclosure. The woman I was involved with got a surgical residency at Rush University Medical Center, and since I can do my job anywhere, I relocated to be with her. When we broke up, I stayed. That was two years ago." When I didn't say anything, he cocked his head. "Too much information?"

"No. I'm glad you told me."

"How about you? Simon told me you were a reporter back in New York. What brought you back home?"

It was the logical question, and he'd been up-front with me, but I still paused, not sure how much to reveal. I couldn't outright lie. That would bite me in the ass if we got involved.

"Things fell apart with my boyfriend, and I needed to put distance between us."

Nick reached for my hand. His touch surprised me, but it felt nice. "Any chance you'll get back together?"

"No chance in hell."

He gave me an impish grin. "Then there's no problem."

The food arrived, and it more than lived up to the hype. Nick took a few bites of his meal and offered me a forkful. "You've got to taste this."

I leaned forward and slurped up the pasta, closing my eyes to take in the flavor. "Umm. Delicious." But it felt as though a bit of parsley had wedged between my teeth. "Wait, did something get stuck?" I gave him my best smile-for-the-dentist grin and pointed.

"Nope. All clear. But you might want to wipe your . . . Hold on." He stuck the corner of his napkin in his water glass, leaned across, and dabbed at the corner of my mouth. A tingle traveled up my spine. His cologne was intoxicating, a blend of pine and ginger. "There. All fixed."

The evening was going so well, I decided to ask the question that had been bugging me. "When I came to your office the first time and introduced myself to your partner, he said, 'Oh, you're the one who . . .' But when you appeared, he stopped talking. What did you tell him about me?"

Nick's neck turned red, and he fumbled with his napkin. "I said I'd met this attractive woman who worked in the building and tried to chat her up, but she pretty much told me to take a hike." His eyes met mine. "I'm glad you changed your mind."

I grinned. "Me too." I tore off a piece of bread, dipped it in oil, and popped it in my mouth.

We passed on dessert but lingered over a final cup of coffee. By that time, the line of people waiting to be seated had spilled out the front door, and I realized we'd monopolized one of the restaurant's prime booths for over two hours.

"We should go," Nick said, clearly thinking the same thing. He asked for the bill, and when it came, he grabbed for it.

"How about we split it?" I said.

"I invited you, remember? But don't worry, you're on the hook for next time."

A pleasant shiver went through my core. Next time. I liked the sound of that.

TWENTY-TWO

As we headed to the car, we passed two girls strolling by, and one of them accidentally bumped into me. It was Heather Barrett, a classmate from Northwestern, and another girl I didn't recognize, arm in arm.

"Megan, is that you? What's it been, two years, three?"

"Four," I answered. "How have you been?"

"Forget me. How about you? I mean, all this stuff with your mom. I can't turn on my TV without seeing her face. It must drive you up a wall."

My gaze darted toward Nick. I hadn't told him who my mother was, and this was an awkward way for him to find out.

Heather gushed on. "God, I hope she doesn't win. I mean, the last thing we need is one more elected official pushing to overthrow Roe, right?"

My stomach backflipped as I fumbled for a response, but before I could say anything, Nick put his hand on the small of my back and threw me a lifeline. "Sorry to interrupt, honey, but Tash expected us ten minutes ago. We need to get going."

"Yes, of course. It was nice seeing you again, Heather, but we've got to run."

We'd parked a block away, and as we walked to the car in silence, Heather's chatter echoed in my ears. Nick glanced at me but didn't ask anything except directions to my apartment.

I climbed in, tucked my purse on the floor by my feet, and buckled my seat belt. "Thanks for coming to my rescue back there."

"I could tell you were uncomfortable. Care to clue me in?" When I didn't respond, he added, "You don't have to." He put the car in drive and maneuvered out of the parking space.

My shoulders relaxed. I might as well tell him. I mean, he could easily figure it out from what Heather had said. "My mother's Helen Watkins."

He gave me a blank look. "No idea who that is."

"The Republican candidate for the ninth district congressional seat in the upcoming election? It's confusing because we've got different last names. And different political views."

We hit a red light, and he faced me. "I stay away from politics as much as possible. But why didn't you mention any of this when we were sharing our family histories? Does everyone at work know? Does Jocelyn?"

"No, and I want to keep it that way."

The light turned green, and we drove on. "I'd think you'd be proud. I mean, running for Congress is a big deal."

We passed storefronts locked up for the night as I considered my response. He was right. It *was* a big deal. With all the hoopla around Jocelyn's situation, I kept forgetting that this time next year, my mother might be helping run the whole damn country instead of just my life.

When we were a few blocks from my place, I took a stab at explaining. "My mother and I disagree on pretty much everything, not to mention her candidacy means I can't get a job as a reporter until after November." I told him about my experience with Diaz.

"So that's why you're working at Arrow."

"That and a reference from Jocelyn Jones can't hurt. But if she finds out who my mother is, she might not want me around either."

We reached my apartment, and he parked in front.

I hesitated, biting my lip. "Well."

"Well," he echoed.

I faced him. "Look, I'm having a great time, and I'd invite you in for a glass of wine, but I don't want you to think—"

"No problem. One glass and I'm off. I've got a big day tomorrow."

My shoulders sagged with relief. The last thing I wanted was to move too quickly with Nick. I'd made that mistake before. We climbed the steps, and I unlocked the door. Luckily, my furniture had arrived so we had somewhere to sit.

"I'll be right back with that wine. Make yourself at home." I fled to the kitchen, my legs unsteady. Inside the refrigerator door, I found a bottle of pinot grigio I'd bought earlier in the week. I rummaged around in a drawer for the wine opener and poured two glasses, ordering my hands to stop shaking. The last time I'd been on a first date was with Luke. I took a deep breath and came back into the living room.

"How about some music?" he asked when I handed him the glass.

He played in a rock band, but that didn't seem to fit the mood, so I played it safe with middle-of-the-road mellow. "Alexa, play songs by Ed Sheeran." I sat beside Nick on the couch, our knees slightly touching.

He raised his glass. "To our first, but I hope not our last, date." We clinked, but I'd barely taken a sip when the doorbell rang. Who would drop by at nine o'clock on a Friday night? *Please don't let it be Mother again.*

It was Mateo, hands clasped behind his back. "Hey there," I said. "Shouldn't you be doing homework?"

"It's Friday."

"So it is. What's up?"

"I told my friend Ellie what you said."

"Who? Oh, yes, Ellie." I flashed to the conversation we'd had about being a feminist, about how both the coach and the class bully had told his friend she couldn't be on the basketball team.

"She asked the coach about Title IX like you said, told him he *had* to let girls play, that it was the law, and if he didn't, she was calling the newspapers. It was so cool. She did it during fifth period, and everyone in gym class clapped.

Now she's part of the team, and with her free throw, we might even win division."

I'd made a tiny difference. That was okay. It counted. It all counted.

"This is from Ellie." He held out a folded piece of yellow paper. I took it, and as I read the words, my eyes clouded over.

Nick's voice sounded behind me as he joined us in the doorway. "How about introducing me to your friend?" He must have spotted my tears because he lifted my chin, a look of concern tracking across his face. "Hey, what's wrong?"

"Nothing. I'm good." I handed him the girl's note. "Seems I'm somebody's 'roll' model." I sniffed, then grinned. "Nick, this is Mateo. He lives upstairs."

"Nice to meet you, Mateo." Nick stuck out his hand. "Glad there's someone who can watch out for Megan when I'm not around."

I lightly punched Nick's arm. "I can watch out for myself, mister." I knew Nick was trying to puff the boy up, but it sent the wrong message.

"Are you her boyfriend?" Mateo asked.

"No," I said.

"Not yet," Nick said at the same time, shooting a goofy grin my way.

"Kissing makes worms grow in your brain, you know," the boy offered out of nowhere.

Nick gave a low chuckle. "Whoa, where did you hear that?"

"On the internet. I saw pictures. They've got suckers for feet, and when you kiss, they get swooped into your mouth and crawl through your nose and into your skull and make you go crazy."

Okay, he was right about one thing. Kissing someone you liked *could* make you go a little crazy, but still. "Don't believe everything you read on the internet," I said.

"Why would they say it if it wasn't true?" Before I could respond, Mateo bounded up the stairs.

"You've got a lot to learn!" I playfully called after him.

Nick and I stepped back inside, and I shut the door. He made a remark about worms and kissing, but I wasn't listening. I was too busy staring at his lips as they moved, obsessed with how full they were. We were standing close enough for the warmth of his body to sear into mine. Did he lean toward me or was it the other way around? Before I knew it, he'd cupped my face in his hands, murmured my name, and lowered his face so our lips were only inches apart.

"You smell like spring." He tilted my chin, and I gazed into his dancing eyes. His voice dropped to a whisper, a smooth hush of silk. "Your lips are so smooth, like the petal of a rose."

I had trouble swallowing. God, this was happening. Right here. Right now. Nick Russo was about to kiss me.

He started with a slow, delicate one, a gentle caress. When I gave a slight moan, he took me in his arms, his rough stubble scratching my cheek. I closed my eyes and reached behind him, knotting my fingers through his thick, curly hair. My breath caught in my chest and my legs turned to limp noodles as he lowered his lips once again to mine. God, who knew his mouth would be so intoxicating?

I'd been kissed before, but this was different. This kiss was like standing on the ledge of a thirty-eighth-story window. This kiss was the beginning of something. I felt a rush of helplessness as his mouth met mine. I was spinning, clutching him, and then I kissed him back, a shudder running through my veins.

And that scared the living shit out of me. My brain sounded an alarm, and I backed away. What was I doing? Hadn't I learned my lesson? We stared at each other, breathing like we'd run the hundred-yard dash.

"Whoa." Nick rubbed the back of his neck. "That was some kiss."

Under-frigging-statement of the year.

His eyes held a hint of a question. "Too much too soon?"

"I'm not sure I'm ready." To what? Risk my heart? Fall in love again? Luke had never kissed me like that, not even in the beginning. Never sent me reeling. Never made me want to tear his clothes off, drag him to the bedroom, and lock the door.

Nick stood still, hands by his side, waiting for me to explain.

"The man I told you about in New York? I came home in the middle of the day and found him in bed with our neighbor."

"That explains a lot."

"You cheat on me, you're history."

He touched my arm. Gently, as if he might spook me. "I would never hurt you that way, Megan. You can trust me."

"Give me time to get there, okay?"

"Don't worry." He lifted my hand and kissed my palm, and the wave of heat rushed back. "Take as long as you need." We stood close, eyes locked, foreheads touching. "I'm going now. I'll call you tomorrow."

He left, and I'd gone to the kitchen to put the wine back in the fridge when the doorbell rang again. I opened the door a sliver. Nick was back.

He was right, I shouldn't have sent him away. I needed to plow through my fear and take a chance. "Missing me already?" I asked, a bubble of a laugh slipping out.

"It's not over."

Of course it wasn't over. It had barely begun.

Then I saw the phone in his hand. It had been three weeks since the first posting, one week since the last one. So much for hoping this would all go away.

"What does it say?"

Nick held out his cell. "It posted an hour ago."

Nothing stays hidden forever, Jocelyn.
Guess you thought you got away with it.
You didn't. It's plagiarism and I've got proof.

I couldn't take my eyes off the screen. Now we knew. The troll was targeting Jocelyn. And now the charge was out in the open. Outright plagiarism. The worst accusation you can fling at a respected journalist.

Nick tucked the phone in his jeans. "There's more."

"Meaning?"

"She tweeted back."

"Shit."

"You got that right. And it's hitting the fan."

TWENTY-THREE

Jocelyn hadn't minced words.

Stop hiding behind a handle,
you sniveling scumbag.
Show yourself or shut the hell up.

Her public jab reignited the scandal, and Twitter blew up. Eight hundred retweets in one hour. Soon celebrities from sports figures to Instagram influencers to movie actors chimed in, sending the views into orbit. *BuzzFeed* and *Jezebel* printed a recap of all three tweets and speculated on the fallout. Many of Jocelyn's fellow journalists decried the troll for hiding behind a pseudonym and flinging innuendos with no proof. But just as many called Jocelyn a rich, white newscaster trying to stifle a whistleblower.

Interviews we'd booked for next summer were suddenly cancelled—a *Vanity Fair* cover story, a feature in *Time* magazine, a scheduled appearance on *Ellen* and another on

Jimmy Kimmel Live—on the off chance the accusation was true. There was even speculation on social media that her publisher might cancel her book deal altogether, although others took a more jaded view: the public, ever hungry for scandal, might buy even more copies of her memoir, scouring the text to spot her lies.

Simon came back from his honeymoon on Monday and called Nick and me into his office.

He leaned on the corner of his desk, arms folded tight across his chest. "This is one hell of a mess," he ranted, lines of worry tracking across his forehead. "The only way I see to salvage this situation is proving there's no basis for the allegation. Jocelyn insists it's not true, and she's damn convincing. I talked with a lawyer and a police detective, and they both say since there's no overt threat or blackmail demand, there's nothing they can do."

God, it just got worse and worse.

Simon went on. "Jocelyn has okayed a blank check, says to do whatever we think best. If we find out the accusation is false, Frank's prepared a full-scale counterattack we'll release to the media. If we find out it's true, meaning the troll's got hard evidence, well, we'll know Jocelyn lied to us, and I'd have serious reservations about keeping her on as a client. But let's not get ahead of ourselves. Nick, any progress identifying the person behind this?"

"We've got a lead we're following. One of my guys planted a reply to the troll's last post, suggesting he had evidence against Jocelyn too, and whoever this is clicked through. It's a rookie mistake, and they fell for it. That click transferred them to a dummy site we set up and let us capture their IP address. They're in a residential area south of St. Louis."

My hands tingled. It was the break we'd been waiting for. But the troll had been so careful up until now. Had they changed tactics, wanting us to find them? Were we playing into their hands?

"A PI colleague in Missouri, Harry Egan, is narrowing it down further. So now that we've got a location, what's the plan?"

"Jocelyn and I discussed that early on. She trusts you, Megan. She was adamant that once we found the troll, she wanted you personally to meet with them. Pretend you work for an independent news magazine, promise you'll put them on the cover. Say you can get them on TV. But first, insist on verifying the story. That way, they'll have to show you the evidence."

A bead of sweat crawled down my spine. "I can't."

His face darkened. "Why the hell not? Weren't you an investigative reporter back in New York?"

"Yes. But I never went undercover. I'm not an actress. He'll spot me."

"Come on, Megan." Nick gave me his best smile. "Do it for Jocelyn. We'll team up. I'll say I'm your staff photographer. We'll catch the bad guy, make him confess, and save the accused from being burned at the stake."

A fitting analogy since this was a modern-day witch hunt. No presumption of innocence. No opportunity to defend herself against the frenzy of a mob with pitchforks, out for blood. Granted, after what Jocelyn had told me, I knew there was a chance she'd reported a story using someone else's research. But there was a big difference between not sharing sufficient credit with a member of the team and outright plagiarizing another journalist's work. She deserved the benefit of the doubt until we had real proof of what happened.

As for this plan Simon and Jocelyn had hatched, I had misgivings. "What if they ask for identification? This is someone hiding behind a Twitter handle and purposely covering their tracks. How likely is it they'd confide in two strangers who show up at their front door unannounced?"

"Your Facebook profile says you're a reporter, so you're good," Nick offered. "I'll create a fake name for myself, print a bogus ID, and rig up a web page showcasing my photographs. Hell, I'll even loop a camera around my neck and take a few shots while we're there."

I ignored the fact Nick had checked me out on Facebook and concentrated on the matter at hand. "What if he asks how we found him?"

"How about the truth?" Nick answered. "We'll show Harry's business card and say our newspaper hired him once we tracked the IP to Missouri."

"Why are we making this so complicated?" I asked. "Why don't we admit we work for Jocelyn? Tell the troll if she inadvertently didn't credit them on a news story, she wants to correct her mistake."

"In other words, ask the troll why we can't settle this like reasonable adults?" Simon raised his eyebrows and exchanged a look with Nick, not bothering to hide his sarcastic tone. "If all they wanted was an acknowledgement, they'd have contacted Jocelyn directly. They're using words like *revenge, violated, angry*. Does that sound like someone who wants to play nice?"

"I'm with Simon on this one," Nick chimed in. "It's gone too far at this point. I don't see anyone settling for an apology and a shared byline. Plus, if we say we work for Jocelyn, they could go online and accuse her of trying to silence them, which means even worse PR than she's got now."

What they proposed made sense. So why was a bell ringing inside my brain, warning me we could be walking into a trap? Before I could counter with another argument, Simon slapped his knees and stood.

"It's settled then. Nick, get the two of you booked on a flight, and I'll let Jocelyn know. And Megan?" He pointed a finger at me. "Convince her to stay off the internet and let us handle this. She's making it worse by goading the guy."

Once we got clear of Simon's office, Nick pulled me into an empty corridor and wrapped his arms around me. "I've been thinking about our kiss the other night."

I glanced over my shoulder. "Shh. Someone might hear you."

"You think people don't already know?"

"I want to keep my work life and my private life separate. Particularly from Simon."

Nick dropped his hands down. "Got it. The last thing I want is you feeling uncomfortable. But I'm pretty sure

Simon wouldn't have a problem with us dating. After that whirlwind marriage of his, I think he's a romantic at heart."

————————•————————

Two hours later, Nick sent an email. "No name yet, but Harry's getting close. Pack your bags. I'll be out of the office the rest of the day meeting with other clients, but I've booked us on a flight tomorrow afternoon at one. I've alerted Simon."

A frisson of excitement started at the base of my neck and traveled through my limbs at breakneck speed. My legs fidgeted under the desk. In another day or two, we'd have answers. Hopefully, Jocelyn's reputation would be vindicated, and I'd write the story of how we'd traced the troll. No newspaper editor in his right mind would turn down the scoop, no matter who my mother was.

I'd be back in the game.

"Yes!" I pumped my fist in the air and danced around in my chair.

The murmur of voices brought me out of my reverie. Several fellow employees stood in clumps, whispering and nodding in my direction. Before I knew it, Jocelyn materialized at my cubicle, her face lit up.

"You found him."

I stood. "Somewhere near St. Louis."

"Thank God it's over."

"It's not over yet. We'll know more once we've interviewed them. But we're getting there."

"I'm depending on you, Megan. Don't disappoint me." She put her hand on my shoulder and stared at me for several moments before she spoke again. "I'm so proud of you. And grateful. You never once doubted me. That kind of loyalty deserves a reward. Let's go to lunch and discuss your future."

A harrumph sounded from the other side of the cubicle, but I ignored Zachary. This was shaping up to be one of the best days of my life, and I'd be damned if I'd let him ruin it.

"Let me ask Simon, make sure he's okay—"

"Nonsense. You have to eat, don't you? Don't worry. I'll get you back in plenty of time."

Before I could catch my breath, she hustled me into a taxi waiting outside, and we took off for the Walnut Room.

———◆———

We turned onto State Street, and I glimpsed the Great Clock, the iconic eighteen-foot verdigris symbol jutting out from the corner of Marshall Field's, the renowned department store in the heart of the Loop. Back before it was rebranded as Macy's, this had been a favorite destination for my mother and me. In August every year, we rode the El downtown to this store and bought back-to-school clothes and Frango mints. I hadn't been back in years.

As we strode through the art deco atrium, I tipped my head back and gawked at the Tiffany mosaic ceiling six stories up. A crush of shoppers eddied around me:

women pushing strollers with sleeping toddlers, teenage girls giggling as they fingered the sample perfumes, a well-dressed older woman examining a display of scarves.

"Stop dawdling. We're running late." I followed Jocelyn into the elevator, and we rode to the seventh floor. "I've asked a friend of mine to join us."

The hostess led us to a table beside the center fountain where a slightly overweight older gentleman with a full head of silver-gray hair and steel-rimmed glasses stood and greeted us. Before he straightened the sleeves of his pin-striped suit, I caught a glimpse of engraved cuff links. Jocelyn embraced him.

"God, how long has it been since we've seen each other?" he said, holding her at arm's length.

"At our age, that's an indelicate question," she replied, a twinkle in her eye. "Abbott, let me introduce the young woman I told you about. Megan Barnes, this is Abbott Sinclair."

"Mr. Sinclair." I glanced at Jocelyn, searching for a clue about who this man was and why he'd joined us, but her gaze remained squarely on him.

"Abbott knows everybody who's anybody in the newspaper business in Chicago," Jocelyn explained.

We took our seats and ordered, and I watched in silence as these two old friends reminisced about various times their paths had crossed: working on the ERA ratification, covering the 1984 Democratic convention, in the wings at Obama's victory speech in Grant Park. I spent my time half listening, half gazing at the familiar gleaming wood paneling and chandeliers which sparkled like crown jewels around the cavernous room.

This restaurant had been a December tradition. My mother and I would shop on Michigan Avenue, visit Santa, and finish up in this room, where I'd drink hot chocolate and eat sugar cookies and gaze in wonder at the magnificent forty-foot-high Christmas tree with its thousands of flickering lights.

"We must be boring you with all our shop talk," Mr. Sinclair said.

I tuned back into the conversation. "Sorry. Reliving holiday memories of this place. Did I miss something?"

"I was singing your praises to Abbott here, telling him how much you've stood by me through this ordeal. How we're this close to exposing the bastard."

I hadn't traced the troll. That had been Nick and his team. But I had provided Jocelyn with moral support, so I guess that was enough in her book.

"You should sue him for damages, Jocelyn," Sinclair suggested. "It's unconscionable he could walk away scot-free." His voice was deep and sonorous, his manner that of a world-class orator.

Abbott Sinclair was obviously a one-percenter, used to taking down anyone who got in his way. Jocelyn was part of his circle; ergo, she was innocent and should fight back.

"Hmm. I've been so preoccupied with shutting him down, I hadn't thought that far ahead, but you could be right. What do you think, Megan?"

"It might be better to—" I started, but Sinclair cut me off.

"Call that producer at CBS you're tight with and go on *60 Minutes*. He'll jump at the chance to haul this guy's ass over the coals. If you ask me, the time's ripe for an exposé of these cyber creeps—you'd be the perfect poster child."

My stomach twisted into a knot. I wanted to tell him to shut up. He knew nothing about the situation, yet here he was, advising Jocelyn to do a full-court press against her attacker instead of letting the story die a natural death and moving on with her life. Granted, the troll had hurled ugly barbs across cyberspace. But after what I'd learned about Jocelyn, there was a chance there was a grain of truth in his innuendos. It was way too early for Jocelyn to get overconfident and launch into full revenge mode.

"I'll think about it, Abbott. But that's not why I brought you two together today. After Megan finishes her assignment for me, she wants a job as a reporter at the *Tribune*." She winked at him. "Any chance you can help her?"

Sinclair glanced my way, and his gaze moved slowly from my eyes down my face to my breasts and back again. A nasty, metallic taste crawled up the back of my throat. So that's the kind of *mentor* he was. Pervert. I considered walking out, but that would embarrass Jocelyn, so I stayed put. Evidently, she hadn't noticed his leer.

"Aren't you poker buddies with an editor there?" she asked.

She'd told me *she* was the one who knew the editor. He licked his lips and took a sip of water. "Yeah. It shouldn't be a problem getting her an interview with Peterson. You married, Megan?"

I swallowed wrong and had a coughing fit, covering my mouth with my napkin. What kind of a question was that?

Jocelyn spoke up, but not before giving Sinclair a half laugh. "Abbott, you know you can't ask that nowadays."

He scowled. "God, spare me the PC crap." His tone reminded me of barbed wire. "It's a legitimate question. I'm asking whether she's willing to travel or needs to stick close to home."

I fixed him with a stare. "I worked three years as an investigative reporter in New York, so I know what the job entails. No need to worry."

"Good, good. Well, as soon as you're free, give me a call." He pushed his business card across the table with a grin. I left it sitting there during the meal, and eventually, when Jocelyn left for the restroom, I dropped it in a dollop of salad dressing on my plate as they cleared the dishes.

I grinned as I imagined it tossed out with the rest of the day's garbage.

———————•———————

Jocelyn and I waited at the corner of State and Randolph for our Uber. The wind whipped strands of hair across my face as I pulled my jacket tighter around my body and shoved my hands into my pockets. They didn't call this the Windy City for nothing. Jocelyn said something, but the clatter from the overhead train drowned her out. "I'm sorry, what was that?"

She leaned in closer. "Keep Abbott's card in a safe place. He's someone you should know. He can open doors."

Her words shocked me. "There's no way I'd ever ask that man for a recommendation. He looked at me like I was a slab of meat, all laid out on a platter, ready for him to take a bite."

"So what? Use that. Flirt around with him until he gives you what you want."

"How can you say that?" I shot back. "I won't work with misogynists."

"Oh, spare me the righteous indignation," she said.

Two young guys on skateboards raced by, almost knocking Jocelyn down. She scowled at them as they disappeared around the corner. When she spoke again, her tone was sharp as a tack. "You may not approve, but journalism's a cutthroat business. You use what you've got."

Our ride pulled up to the curb, and we climbed into the back seat. I thought our conversation was over, but Jocelyn launched into a lecture as soon as we took off. "You need to realize when you get up in the morning, your one goal is to land the story before the other guy. It's not about how talented or how driven or how smart you are or the fact that you're a woman. It's about whether you'll do whatever it takes to succeed. The world won't hand you opportunities. You have to take them. The sooner you learn that, the better off you'll be. You'd be surprised at what I had to do to get where I am."

I hadn't seen this side of Jocelyn before—opportunistic, selfish, bordering on ruthless. She might have fraternized with the likes of Abbott Sinclair to advance her career, but I wasn't going to.

"Things have changed," I shot back. "What about those lawsuits at Fox News? Harvey Weinstein? Women don't have to put up with that kind of sexual harassment anymore. I'd think you'd be happy about that."

"Don't be naïve." Jocelyn booted up her phone and glanced through her messages. "The people in power always come out on top."

A reporter's role was to make sure that wasn't true. To hold people with money and influence accountable for their actions. How could Jocelyn have functioned as a journalist all these years if she truly felt the powerful controlled the game board?

I didn't believe that for one minute. If I did, I'd never have become a journalist.

TWENTY-FOUR

Nick and I caught the afternoon flight from Midway and landed in St. Louis an hour or so later. On the way to the car rental, Nick phoned Harry. "That's great news," I heard him say, followed by, "Got it. Thanks for the tip." When he hung up, he briefed me. "He hasn't pinpointed the exact location yet, but he should have an answer in the next few hours. So unless we've miscalculated somewhere along the way, we'll knock on the troll's door early tomorrow. Sure you don't mind camping out in Harry's spare bedroom?"

"It'll save time if we don't have to drive back and forth to a hotel. What was that last part about?"

"Seems there's been massive flooding up and down the state all summer, and the Mississippi River's at critical levels. He told me an alternative route to take."

I transferred my duffel bag to my other shoulder and checked my messages, expecting Jocelyn might have phoned. But so far, she was sitting tight.

Nick filled out the rental paperwork, and we found our way to a cherry-red Camry parked nearby. I tossed my stuff in the back, climbed in the passenger's seat, and fastened my seat belt. As Nick drove out of the terminal area and onto Highway 170, I drummed my fingers on the side console.

"Still nervous about our cover story?"

"We could make everything worse."

His hands tightened on the steering wheel. "I'm not concerned about us. What worries me is the troll saying he's got proof of the plagiarism. There might be notes they kept, eyewitnesses, video, who knows what? If that's true, what are we supposed to do? Jocelyn's our client. Talk about a rock and a hard place."

I still believed Jocelyn. But then, I knew her backstory, which I hadn't shared with Nick. To him, she was just another client. I took a sip from my water bottle.

"No matter which way it goes, at least we'll have answers," I said.

———•———

Harry lived southwest of downtown St. Louis in a suburb called Kirkwood. We drove through a bustling downtown district, past a historic train depot from the 1890s, and eventually arrived at a one-story family home with slate-gray shingles, a front lawn dotted with mature birch trees, and green window boxes filled with lush geraniums. A man, square as a spark plug with a nose that looked as though he'd been in a fight or two in his day, burst out the front door and greeted us. The stubble on his jaw and his long ponytail had flecks of gray, and he wore faded Levi's, Birkenstocks, and an old Pearl Jam T-shirt. Harry didn't fit my idea of a top-notch investigator, but Nick had vouched for him, told me the two of them had met at an industry convention last year and the guy knew his stuff. That was good enough for me.

He showed us to our respective bedrooms, and after I'd freshened up, I joined the two of them at a dining room table littered with stacks of papers, several printouts of area maps, two laptops, and what smelled like the remains of a tuna fish sandwich.

"What have you found out?" Nick asked.

Harry shuffled through folders and consulted his notepad. His voice was raspy, like a long-time smoker. "I took the IP address your guy gave me, and like you said, it's located in a twenty-mile radius south of the city. Of course, it's a big territory, and since we've got no legal standing to force the ISP to turn over the actual location, I called a guy who knows a guy whose cousin hangs out on the dark web."

"And?" Nick pressed.

"I've got an address."

Nick looked puzzled. "How did—"

"You don't want to know."

"Please tell me you didn't break the law."

"Skirted it. Hey, you said money was no object, and a woman's reputation was at stake."

"Okay. Let's hear the rest of it."

"I researched the property rolls. It's a single-story house owned by Amina Petrovic. Odds are she lives there, although she might be renting it out. Anyway, I figured we'd start with her, so I did a deep dive into her background. She's the widow of Mak Petrovic, a reporter who died during a bomb attack in Bosnia in 1995. Not long after that, this Amina and her three-year-old child Dragan fled to England and eventually to the United States. There's a large population of Bosnians in St. Louis, so they may have family here, but we haven't confirmed that. I don't know for sure, but my gut tells me Dragan may be living in the house with the mother. Which points to one of them being our troll, most likely the kid."

I did the math. The troll harassing Jocelyn was someone my age? "What have you found out about this Dragan?" Nick asked.

"No record of employment I could turn up. Zilch. Which looks suspicious. God, where are my manners?" Harry stood up. "What can I get you guys—soda, beer?"

"I'll take a glass of water, thanks," I said.

"How about you, buddy? Fair warning. In this town, it's Budweiser or Budweiser."

Nick laughed. "Then I'll take a Budweiser."

Harry disappeared into the kitchen, and when he returned with the drinks, he and Nick scrolled through all the social media sites, searching for any further hits on Dragan or Amina. I retreated to the living room and worked on my own, scouting for mentions of anyone with the same last name. Before long, I'd discovered scads of photos and postings of a middle-aged man named Ivan Petrovic.

Resembling a modern-day Paul Bunyan, he sported a shaved head and sleeves of tattoos down both arms. He rode a Harley and worked as a bricklayer.

Somewhere along the way, I'd forgotten the KKK might be involved in all this. When I dug deeper, I found a whole slew of recent reports on Klan activity in and around the area. They'd distributed hate flyers during the Ferguson incident in 2014. Two years later, there'd been a murder case involving the assassination of the head of the Traditionalist American Knights an hour south of St. Louis.

Was I seeing connections where there weren't any? I took my laptop to the dining room and walked the guys through what I'd found, filling Harry in on what Zachary had overheard back in the beginning. "What do you think?"

"No offense, but it sounds like a half-baked conspiracy theory to me," Harry said. "But hey, you two are driving the bus. If you think there's something there, I'll dig into it." He stood. "I'm taking a break." He grabbed a pack of cigarettes off the table and went outside.

Once the screen door slammed, Nick stroked my arm. "You're connecting dots that aren't there. Fact: there's an active KKK presence in Missouri. Fact: this Ivan doesn't resemble your average middle-aged schoolteacher, and he's got the same last name as the troll. And he's bald. And working-class. And he likes motorcycles, same as hundreds of other guys, including Harry. None of that makes him a Klan member."

He was right. When had I started stereotyping people? A good journalist doesn't make assumptions. They follow the facts. Ever since Luke had blindsided me, I'd begun to doubt everyone. I needed to stop jumping to conclusions. I'd done that with Nick too, at first. Thank God he'd given me another chance.

"Come here." Nick gave me a quick, fierce kiss.

My pulse skyrocketed at the feel of his lips on mine, but I didn't kiss him back. "Tempting, but we need to focus."

Harry rejoined us, and after another half hour of research, we cleared the dining room table, and Harry cooked up a batch of fish, sautéed vegetables, and a summer salad. I was too keyed up to eat much. Tomorrow we'd face the troll, and I was on high alert, like a feral cat stalking a mouse through a cornfield. One slip, one false note, and we could send our prey scurrying back into their hole.

I tucked my laptop under my arm. "I'm gonna turn in."

"I'll be doing the same once Harry and I finish going over a few things. Hey, don't worry. Our cover story's solid. We'll be fine."

I gave him a weak smile, grabbed more water from the fridge, and retreated to my room. But I couldn't sleep. Staring at the ceiling fan rotating lazily over the bed, I retreated into half-conscious dreams where a faceless troll greeted Nick and me at the door with a sawed-off shotgun and ordered us off the porch. That startled me awake, and one more time, I scrolled through dates and events from Jocelyn's memoir in my head, correlating them with what Harry had shared about the Petrovic family's history.

And a click went off, so major I threw back the covers, switched on the desk lamp, and found the notes I'd stored on my computer. I opened a new browser window, typed into the search box, and prayed it wasn't true.

But it was.

Hot fire and brimstone.

I threw on a robe and searched for Nick. I found him dozing in front of the television, the flickering light casting an eerie blue glow over his face. Harry was nowhere in sight. I shut off the set, flipped the lights on, and shook him awake, anxious to share what I'd found but also upset at its ramifications.

"Change your mind about wanting company?" he drawled, rubbing his eyes.

"It's worse than we thought." I flipped to the pages of my notebook where I'd copied the timeline of Jocelyn's career. "From late 1994 until the end of 1995, Jocelyn was based in Sarajevo."

"So?"

"It's the same year Dragan's father died. And during that time, she filed a whole slew of reports on the massacre of thousands of Bosnian Muslims in the Manjaca prison camp. Don't you see? This Petrovic and Jocelyn were both reporters, and they were both in the same area of Bosnia at the same time. That's the story the troll's accusing her of stealing."

"And that makes it worse why?"

"She won the Pulitzer for it."

TWENTY-FIVE

The three of us took off in Harry's car at nine the next morning. The GPS took us through affluent neighborhoods with well-manicured lawns and sidewalks. Then the area morphed. The houses became run-down with roofs in need of repair, junked cars in the yard, and the occasional fluorescent-yellow foreclosure notice stuck in the front window. Eventually we pulled up in front of a small ranch house with an attached garage and a striped awning which shaded a large front window. The gray paint had peeled in spots. The lawn was overgrown, and the shrubs along the walk had withered.

My pulse echoed in my ears. We were so close. *Please don't let this be a dead end.*

"Are you sure this is it? It looks deserted," I said.

"Someone's been out here today." Nick pointed at the leaning mailbox with its raised flag. He swiveled to face me. "Let's go meet our troll, Watson."

I was still anxious, but once I heard his calm, reassuring

tone, my neck muscles relaxed. We left Harry behind in the car, and the two of us climbed the front steps. Nick rang the bell, and after several minutes, a moonfaced woman wearing a faded chenille bathrobe and scuffed slippers opened the door. Blue veins showed through her skin, and the plastic tube in her nose led to an oxygen tank trailing behind her. She peered at us through smudged bifocals.

I gave her my best smile. "Ma'am, we're sorry to disturb you, but we're here to speak with Dragan Petrovic. Are you his mother?"

She scanned the street and glared back at us. "Who are you and what do you want?" Her heavily accented voice barely registered above a whisper as she steadied herself against the screen.

I flashed my fake ID. "We're reporters. We think your son can shed light on a story we're investigating."

The woman's racking cough lasted half a minute before she wiped spittle from the sides of her mouth with the handkerchief tucked in her sleeve. "Wait here," she spat out, and slammed the door in our faces.

I raised my eyebrows at Nick. "Well, that went well."

"Patience, grasshopper."

Some time passed before the door opened again. This time, we were greeted by a young woman with a pale pink complexion, all wide-eyed and innocent, her banana-blond hair shoved under a grungy baseball cap. She could pass for a teenage boy, all sharp angles, no makeup, no breasts or hips to speak of. She wore a T-shirt with the Slashdot logo, black leggings, and ballet flats. A smattering of freckles danced across her nose. Exactly how many family members did we have to work our way through before we got to the troll?

"My mum said you wanted to see me," she replied, her voice deadpan, not even a hint of curiosity. I detected a hint of a British accent.

"We must not have made ourselves clear. We're here to see Dragan Petrovic, who's been tweeting as @freethetruth." I assumed the girl would step aside and reveal her burly brother standing in the wings.

"How did you find me?"

My brain did a backflip. This was the troll? Our cover story flew right out of my head, but luckily, Nick came to my rescue.

"We're investigative reporters. Finding people is what we do. Can we come in? There's a chance we can help each other."

She leaned against the doorframe. "Who'd you say you were again?" On her left wrist, she sported a braided friendship bracelet with a tiny charm of a fire-breathing dragon.

Pull yourself together. I stuck out my hand. "Megan Barnes." Dragan's left eyelid twitched as though my name rang a bell. Had she recognized me from somewhere? "And this is my photographer, Nicholas Ricci." I handed over my ID, praying it would appear legit. The girl scrutinized it and did the same with Nick's credentials.

I wanted to make doubly sure we had the right person, so I questioned her one more time. "You're Dragan Petrovic?"

She shrugged. "People always get the name wrong. Rhymes with ray gun." She opened the door and ushered us into a living room the exact opposite of my mother's pristine home. The tiny space smelled musty and had a claustrophobic feel, with three overstuffed chairs, a massive burgundy couch, and five curio cabinets packed with family photos, vases of plastic flowers, and assorted china figurines. A shabby calico cat raised its head as we came inside, then curled back beneath the window air conditioner. Mrs. Petrovic was nowhere to be seen.

I fell back on the cover story we'd practiced. "I don't know if you've heard of Consortium News, but we're—"

"I'm familiar with the paper. You must be here to talk about Jocelyn Jones." When Nick and I exchanged a look, she added, "The only tweets I did under that handle were about her."

Dragan motioned us to the adjoining dining area, and we sat at a long rectangular table covered with a lace cloth. "Why did you send the posts?" I asked.

"What I said. Justice."

"You believe Jones plagiarized a story?"

Dragan's eyes narrowed. "I know she did."

"Well, we'll need more than your reassurances if we're going to help you get a wider audience for your claim. Which story are we talking about, and what proof do you have?"

"Before we get to that, what's your offer?"

A spasm hit between my shoulder blades. *Note to self: do not underestimate this girl.* I snuck a peek at Nick. This wasn't part of the plan. We'd assumed the troll would be a nerdy guy tweeting from his bedroom who'd jump at the chance to talk to a national news outfit. But this girl was smart. Savvy. Prepared.

I leaned forward and gave her my best sales pitch. "If what you say is true and if you give us an exclusive, we'll feature you in a lead article and publish all the hard evidence you share with us in full." When she didn't react, I sweetened the pot. "We also have overseas affiliates who'll publish your claims that same day. You'll have coverage in every major country in the world."

Nick jumped in. "And we'll station someone at Jones's house and confront her when the story breaks. Get her unfiltered reaction before she hides behind lawyers and PR experts."

"You're thorough, I'll give you that." Dragan's voice had not changed from its steady, low-pitched monotone. I couldn't get a read on her. On the one hand, she hadn't thrown us out of the house. On the other hand, she hadn't jumped at our offer either.

She stared at me as if daring me to up the ante. My mouth was dry as a stone. I swallowed and improvised. "And once we run it, every other news outlet in the country will want a follow-up interview with you. You'll be famous, at least for a while."

"I don't care about fame. How much money will I get?"

My body tensed. We'd never discussed a pay-off for the troll, but Jocelyn might agree if there was no other way to keep this girl quiet. Even if her evidence was sketchy, she could ruin Jocelyn's reputation if she kept this up, particularly if this all tied back to the prison camp exposé. How much money was Dragan talking about?

From the appearance of the house, she and her mother were struggling to scrape by. Plus Mrs. Petrovic, given her physical condition, must have hefty medical bills. Was it possible this whole mess was nothing more than a garden-variety blackmail scheme? Or worse, an elaborate trap? What if we revealed the fact that Jocelyn sent us, agreed to a payoff, and later this girl broadcast the deal all over the internet as proof her accusation was valid?

My voice turned prickly. "You said you wanted justice. Now you're after a bounty?"

Nick touched my arm. "We don't pay our sources." I picked up his cue. *Don't get emotional. Stick to the story.*

Dragan didn't blink. "Relax. I'm not after money. I wanted to make sure you're legit. Come with me." We trailed her down a hallway, and I pictured a bedroom filled with vintage comic books, rock-band posters, and a cubbyhole with a laptop computer. The rabbit warren of an internet addict. Instead, we followed her into a dim basement. At the bottom of the stairs, she flipped on a bank of light switches.

"Holy shit," Nick muttered under his breath.

The open space took up the entire length of the house and resembled the inside of a small space station. Video screens covered the entire back wall, displaying news feeds from CNN, MSNBC, and Fox. A gray laminate work surface in the shape of a horseshoe sat in the center of the room, supporting a grid of five additional monitors, each as large as my TV set at home. On the screens, I glimpsed Excel spreadsheets, statistical grids, detailed maps of cities, and scans of newspaper and online articles. A phone system with three extensions sat on one side, several printers on the other, and a single black leather chair with a high foam back stood behind the desk like the throne of an imperial commander.

One screen on the end showcased a panoramic view of Dragan's front yard, including real-time footage of Harry, leaning against his car, smoking a cigarette. She must have seen us arrive, sent her mother out first, might even have run the license plate before she answered the door. Well, so what? Harry was a licensed investigator. It made sense we might have hired him.

"What is this place?" whispered Nick, his eyes as wide as a kid's at Christmas.

Dragan chuckled under her breath. "My own private domain. Mum's set in her ways. Doesn't even have a cell phone, much less a computer. So I limit my design aesthetic to the basement. This way." She led us to an oblong table which could have been a futuristic work of art with neon lights glowing beneath an opaque crystal top. The four scooped seats appeared to float in midair. I instinctively put my hand out for leverage before I sat.

"What in the world do you do?" Nick said. I'd had the same question but had been too off-balance to ask.

"I own the patent for a computer program that gauges what voters think about particular political candidates. I pair that information with news feeds, the opposition's positioning, and past election data, and advise my clients how they can tweak their campaigns to optimize results." She smiled. "And thanks for asking. I love showing off."

Nick's gaze darted every which way. "It's frigging awesome. So it's just you and your machines?"

Dragan chuckled again. "I'm not *that* good. I've got a network of coders and data analysts scattered across the world, most of them working out of their basements too. But that's off the record, okay? My clients think my company is housed in a high-rise in downtown Manhattan. They'd have a coronary if they knew the recommendations came from dozens of gig workers lounging around in their pajamas."

This girl was some kind of genius. Which meant her tweets were part of a meticulous and well-planned strategy. Doubts crept in. What exactly did she have on Jocelyn?

"I'm curious. Are you by any chance related to Ivan Petrovic?" I tried for casual, but the tone came out wrong. Too direct.

As sudden as striking a match, Dragan's whole demeanor changed. Her eyes moved back and forth as though connecting dots. "Why?"

She obviously didn't want to talk about him, but I pressed. "We stumbled on him during our research and noticed he lived here in St. Louis. Is he connected to this?"

"He's my father's brother. My family's originally from Sarajevo, but I assume you already know that. Ivan lived with us there before he joined the resistance. And when Mum and I moved to America, he joined us." She addressed her next words to Nick, ignoring me altogether. "He's like a lot of people who lived through the war, my mum included. They don't trust people. They've learned even their closest friends might betray them. If you want to talk to him, I'll make the introduction. Otherwise, he'll shut the door in your face."

I made a mental note. Research Ivan further. Follow every lead, no matter how small.

"How about we get back to business?" I said. Did this person have actual evidence against Jocelyn, or was this all hearsay?

Dragan answered. "Should I go ahead and launch into the story?"

"That's fine. And if it's okay, I'm going to take notes." I flipped open the notebook Mom had given me and clicked open my pen.

"Or I could give you a copy of the tape I'm making." She pointed at a CCTV camera mounted nearby with the light on. A chill raced through my body. It was as though Dragan had expected us to knock on her door and planned accordingly.

She leaned back in her chair, tucked one ankle behind the other, and began. "My father was Mak Petrovic. He worked as a reporter at a local Sarajevo newspaper, but he got laid off and took a job as a freelance stringer for the Associated Press. This was in 1995. The war had been raging for three years by then, and life was extremely difficult. We lived in a tenement building with a dozen other families. Food was scarce. No one could play in the streets because of the constant bombings. Of course, I was a baby, so I don't remember any of this, but Mum has told me stories."

Dragan's voice was casual, but what she was describing was horrific. Her mother's demeanor at the front door made sense now. A woman who'd lived through years of brutal civil war would be on alert for anything or anyone who might threaten her family.

"One day, my father came home all excited. He had a lead on an important story, one that would make his reputation, but he had to leave us and travel to the prison camp in Manjaca. My mother begged him not to go, but he argued that if he filed an eyewitness account of the atrocities happening there, he could get his old job back. Maybe even get hired full-time by an international news outfit. We could move to England where my mum had family." She paused. "Anyway, he packed his suitcase and caught a ride to the countryside with a friend. Two weeks later, that same friend knocked on our door and told us my father was dead."

I grew increasingly uneasy. I'd been right. This tied back to the prison camp.

"But if your father died before he filed his article, it's anyone's guess who he interviewed or what he found out," Nick said.

Dragan ignored his comment and continued. "Late last year, I decided to research both my father and my homeland. I scoured the internet for stories about the Bosnian War, and it wasn't long before I ran across Jones's reports, and, in particular, her coverage of the July massacre at the same camp my father mentioned in his letters. When I asked my mum about it, she teared up. She rummaged around in her bedroom closet and brought out a shoebox with three notebooks inside."

Up until now, this had been a fascinating tale, but one with no concrete evidence backing it up. Her mention of the notebooks changed that.

"The same friend who'd told us about Dad's death had given her his journals, and she'd carted them around for years—first to England, then here to the States. I read them through. It didn't take an expert to catch it."

I had a handle on what had occurred back then, both from my sessions with Jocelyn and from reading her memoir. "Okay, it's feasible Jones could have filed reports about that camp at the same time as your father," I countered. "But that doesn't prove she plagiarized his work. There must have been a half dozen reporters sniffing around, sending in stories to their respective news organizations. Stands to reason they'd cover many of the same events."

Dragan's expression changed from guarded to downright stony. "That doesn't explain how certain phrases, entire sentences, even whole paragraphs written by two separate people could be identical."

Don't take what she's saying at face value. Dig deeper.

"You're saying Jones got hold of your father's notes and, in the middle of a tumultuous war, copied them, then snuck them back into his belongings where this friend discovered them after he was killed? That doesn't sound plausible." Had we come all this way to listen to a conspiracy theory from a highly intelligent but obviously overzealous daughter?

Dragan's jaw clenched. "I agree with you. That scenario doesn't make any sense." She leaned forward. "But what if Jones collaborated with my father—who, incidentally, was an educated man and wrote and spoke fluent English—and they shared what they found down to the smallest detail? What if she heard he'd been killed, took his report, combined it with her own, and pretended it all came from her? Didn't share a byline. In fact, didn't even mention him. Particularly after she won every major prize in journalism for her *brave reporting.*" She put the last two words in air quotes.

Dragan and I glared at each other.

Don't flinch. She's bluffing.

The air was thick with tension. Luckily, Nick sensed it and jumped in. "Why don't we all take a breath? I mean, we're all on the same side, right? Don't take Megan's remarks the wrong way, Dragan. She's asking the same questions our editor will ask us. We should take a look at those notebooks."

He was right. The notebooks were the crucial component here. Without planning to, he and I had fallen into good cop, bad cop roles, but it seemed to be working.

"I'll give you one to send to a lab, or whatever you do, to verify the paper and the ink and confirm the timeline. And I'll share the side-by-side comparison I did, pinging between the complete set of my father's notes and what Jones wrote. It'll save you time."

Dragan had an answer for everything. Her whole story was well polished. Too polished? When we got back to Harry's, I intended to comb through those transcripts and search for any inconsistencies.

"What's your email?" Dragan asked.

Luckily, we'd anticipated that and rigged a fake Gmail account ahead of time which routed to Harry's computer. I tore a sheet from my pad, wrote the address, and Dragan tucked the note in her pocket. She crossed the room, opened a drawer, and returned with a well-worn journal the size of a small paperback book. "This is the one that details conditions at the prison camp. It's hard to decipher my father's scribbles, but at least you can see I'm not making this up."

The pages were yellow and faded, and the handwriting cramped. There were margin notes, some barely legible, and the inside front flap showed her father's name and the year 1995 written in black ink.

I worked to steady my breathing. This looked legit. What Becca said earlier echoed in my ears. What if the most logical explanation is, she *did* steal a story?

Nick glanced over at me and raised his eyebrows. "Pretty convincing all right." He unwound the camera from around his neck. "Do you mind?"

"No pictures of me, please."

What was that about? Did she value her privacy and not want her picture online, or was there more to it? Nick zoomed in and took a half dozen snapshots of both the outside cover and the handwritten pages.

But something still didn't add up. "Your mother showed you these notebooks a while ago. Why did you wait until now to accuse Jocelyn?"

"Mum's reluctant to dredge up the past. It's filled with painful memories for her. But the doctors say she's running out of time. I want her to see my dad get the credit he deserves before she dies."

"Wouldn't it have been easier and quicker to call Jones, give her a chance to make it right, instead of making your accusation so public?" I asked.

"I tried that. I reached out through her publisher. Sent emails, left voice messages. Nothing. So I resorted to Twitter, but only used her initials in the first two posts. I didn't want to hurt her, only get her attention. When she didn't bother to respond, I decided, *sod this*, and sent the third tweet revealing her name. But instead of apologizing, she lashed out. The only thing she understands is flat-out war."

I knew those initial messages never got to Jocelyn. One of Kate's assistants read them, wrote Dragan off as a crackpot, and threw them in the digital trash can. We'd spent time searching for the troll when all we had to do was go through the records at Jocelyn's publisher. But I still had my doubts. This story fell into place down to the last detail. Like a well-rehearsed stage play.

"We'll need to have our fact-checkers examine all this before we publish," I said.

"You've got doubts. I get that. I'm challenging a powerful, admired icon. Maybe this will convince you." She grabbed her cell out of her pocket. "My father recorded this a few days before he died." She punched a button and held the phone up so we could hear.

I held my breath as a man with a thick accent spoke, followed by a woman speaking in clear, succinct tones. The conversation lasted several minutes as the two talked about an upcoming interview, made plans to meet the next day, and laughed together like old friends.

And suddenly I was slipping, falling, swirling, grabbing debris, clutching rocks as I careened down a mountainside. Because Dragan had told the truth about one part at least. There was no mistaking the second voice on the tape.

It was Jocelyn.

TWENTY-SIX

"**J**eez. Then what happened?" Harry asked. While he drove, Nick filled him in.

"She loaned us one of the notebooks and gave us a copy of the tape so we can run a voice match. But that's a formality. It's obviously her."

I huddled in the back seat, questions cycling through my brain. Nick swiveled around. "You okay?"

Was he joking? The shock of hearing Jocelyn's voice coming out of that phone had upended me. All the evidence Dragan gave us pointed to one conclusion—Jocelyn had neglected to give Petrovic credit for his contributions, or even worse, she'd outright stolen his entire story. But if Luke had taught me anything, it was that people could lie to your face and get away with it. Was there another explanation?

"Didn't it seem a little too pat?"

Nick frowned. "You didn't believe her?"

"An attractive young thing instead of a sweaty troll? A

dying mother wheeling around an oxygen tank? That setup in the basement? None of that struck you as odd?"

"It *all* struck me as odd. But you have to admit, her facts hang together."

"Nick, think about it. Does Jocelyn seem like a person who would do this?"

"I've never met her. My impressions are all filtered through what you've told me. But if you ask me, nobody gets to her position without trampling a few people along the way. And in the middle of a war zone? Who's thinking clearly when bombs are exploding around you? So no, I'm not automatically assuming she's innocent."

What if this whole story was an elaborate trick? But Dragan hadn't asked for money. If profit wasn't the motive, what did she stand to gain? Was it as simple as she said, that all she wanted was justice?

"I'm going to dig around more."

Harry turned to Nick. "Where'd you leave it?"

"That we'd contact our editor and get back with her in a few days. That means you need to send the notebook to a local lab tomorrow. She promised not to talk to any other media sources until she heard back from us. I'll update Simon and see what he wants to do next."

I flipped through my notes. "What about her uncle, the guy I showed you online? She got nervous when I mentioned him. There could be something there."

Nick shook his head. "You're a drowning woman clutching at wisps of seaweed."

"I'm not abandoning Jocelyn based on that girl's say-so."

But it wasn't only Dragan's word against Jocelyn's. There was the notebook and the tape. I couldn't ignore what appeared to be hard evidence.

By the time we got back to the house, Dragan had sent over the analysis between her father's notes and the article Jocelyn had filed. I studied the screen, eyes darting back and forth, foot tapping under the table. Try as I might, I couldn't spot any major discrepancies between the two texts. Other than two verb changes (*hurried* instead of *ran*, *asked* instead of *questioned*), they were the same. One detail Jocelyn had written—how she'd fallen outside the camp, slipped on something wet, and discovered it wasn't mud covering her hands, but blood—stood out like a flashing stop sign. Mak had written the identical detail in his notebook, word for word.

Nick read over my shoulder. When I got to the end, he gently placed his hand on top of mine. "That's it, then. She didn't write any of it. She outright copied every word he wrote, didn't even try to cover her tracks. I'm sorry. I know you believed her."

I wandered to the kitchen and poured myself a glass of water, but couldn't swallow, my throat as tight as a coiled rope. When I returned to the front room, I reexamined the transcript, hoping I'd notice something we'd missed, desperate not to believe what I now knew was true.

It wasn't long before Nick appeared in the doorway. "I touched base with Simon. He wants us on the first plane home, says this has gone on long enough. He'll brief Jocelyn on what Dragan has and get her focused on damage control.

As for me, I'll write up a final report and then I'm washing my hands of this whole mess."

"You thought she was lying from the beginning."

"No. But I sensed she knew more than she let on. Hey, being a cynic is part of my job description. Yours too."

My byline carried weight, she'd said. I understood what might have happened. She'd been under a deadline. The genocide going on in that camp had to be exposed, and she was in the position to reach a worldwide audience. Petrovic was a no-name freelancer writing about events in his own backyard.

Nick hadn't heard how Jocelyn's father had betrayed her, didn't know about Robert and how he'd died. If I told him now, he'd say I was making excuses. I waited a beat before answering.

"I'll concede Jocelyn and Mak knew each other in Bosnia, and they were both at Manjaca at the same time. But for the sake of argument, let's say Dragan, maybe with the help of her uncle, reverse engineered the notebook. Downloaded Jocelyn's report, copied it line by line, and distressed the pages so they'd look old. And then pretended *her* version was the earlier one. Like a conjuring trick. What if—"

Nick took hold of both my hands and squeezed. "Megan, stop. You're spinning a wild fantasy so you don't have to face the truth. Listen to me. Nobody is behind this. Your hero worship of Jocelyn needs to end right now. Put on your reporter hat. She plagiarized the story." His expression was laser-focused. "It might be the one time in her career she did anything like this, but it doesn't matter. It was wrong. It was unethical. And no amount of spin will change the facts. You know it in your heart, but you don't want to admit it. Cut yourself off from her before you turn into someone who's lost all sense of the truth."

Bile rose in my throat. Nick was implying Jocelyn had been lying this whole time, that I'd been so blinded by my admiration for her I'd lost my perspective. Journalists call it confirmation bias, the tendency to believe information that validates our worldview.

A steel vise slowly squeezed my skull. I grabbed the notebook and my laptop, retreated to my room, and locked the door. Sitting on the bed, I worked my way one more time through the parallel narratives, concentrating not on the words themselves but the cadence, the tone, the idiosyncrasies.

In school, I'd learned every writer has their own distinct voice, as unique as a fingerprint. From reading the memoir and viewing old YouTube videos, I was familiar with Jocelyn's—short, succinct, an almost staccato style. Heartfelt? Yes, but not flowery, not nuanced. Petrovic's writing was different. For one thing, since English was his second language, his word choice was often unusual. His sentence structure was more complex, more formal. He wrote longer sentences, used more metaphors and allusions in his writing. There was also an emotional element to his observations. The atrocities he described felt personal.

I ran my hand over the faded ink in the journal. The pulse of the writer's heart beat beneath the flowing script.

When I came to the end, I discovered a pocket on the back flap I hadn't noticed before. Inside was a Polaroid snapshot of a young woman in front of a church, wearing a white peasant blouse, a kerchief tied over her hair, holding a baby. I pictured Mak gazing at his wife and child every night, memorizing their faces, whispering their names as he drifted off to sleep. I stared at the woman for a long time, remembering the frail ghost who'd greeted us this morning at the door.

Her eyes pleaded with me. Stand up for my husband. He died in the fight for justice. Please. After all these years, get him the credit he deserves.

The fan whirled overhead as thoughts bounced around my brain like billiard balls. When I couldn't lie still any longer, I went to the bathroom and splashed cold water on my face until my cheeks stung. I reached for a towel, and that's when I caught sight of myself in the mirror. Someone I didn't recognize stared back.

As a reporter, I'd always depended on my brain—to ferret out the clues, to make sense of the facts, to fit the puzzle pieces into a final pattern. But this time, my brain had let me down. I'd ignored the inconsistencies, pooh-poohed the connections, followed innuendos and vague hints because I didn't want to find the answer. Because in my gut I knew the answer.

Through the walls, I heard Harry and Nick talking, probably saying out loud what I'd been afraid to—that Jocelyn had committed plagiarism, that she'd have to give back the Pulitzer, that her reputation would never recover.

The bedroom was stuffy, as though all the oxygen had escaped and I couldn't get air into my lungs. I threw on my running shoes and rushed out the front door, not even stopping to tell Nick where I was going. The sun was disappearing over the horizon, throwing the unfamiliar neighborhood into shadow as a light mist coated my hair.

My emotions raced along with my legs. I'd been dead wrong. I'd gone to bat for Jocelyn, believed in her, defended her not only to Nick but the entire team at Arrow, Stein, Becca, even my mother.

And all along, she'd been lying. Right to my face.

I jogged faster. Faster. Up one street, down another. Anger, mixed with hurt, swelled inside me like an expanding balloon, ready to burst.

Blind to where I was going, I rounded a corner and slipped. I fell forward, catching myself only seconds before my face hit the pavement. I'd scraped skin off both my palms and bruised my right knee in the fall. Tears sprang to my eyes, and my lungs burned fire. I stumbled to the curb and buried my head in my hands, blood roaring in my ears.

Nick had nailed it. I was lost. I flung back my head and sobbed into the darkening sky.

And then I heard my mother's voice from years ago, one of her crazy mixed metaphors. "You can't put the eggs back in the carton after you've served them for breakfast. What's done is done. Figure out how to make it right."

I stood, my legs heavy as concrete, and made my way back.

TWENTY-SEVEN

When I reentered the house, Harry and Nick were plunked on the sofa in the den, beers in hand, feet on the table, watching the Cardinals/Brewers game. I hovered in the entryway, my injuries hidden in the shadows.

Nick turned around. "Come join us." He patted the space beside him.

I stayed where I was. "Too slow-paced for me."

"But that's what's good about it." He stretched his arms above his head. "I booked a flight out at eleven o'clock tomorrow morning. We need to leave by eight."

My gut twisted. I was out of time. I thought about telling Nick my plan but decided it was my problem to solve. "I need to go out. Where are the rental car keys?"

"On the table near the front door. Where do you need to go? I can drive you."

I waved away the suggestion, improvising on the spot. "Watch your game. I need to swing by CVS for some tampons." I knew that would make him back off.

"There's one about five miles away on the left," Harry said. "You can't miss it."

"See you in a bit." When I got in the car, I punched Dragan's address into the GPS.

———•———

A black SUV was parked in her driveway. Damn. I'd counted on her being alone. I parked on the street and rang the bell. Dragan startled when she saw me. "This is a surprise."

"Can we talk?"

She stepped aside and let me in. Dragan's mother sat at one end of the dining room table and Ivan Petrovic at the other. Dragan introduced her uncle and his wife and children—an attractive middle-aged woman with deep-brown skin, a teenage boy, and two twin girls around eight years old. The aroma of roasted lamb lingered in the air, and a serving of baked apple crisp sat at each place.

"I didn't mean to interrupt your family dinner. I can wait in your office."

"Nonsense. Make yourself at home." Dragan's earlier adversarial attitude toward me had taken a one-eighty. She disappeared into the kitchen and returned a minute later with another dish. One of the little girls retrieved a chair from the living room, and everyone scooted closer to make room for me.

All I could think as I spooned the dessert into my mouth was what an ass I'd been. Here I sat, chatting with the guy I'd painted as the grand pooh-bah with the Klan, the mastermind behind an elaborate plot to discredit Jocelyn. In reality, he was a friendly, quiet man wearing a Bob Marley T-shirt, sharing a family meal.

My cell phone buzzed, and I snuck a peek. It was Nick asking if I'd gotten lost, but I ignored him. Once everyone had finished their dessert, Dragan and I retreated downstairs.

Instead of making excuses, I dumped the entire story in her lap, including my background as a journalist, how I'd wound up working for Jocelyn, and how the owner of my PR firm had sent us. And I didn't stop there. I said Jocelyn had painted herself as a victim, insisting she'd never stolen a story, and I'd believed her. That I'd come to St. Louis expecting I'd find a vindictive troll who didn't have a shred of actual evidence.

I glanced at her, but her face was a total cipher and I raced on. "When I left here today, I tried to convince myself that you and Ivan had concocted a giant scam to wreck Jocelyn's reputation. But after we got back, I examined the notebook and the transcripts and listened again to the recording, and well, I believe you. Jocelyn plagiarized your father's story."

"Why did you come here tonight?"

"First, to apologize for how I treated you. Second, to say I can help get your father the recognition he deserves. If you'll let me." I shut up and waited for her response.

Seconds ticked by. Finally, she spoke. "If you're trained as a journalist, why would you accept Jones's story before you'd researched all the facts?"

It was a moment before I answered, and when I did, I had to force the words out. "Because she was someone I admired." My voice broke. "She treated me as though I was special, and I loved how that felt." And the realization hit me like a blow. I'd been looking for that kind of validation from my mother my whole life and never got it. But I didn't say that last part out loud. I could barely admit it to myself.

"At least that's honest. And as long as we're leveling with each other, I lied to you too."

I stiffened. I'd offered myself up as an ally, and now she was admitting she hadn't told me the truth? My pulse quickened. "What does that mean?"

"I knew Jocelyn wouldn't tolerate my taunts for long once I printed her name. She's a smart woman. Savvy. I figured it was only a matter of time before she traced me, so I made a move. I responded to a few replies on Twitter that looked like plants. Obviously, yours was one of them."

"I noticed you had a reaction when I introduced myself. You'd researched Jocelyn's contacts and knew she'd sent me."

"No, that wasn't why. I remembered seeing the name Megan Barnes before. After you left, I checked my feed. Your mother's name popped up, along with specific references to her daughter. I dug around on the internet, and that's when I discovered your affiliation with Arrow. Once I examined their roster of clients, the pieces fell together."

Information was coming so fast, it was hard to process. "Can we go back? What's this about my name showing up in connection to my mother's run for office?"

"She's getting flak from her party's bigwigs about why you're not out campaigning for her. Her platform centers on family values, but she's divorced, and her only kid is MIA. Her lead's eroding."

I knew the voters would notice I wasn't on the campaign trail, but I'd convinced myself it wouldn't make that much difference. Now I realized I'd seriously jeopardized my mother's chances, the same way she'd hurt my own job prospects.

"Anyway, that's how I realized who you were, and that Jocelyn must have sent you," Dragan shared. "Which meant I'd gotten her attention, which is what I wanted all along."

"You're definitely on her radar now. But don't think that means she'll admit her guilt. She's much more likely to want to buy you off."

"I told you before, I'm not for sale. The only payment I'm interested in is her giving my father credit for this story. His name should be listed on the Pulitzer alongside hers."

She acted like that was a simple request. "I'd love to tell you she'll do that once she sees your evidence, but I doubt it. It's a lot more likely she'll search for ways to discredit both you and your father and raise questions about the legitimacy of the notebooks. She's got powerful friends. And a long reach."

A muscle throbbed in her throat. "I've come too far to stop now."

Jocelyn had a determined enemy in this girl. Instead of declaring all-out war, maybe I could negotiate a cease-fire. "Why don't we take this one step at a time? Let me see if I can get her to agree to your terms. If she does that, we can settle all this amicably."

"I'm okay with that. I don't need to destroy her. But what if she doesn't agree?"

We both knew what I'd suggested was a long shot. "I'll write the truth and cite the notebook and the recording as evidence. We'll get your statement notarized and publish the story. Once the major news services pick it up, that's the version the public will remember, no matter what excuse Jocelyn concocts later."

Dragan rose and paced the room, shaking her head. "I appreciate your offer, but wouldn't I be better off taking my evidence to someone here in St. Louis? You work for a PR firm. What newspaper will listen to you?"

That did make more sense from where she sat. But I couldn't stand the idea of another reporter getting this scoop. I wanted my byline on this.

"The article will carry more weight if I write it because I've worked alongside Jocelyn and gotten close to her." And I knew who would help me. That editor at the *Register*, Alex Diaz. He'd jump at the chance to publish an important story like this. "And don't worry," I reassured her. "Jocelyn isn't the only one with friends."

TWENTY-EIGHT

D ragan and I agreed on a plan. We'd give Jocelyn one last chance—admit Mak was the co-author of her prison camp report and contact the Pulitzer committee to add his name to the award. In exchange, Dragan wouldn't give any interviews or cause Jocelyn any further trouble. But if Jocelyn persisted in denying Mak's contributions, or worse, threatened retribution against Dragan, I'd write the story and expose the whole mess.

"You're awfully quiet," Nick said on our way to the airport the next morning.

I hadn't slept much the night before, too preoccupied with my next steps. I wanted to keep my arrangement with Dragan a secret from Nick until I met with Jocelyn. "You know she'll go ballistic when she hears about that tape."

"Let Simon handle her."

"No, I'm the one who met Dragan and saw the evidence. Plus, a part of me understands why she did it. If I can reach her, maybe she'll admit the truth."

Nick squeezed my hand. "I wouldn't bet on it, but it's nice of you to offer her a last chance."

He dropped me off at my apartment around two. "I've got to contact a few of my other clients and touch base with Simon, but I'm only a phone call away. Want me to come by later with takeout?"

It'd be heavenly to spend a quiet evening with Nick and forget about what I had to do, but Dragan and her father deserved more. "I'll take a rain check. I'm going to turn in early and forget all about this until tomorrow."

I leaned over and kissed him, then scooted inside my apartment and took a long, hot shower. I'd lied to Nick. The truth was I'd be up all night working on the story. Much as I hoped Jocelyn would tell the truth once she heard what Dragan had to say, a part of me feared she wouldn't. Which meant I needed to file my article right away before Jocelyn got a chance to spin her version of the facts.

I emailed Simon, told him I'd be working from home that afternoon, then texted Jocelyn about meeting the next day at her place. The hours ticked by without a word from either of them.

I made a few notes but found it hard to concentrate, like knowing a bomb is going to explode but not knowing when or where.

At six thirty, the doorbell rang. When Nick had dropped me off, the day had been clear, but now, when I glanced out the window, I saw the weather had changed: the leaves on the massive oak tree flapped in the wind and the sidewalks shone wet in spots. A streetlamp illuminated a taxi parked at the curb, its wipers going. The doorbell rang again. I peeked through the peephole, and every muscle in my body tensed.

Jocelyn.

Funny thing about role models. Once you draw back the curtain, they aren't that different from the rest of us. She looked like every other celebrity caught in a scandal: haunted, hollow-eyed, desperately looking for a way out.

I opened the door, and she barreled past me like a one-woman SWAT team. My temples throbbed. Where did she get off, barging in like she owned the place? "Don't mind me, I just live here."

"What did he say?" she demanded.

My mind wasn't firing on all cylinders. "Who?"

"The damn troll, of course. Isn't that where you've been?" she spit out.

Jocelyn still assumed Dragan was a guy. I needed more time. "Can't this wait until tomorrow? I only got back a few hours ago, and I'm wiped out."

Her gaze turned stony. "You? I haven't slept in thirty-six hours." And she looked it. Her eyes were bloodshot and puffy, her hair matted, her skin gray as ash. I smelled the booze sweating through her skin, and a button on her blouse hung by a thread. "Why didn't you keep me posted? I left messages while you were gone, but you ignored me."

"I assumed Simon would update you." Actually, I'd purposely ignored her emails ever since we'd met with Dragan. I moved a stack of books from a chair and set them on the nearby coffee table. "Why don't we sit?"

"I'm not staying that long. What did you find out?"

I sighed. She wasn't going away. "Well, first off, the troll isn't a guy. She's a woman my age by the name of Dragan. She was born in Bosnia."

I watched closely, but she didn't so much as flinch at the mention of the country, only laughed as though she had no idea what I was talking about. "That's rich. I'm in a catfight with a kid young enough to be my granddaughter."

She said it with such disdain, I winced. "She doesn't want a fight. All she wants is justice for her father. His name was Petrovic. Mak Petrovic." I pronounced the name slowly, once again keeping my eyes glued for any sign of recognition. She seemed genuinely clueless. Either Jocelyn was a fantastic actress, or she'd wiped out all memory of Mak.

Her eyes narrowed to slits. "You sound as though you've switched sides."

"Maybe I'd better start at the beginning."

"Maybe you'd better," she said, crossing her arms.

She wanted to intimidate me, remind me what I had to lose if I betrayed her. That might have worked a month ago, when I was a baby moon orbiting the magnetic field that was Jocelyn Jones. But now I knew who she truly was, so I was through backing down. I swallowed the words I longed to scream: *I'm not the one at fault here.* Instead, I ran my tongue over my chapped lips and described the meeting with Dragan, the story of Mak's last days, and then the notebook, the transcript, and that irrefutable recording.

Her lips tightened as soon as I mentioned the tape. "You listened to it?"

My hands shook, but I held her gaze. "It's you."

"How much will it cost to keep her quiet?"

"She's not doing this for the money."

"She's got a pulse. That means she's got a price."

I braced myself against a chair. "Yes, she does. Tell the truth."

Outside, the weather had turned nastier. The front window frames rattled, and the pelting rain sounded like someone throwing pebbles against the glass. Thunder rumbled, and chimes clanged from my neighbor's porch. Jocelyn paced the room, hands clenching and unclenching. I could almost see inside her brain as she ran through different scenarios, examining all the angles. Hopefully, she'd realize she needed to admit what she'd done and concentrate on dealing with what came next.

She faced me, her eyes like laser beams. "Okay. This girl has proof I knew her father in Bosnia. I don't remember him, but it's possible. I met dozens of locals while I was there."

"You didn't just know him. The report you filed dovetails with what he wrote in his notebooks. Word for word. Admit it. Not to me." My tone softened. "To yourself."

She didn't move, didn't say anything. I knew Mak wrote the story based on my analysis of the manuscript, but for some reason, I wanted to hear her say it. "No one else is here. Level with me. You copied his account, didn't you?" I willed myself not to blink. An invisible trip wire lay between us. Once it was triggered, everything would be set in motion.

My insides felt hollowed out, but I returned her stare.

"I—" Her voice cracked, and she broke eye contact. She glanced away, her eyes flicking from side to side.

I pressed. "All those years ago, that moment right before you filed your story, you had the choice. You could have pulled back the copy, listed his name right alongside yours, and you chose not to." My voice cracked. "What went through your head? Tell me. Help me understand."

After a minute, her expression changed from frightened to deadly calm. We locked eyes again, and this time, she didn't hesitate.

"I'm the one who wrote that story. Petrovic had nothing to do with it," she stated in a clear, steady voice.

But we both knew it was a lie.

Which meant if I were any kind of journalist, I had to ignore my admiration for her and write the truth, even though it would destroy her.

"I answered your question." Her angry voice cut through the room. "Now what?"

A ball-peen hammer smashed against my chest, right behind my lungs. "You didn't even cover your tracks. You copied what he wrote down to the last comma."

"Stop saying that!" Her face reddened. She lunged at me, clamped her hand around my arm, and dug her nails into my skin.

I pulled away, but she held on, so close I could hear her labored breathing.

"Let. Me. Go." I drew the words out, my teeth gritted.

When she didn't move, I added, "Right now."

She staggered back, visibly shaken, and brushed her hair back from her face. "I apologize. I don't know what came over me." Her voice changed. Now it was soft and soothing, like the siren's song right before she dashes your ship on the rocks. "You've been incredibly loyal to me, and I'm grateful. But you're out of your depth negotiating with this blackmailer. It would be best if I meet one-on-one with this Dragan and convince her it's not in her best interest to cross me." She scanned the room as though I had the girl hidden behind the sofa.

I willed myself not to look at the kitchen table where the notebook sat in plain sight next to my bag. "I can't believe you did this. It's the bedrock principle of journalism—you don't take the work of someone else and pass it off as your own." My words stuck at the back of my throat. "But I'm not telling you anything you don't know."

I'd tripped the wire, and now there was no going back.

The corner of her mouth twisted, and her face reddened. "Where do you get off, lecturing me on my profession? I'll have you know that by the time I was your age, I'd profiled the governor of New York and exposed a corruption scandal at the Pentagon. Where are your award-winning articles, Megan? Your scoops? Face it, you're a nobody."

The hammer in my chest hit a final time. So many people had warned me—Simon, Zachary, Becca, even Kate that night at the party. But I didn't listen. I'd convinced myself I was different. Special.

Turned out I wasn't.

"You're one to talk. You used me to puff up your ego,"

I said. "I was your own personal lapdog. I came when you called. I attacked anyone who threatened you. I all but wagged my tail when you gave me a compliment."

"And you filled the role impeccably, my dear. That day at the rally? You grabbed your chance, glommed onto me. You came to my house and pressured me for a referral, and when I wouldn't agree, you accepted a job you weren't qualified for to get close to me. Don't think for one minute I didn't notice you at the women's conference, leveraging our connection so you'd seem more important."

Her words stung. Because I knew they were true.

"If you don't admit what you did, Dragan's given me the go-ahead to publish the story. And it's not her word against yours. There's the matter of the evidence." Which was inches away from us, hidden in plain sight.

"You wouldn't dare. You're bluffing."

For weeks now, I'd questioned Jocelyn, heard her secrets, and observed how she acted under pressure. I'd learned her history from Stein. I'd read her memoir. I'd seen how she manipulated Sinclair.

I understood her.

She sat on the top rung of her profession with a Rolodex of influential friends. She could blackball me from any newspaper job I went after. She truly believed I'd never stand up to her. Which meant I had the advantage.

Because she'd failed to understand me.

"We don't have anything left to say to each other," I said.

"You have no idea how big a mistake you're making. I can be a dangerous enemy," she hissed.

"I'm not afraid of you." I sounded confident, even though the hairs on my arms stood up.

"Oh, no? Don't underestimate me. And by the way, don't bother going into work tomorrow. I'm calling Simon and telling him to fire you." She whirled and bolted out of my apartment, holding her purse over her head as she scurried to the taxi.

I stood in the entryway until the cab disappeared. What had I done? Would Jocelyn dig up dirt on me? Although really, there was nothing she could find except my firing in New York, and she already knew about that. No, she was a woman with everything to lose, backed into a corner, throwing out idle threats to intimidate me.

I went inside and poured myself a glass of wine. As I sat motionless on the sofa, I unconsciously played with the necklace around my neck, the one Jocelyn gave me. What had she said that night at the party? We each have two sides. Yin and yang. Light and dark. We have to constantly battle so one doesn't overpower the other.

I walked to the bedroom, unfastened the clasp, and tucked the necklace at the back of my jewelry box. I lifted out the gold chain from my mother and slipped it back on.

Then I logged on to Arrow's server and quit my job.

TWENTY-NINE

I wrote until two in the morning, fingers flying over the keys, and took the story to Diaz the next morning. When I entered the newsroom, he was hunched over his desk, tie askew, rubbing his right shoulder as though in pain. The last time we talked, he'd told me if I turned up a scoop, I should bring it in. I was about to make his day.

He must have sensed me hovering in the doorway because he glanced up. "I remember you. Cornered me in the rib place. Barnes, right?"

"Megan. I've got an article here I need you to publish."

"Your timing sucks. The midterms are three weeks away, and I'm buried. Can it wait until after the election?"

"No, it's got to be now. But trust me. You want to be the paper that breaks this story." I handed over the folder and watched as he read.

When he got to page three, his eyes widened. "Jesus, kid. Are you sure? You've got proof? Because there'll be blowback, I guarantee it."

"I've got the notebooks, the recording, and Dragan's statement. There's no way she can wiggle out of it."

"This will destroy her. Do you want that? I mean, isn't she your—"

"She needs to admit what she did. I'm not the one responsible. I'm just the reporter."

"Well, we'll need to cross our *t*'s and dot our *i*'s on this one." He gathered my pages and tucked them back inside the manila folder. "I'll run this by our legal team. Forward the lab report when it comes through and get me a copy of that tape. We'll need to verify Jones's voice."

"How long will all that take?" Jocelyn's threat still rang in my ears. If I gave her too much time, she might turn up an angle to shut down Dragan.

"Are we working against a deadline here? I gather Jones doesn't know you came here today?"

"I told her I'd publish the story. She doesn't know when or where."

"Okay, I'll push. But it could be a week or two. We're a small paper, so we can't afford a lawsuit. I'll keep in touch. Go home and get some sleep. You look like crap."

My shoulders tensed. A week? This was my breakthrough story, the one that would relaunch my career. I'd fantasized Diaz would snatch it from my hands, run into the newsroom, and yell, "Stop the presses!" and that my byline would be splashed across the internet in forty-eight hours.

"Rush it if you can."

"Of course. And Megan? This is great work. You should be proud."

I *was* proud. If only I hadn't had to tear down a woman I cared about in the process.

Nick called on my way home. "I stopped by your cubicle, and Zachary told me you quit."

"Jocelyn came by last night. It didn't go well."

"Why didn't you call me? What's going on?"

I'd set the plan in motion, so there was no reason to keep Nick in the dark anymore. "Come by after work and I'll tell you about it."

"Chinese or sushi?"

"Surprise me."

———————◆———————

When I got home, I phoned Dragan, told her Jocelyn had refused to admit to stealing her father's story, and that my article was in the hands of the editor I knew.

"I'm glad we offered her the chance. But my time's running out. My mum isn't responding to treatment, so I have to put her in hospice soon."

"I'm so sorry. I'll stay on top of it." I fiddled with my hair, winding a strand around my finger. "There's something else you should know. Jocelyn's last shot was a thinly veiled threat. Will you back out if she turns up anything about you or your family?"

"I wouldn't have started down this road if I didn't intend to see it through. What about you?"

"There's nothing she can threaten me with. Hang in there. It shouldn't be much longer."

———•———

As far as Nick was concerned, he'd been hired to find the troll, and he'd done that. I knew he'd be upset when I told him about teaming with Dragan behind his back, about my confrontation with Jocelyn, and about submitting the story. I was sure he'd tell me in no uncertain terms that I should have stayed the hell out of it. That this fight had nothing to do with me.

But that evening when I filled him in, that wasn't his reaction. "Your quitting Arrow makes perfect sense now. After all, Jocelyn's PR campaign was your only assignment."

I dug into the fried rice, sipped the sake, then shoved a forkful of egg foo young into my mouth and chewed.

Nick pointed his chopsticks at me. "God, I can't believe how gutsy you are. This is major."

I swallowed, then dribbled duck sauce across my egg roll. "Let's see how brave I am if Jocelyn follows through on that last barb."

"Can you think of anything unpleasant she could turn up?"

"I've been asking myself that same question ever since last night. I told her about a time I shoplifted when I was a teenager, but that's hardly a major crime. I'm only twenty-five. Not nearly enough time to seriously screw up my life."

"It'd be a risk on her part too. Even if she found something, you could turn it around and reveal her blackmail scheme in a follow-up article, which would make her look even worse." He poured another cup of sake for both of us.

"You're right, but I'd still be exposed. I can't think of anything she could find, but who knows? She's a smart lady and a hell of an investigative reporter."

"You need to warn Dragan."

"Already done. She's as determined as I am. I do hate the way it's ending, though." I dug into the Szechuan broccoli, which was spicier than usual. My eyes started to water, and within seconds, I was coughing my lungs out. Once I'd recovered, I poured both myself and Nick a glass of water.

"You know, these last few months, there were times I pinched myself, amazed I was working side by side with the famous Jocelyn Jones. I never imagined we'd wind up enemies."

"You did everything you could to help her. Even after we heard the tape and pretty much knew she'd lied, you kept looking for a loophole."

I did. I'd idolized her, and it had blinded me to who she was. I tried to imagine what my life would have been like if I hadn't gone to Northwestern that day, hadn't encountered that skinhead, hadn't ever met Jocelyn Jones.

I suppose everyone's life is filled with moments like that, events that spin your life in an entirely different direction. The biology class where I'd first met Becca. The day I'd discovered Luke had cheated. The night I'd seen my father in a parking lot, kissing a woman who wasn't my mother. But fate sent those moments my way. I didn't want a life where things happened *to* me. I wanted to be the one in charge.

I'd accused my mother of treating me like a child, but could I blame her? I'd run back to Chicago the minute my life got tough. I'd jettisoned my career and settled for the first glamourous job that landed in my lap. I'd avoided my mother instead of searching for common ground between us.

If I wanted to be treated like a grown-up, I should probably start acting like one.

I'd made a start. I'd found an apartment of my own. I'd stood by Becca when she needed me. And when I'd realized Jocelyn had lied to me, I'd swallowed my pride and teamed up with Dragan to print the truth.

Jocelyn might have been a lousy role model, but she'd taught me one thing: go after what you want. I studied Nick, who sat across the table from me. The guy who spotted me alone at the picnic and put me at ease. The colleague who located the troll. The friend who made me laugh so much it hurt. The lover whose kiss made my blood race through my veins.

Nick, who wasn't *exactly* like me, but a *lot* like me. Very close. Close enough.

I dropped my chopsticks, reached for his hand, and led him into the bedroom.

———— • ————

The next morning, I fixed us each a cheese and spinach omelet, and after breakfast, walked him to the door and kissed him lightly on the lips. "Thanks for a great evening."

He shot me a flirty grin. "Don't forget this morning."

"No, I remember." I smiled. "Very clearly."

He shifted his weight from one foot to the other. "Megan, I—"

I put my finger to his lips. I didn't want to talk it to death. I wanted the excitement of not knowing exactly what was happening to last a little longer.

"No, let me say this," Nick said. I waited, expecting a not-so-subtle innuendo. "I've been thinking. Would Jocelyn go after someone close to you? I mean, your mother's vulnerable, isn't she? What with the election and all? And what about that friend you've mentioned, Becca?"

My stomach dropped like a broken elevator. It made sense. If Jocelyn got desperate enough, she might do anything. Giving her more time was not a good idea. I should push Diaz, get that story published.

"Sorry, but it's better if you're prepared," he said.

I squeezed his arm. "Let's hope it doesn't come to that. I'll call you later."

He was almost to his car when he spun around. "I almost forgot. I love your freckles!" he yelled, loud enough to alert the neighbors. And I knew he didn't mean the ones across my nose.

"*Now* is he your boyfriend?" Mateo hooted from across the street where he was shooting baskets with another neighborhood boy.

"Yes, I am, and don't you forget it," Nick shouted back at him as he flashed a thumbs-up.

I wrapped my arms around my body, thinking about last night, a smile spreading across my face as I eased my front door closed.

THIRTY

I hated all the waiting, but I couldn't do much until I heard from Diaz. I spent three straight days cleaning every available surface in my apartment, binge-watched the first two seasons of *Breaking Bad*, and scrolled through a month's worth of friends' Facebook posts, obsessing over when my article would hit.

When Nick had questioned whether Jocelyn would come after my mom or Becca, I'd dismissed it. But the more I thought about it, the more I realized I wouldn't put anything past her if she got desperate enough. I called Becca, said Jocelyn and I had parted ways, and I needed to meet with her.

"I'm off at six. I can meet you in the serenity garden to the left of the women's pavilion."

I got there before Becca and perched on one of the memorial benches scattered around the space. She arrived a few minutes later, her gait unsteady and her posture slumped. When she sat, I saw her eyes were red.

"What's wrong?"

She waved me off. "It was a rough day in the ER. Now, what's this about you and Jocelyn? Tell me everything."

I started with Nick and the St. Louis trip, then took her step-by-step through all that had happened, ending with my meeting with Diaz. Said all I could do now was wait and prepare for the media circus that would hit once the article was published.

"I'm happy for you. I don't mean the scoop, but the fact you've booted Jocelyn out of your life." I'd anticipated a massive high five from Becca, so her flat tone and distracted look surprised me. "The stress was doing a number on you."

She was right. The anchor I'd carried around for weeks had vanished. These last few days, I'd slept through the night and the tenseness in my shoulders had disappeared.

"There's something else, though." I put my hand on her arm. "When Jocelyn stormed out, she threatened to dig up dirt on me. And I'm worried if she can't find anything on me, she might target people I'm close to. Like my mom." I paused. "Or you. You know, Rockford."

An older woman with a cane hobbled by and eased herself onto a bench a few yards from us. She opened a paperback book and began to read.

Becca lowered her voice. "Don't worry about me."

"But I *am* worried about you. If Jocelyn keeps at it, she might—"

"I told Sam the truth last night."

I did a double take. "You mean everything? Not just Jimmy, but . . ."

Tears welled up in her eyes. "All of it." Becca stared at the gurgling fountain in the middle of the garden, her hands squeezed tightly together. I kicked myself for being so self-absorbed I hadn't realized how upset she was.

"What happened?"

She didn't reply at first, then sighed. "I sat him down after dinner and blurted it out. I couldn't even look at him. I was afraid I'd see his love die right in front of me." Her voice quivered. "When I stopped talking, he didn't say anything, just grabbed that framed picture of us on the mantel, smashed it against the wall, and stormed out of the apartment."

She'd kept this bottled up inside the whole time I'd been blathering on about Jocelyn and my particular drama. "Oh, Becca. I'm so sorry. But he came back, didn't he?"

"Not until one in the morning. By that time, I'd cleaned up the shards and gone to bed. I heard his key in the lock, then him rummaging around in the closet." She faced me. "You know what I thought? That he was packing a suitcase. That he was leaving without even giving me a second chance."

She pushed back a sob. "I waited for fifteen minutes and poked my head around the corner. He'd pulled out sheets and a blanket and was curled up on the couch." She wiped at her eyes, rummaged in her purse for a tissue, and blew her nose. "At least he hadn't left for good."

"How was he this morning?"

"He'd calmed down some. We both called in late to work, and we talked for over an hour. He kept saying how picturing someone else's hands on my body made him nauseous." She shook her head back and forth. "I hurt him. I hate the fact I did that."

"I'm sure you two will get past this."

"That depends on whether he can forgive me. He did say he'd go with me to counseling."

"That's a good first step. It means he wants to make the relationship work."

"I guess." She stood and slung her purse strap over her shoulder. "I need to go."

"I'll walk with you." When we got to the parking garage, I asked her the question that had been niggling in my brain. "What made you decide to tell Sam? You said you'd decided not to."

Becca glanced at me. "I met your mom for coffee last week and cleared the air about the whole Rockford thing. She said Sam deserved to know."

I frowned. "You told my mother about your abortion? Why?"

"You told me initially she thought *you'd* been the one who was pregnant." Becca put up her hand. "I know, I know, you also told me she bought your story. But what if she didn't? What if she had this lingering doubt, thinking maybe she'd had a grandchild? Anyway, I wanted her to know it was me. She was such a good sounding board, I wound up telling her the whole story."

"Even about Jimmy?"

"Yes. I expected she'd get all preachy about it, but she was pretty open-minded. Said I should tell Sam the truth and trust in his love for me. Pretty much the same words you used that day when you dropped me off."

"I'm amazed she didn't lay a guilt trip on you."

Becca looked long and hard at me, and the firmness in her voice surprised me. "Maybe you don't know her as well as you think."

———————◆———————

Saturday morning, after I finished my run, I sat on the front stoop with a steaming mug of coffee. This was my favorite time of day, breathing in the quiet before the rest of the neighborhood woke up: no barking dogs, no slamming screen doors, no leaf blowers disturbing the peace. Three dozen Canada geese in a tightly choreographed V pattern flew through the overcast sky, headed south. The air was calm at the moment, but I smelled a hint of rain. Mateo waved as he rode by on his bike, the colorful ribbons woven through his wheel spokes flashing in the sunlight.

I thought back to my talk with Becca yesterday. Since she'd told Sam about her abortion, there wasn't much Jocelyn could threaten her with, but that still left Mom. I'd called her repeatedly, but got her voice mail. Then I remembered she was in Washington for the weekend, something about meeting with the bigwigs from the RNC to go over last-minute strategies. Gavin had gone with her, and I had no idea where they were staying. So I was in limbo until Monday.

My phone rang. It was Nick. "How spontaneous are you? Let's head to the lakefront and pretend we're tourists."

Giddiness began in my chest and cycled through the rest of my body. "Give me thirty minutes." I jumped in the shower, threw on some ripped jeans, a black turtleneck, and my old, quilted leather bomber, and tied my hair in a high ponytail.

When he pulled up to the curb, I sprinted to his car, tossing my bag in the back. "Ready for a day on the town?" he asked.

I couldn't get over how much I loved the sound of his voice. "I'm all yours." I fastened my seat belt, and we headed to the lakefront. After we'd passed the third billboard with my mother's face plastered across the front, Nick brought it up.

"She's everywhere. Must be weird."

"Tell me about it."

"After you told me who she was, I got curious and watched a couple of her speeches on YouTube. I have to say, I was impressed."

I glanced sideways at him. "Please tell me you're not a closet Republican."

"You know me better than that. No, I meant her persona. Her charisma. She's obviously a strong woman."

"Which is so weird because she wasn't that way when I was growing up. Dad called the shots. He was the one who went out and earned a living while Mom stayed at home. I promised myself I'd never turn into her. Never settle for her life. It seemed, I don't know, small. Insignificant."

"That doesn't fit with her image now. She never worked?"

"She had a job at a photography studio for a while. But she quit after a couple of years and threw herself into my school activities instead. Every field trip, she chaperoned. Organized the class bake sale. Led my Girl Scout troop."

"In other words, kept tabs on you."

"You could say that." I dropped my voice. "Still tries to sometimes."

Once we reached Michigan Avenue, we drove south to Columbus Drive and turned into the Millennium Park garage. Given the gorgeous fall weather, hordes of folks had descended on downtown, but we eventually found a spot at the far corner on the third level. As we headed for the exit, I took out my phone, twisted backwards, and snapped a photo.

"What's that for?" Nick asked.

"A trick a veteran reporter taught me the first time I got lost in an underground garage. When we come back, the view will be opposite from when we left. This way we'll have a visual of what we're looking for."

"I'm gonna steal that one."

"Too late. It's patented. But I'll loan it to you for the price of a sandwich."

We reached street level, dodged dozens of people emptying out of a tour bus at the curb, and made our way to The Bean, where Nick stretched out his right arm and snapped a selfie of us reflected in the silver bubble. There was a faint chill in the air from the lake, but the bright sun overhead made it seem like summer. At the giant face fountain, shrieking kids splashed around, running in and out of the water, their faces lit with smiles. We studied an exhibit of intricately carved nine-foot-high totems exhibited around the park and wandered through Lurie Garden. When we passed the pool along the Seam Wall, we stripped off our shoes, submerged our bare feet, and played footsie with each other under the water.

"Should we throw in a penny and make a wish?" Nick asked.

"What would you wish for?"

"More days with you." He leaned over and gave me a quick kiss, and my heart did a tango.

After two hours at the art museum, we sauntered back through the park, bought sandwiches, chips, and two pickles from a street vendor, and made our way over to the marina near the jogging path, dodging a dozen or so middle-aged folks speeding by on Segways. Once we'd settled on a spot, Nick opened his backpack and unfurled a blue gingham tablecloth followed by two wine glasses with a split of prosecco and a tiny vase with a bouquet of plastic flowers.

"How did you know I loved daisies?"

"Who doesn't love daisies?" He poured us each a glass. "A toast to my girlfriend, ace investigative reporter." We clinked glasses and ate our lunch as boats bobbed past heading to Navy Pier.

"Ever sailed?" I nodded toward the lake. I'd signed up for lessons the summer between tenth and eleventh grade and gotten seasick the minute the waves turned choppy.

"Never had the chance. Why, is that a dealbreaker?"

I flipped on my side so I faced Nick and rested my head on my hand. "I don't see anything that's a dealbreaker right now." I leaned toward him and brushed my lips against his.

He stroked my hair and kissed me back, his eyes scanning my face. "Are you ever not beautiful?"

I lay on my back and lifted my face to the sun. It was funny. When Nick said it, I *did* feel beautiful.

"We'll run a marathon together sometime. See how I look after twenty-six miles. By the way, when is that run we talked about way back when?"

"Damn. With all this troll stuff, I completely forgot. I'm pretty sure it's tomorrow. Want to go together and cheer on the runners?"

"Absolutely." My eyelids closed, and I drifted off.

"Hey there, Sleeping Beauty. Where'd you go?"

I jolted myself awake and tuned in again to my surroundings. A kid around five ran past us chasing a frisbee, his father tagging along behind. Two teenaged girls in tight leggings and puffer vests roller-skated by. We were on the edge of the bike path, and a man in tight Lycra shorts with a neatly trimmed goatee sped past at breakneck speed.

"Let's pretend we can read people's minds. Did you see that guy on the bike? What's up with him?" I said.

"I'd rather you read *my* mind." Nick wiggled his eyebrows in what he must have thought was a sexy way.

"Come on, play along."

Nick took a stab. "Single? Exercise nut?"

"Where's your imagination?" I nudged him. "Wanted in three states for stealing public funds from the teachers' union. Figured he could hide in plain sight in the big city. Thinks maybe someone spotted him."

Nick sat cross-legged on the blanket. "Everybody's got a secret?"

"Most of us do. Some are worse than others." I pictured Jocelyn's face. No, I refused to let that woman ruin my day. I hopped off the ground and stretched. "Okay, we're tourists. What's the next thing we do?"

"Whatever you like."

"Shopping!"

"I'm a guy. We don't do shopping."

"Don't be a drag." I pulled him up. We threw the remains of our picnic in a nearby trash can and made our way through the crowds to Michigan Avenue.

He hadn't lied. He hated shopping. He groused about how overpriced everything was and had moved on to a tirade about over-commercialization when I teased him into playing a game I made up on the spot. We pretended we'd won three million dollars in the lottery but we had to spend it by five o'clock. By the time we got to the end of the Magnificent Mile, I'd fake-purchased a houseful of furniture, thousands of dollars in computer gear, and more novels than would fit inside my entire bedroom. Nick owned two Rolex watches, three guitars, and an original etching by Rembrandt.

We collapsed on a bench circling the old Water Tower. "You know, you've never spent the night at my place. It's not fancy, but it's clean and it's close to downtown. How about you stay over with me tonight and we can head over to the run tomorrow morning?"

"Sounds nice." More than nice. In fact, I couldn't wait to get my hands on Nick again.

"Want some ice cream?" Nick pointed to a street vendor nearby. "Mint chocolate chip, right?"

"Two scoops, please."

As we licked our cones, I scanned the crowd. "Okay, you get another chance. See that brunette in the denim sundress and the hat? What's her story?"

"Where?" He scanned the crowd.

"Don't make me point. That girl standing near Topshop. Looks pregnant?"

His smile faded like the sun going behind a cloud, and he stood up. "Tell you what. Let's rent bikes and pedal to the beach."

"But I haven't finished my—" Before I knew it, he'd grabbed my hand and we headed off to the Divvy stand. I dropped my half-eaten cone in a nearby wastebasket.

The Lakefront Trail ran south through Grant Park, past the Shedd Aquarium and the Adler Planetarium, and ended at the Nature Conservatory. Nick stopped, straddling his bike, and faced me. "There's something I need to tell you."

This didn't sound good.

"The woman at the Water Tower?" he said. "She's the woman I followed here from New York."

The one he'd been in love with. "You didn't know she was pregnant?"

"I heard she got married, and I was glad. It's what she wanted."

"I take it you didn't?"

"She kept pressuring me, and when I put her off, she got

tired of waiting. I realized later it wasn't that I didn't want to be married. I just didn't want to be married to her."

"Why'd you freak out when you saw her?"

"I'm not sure. We haven't talked in over a year. Maybe it was stumbling across her unexpectedly like that." He pulled on his ear. "I'm not sure I can explain it."

I could see he was nervous, probably anxious about my reaction.

"Everybody's got baggage," I reassured him. "Don't get me wrong, I'm glad you told me. But you and me? That's all that's important."

Out of nowhere, the sky grew dark and a drop of rain smacked my face. Nick studied the clouds. "I think we're in for it."

Within a minute, we were soaked, my hair plastered to my skull. Even with my jacket, I was chilled, my teeth chattering. We threw down our bikes and took refuge in a shelter a short distance away. Shielded from the downpour, we giggled, shaking our heads and flinging water everywhere.

"You're like a rag doll," Nick said as water dripped off my lashes and onto my lips. His voice was soft as smoke. "If you knew the kinds of thoughts I'm having right now, you'd run away screaming."

"I doubt I'd run. But I wouldn't mind a little screaming. Come here, you."

I grabbed his shirt and pulled him toward me as the pelting rain slapped against the tin roof above us. You could have told me the sky was falling and I'd have ignored you.

The only thing I cared about was pressing my body up against Nick, feeling his muscles through his wet shirt, watching his lips as he slowly bent down to mine.

THIRTY-ONE

ick and I cheered on the marathon runners the next day, and I wound up spending Sunday night with him as well, so I didn't make it home until late Monday morning. When I did, I found a missed delivery notice on my front door. Hopping back in the car, I drove to the post office, thinking it was my severance check from Arrow.

It had been over a week since my blowup with Jocelyn, my resignation, and my filing the story with Diaz. The fact he hadn't been in touch made me paranoid. What was the holdup?

I presented the slip, and when the clerk emerged from the back, he handed me a hefty parcel and watched as I signed for it.

I waited until I was in my car before I tore open the thick manila envelope. Inside was a bundle of official-looking documents. On top was the confidentiality statement I'd signed on my first day at Arrow, which I'd forgotten all

about. Panic hit. Could Jocelyn sue me for breaking this
agreement? I should run this by the paper's legal team
since, technically, I'd been an Arrow employee when I'd
interviewed Dragan.

I flipped through the papers underneath. They were
medical records. Stuck on the front was a yellow Post-it note:
Queen takes Pawn. Check.

I sank against the seat and paged through the documents.
Admission papers from an inpatient psychiatric facility
in upstate Wisconsin dated June 1998. The presenting
problem was listed as severe depression with periodic panic
attacks. There were extensive treatment notes, prescriptions
for Prozac, and later Zoloft. The discharge papers were
dated three months later with a referral to a Chicago-area
therapist.

The patient was my mother.

The pages rustled in my hands as I pieced together
the timeline. This happened the summer I turned five. The
summer my parents supposedly traveled through Europe.
The summer I stayed with my father's parents in Indiana.
The whole trip must have been a cover-up.

Whatever happened, if the media got wind of this,
they'd eat my Mom for breakfast.

But how did Jocelyn get this information? I did a quick
Google search on my phone. HIPAA had gone into effect
a good four years before Mom had been admitted. But of
course, that wouldn't have stopped Jocelyn. There's always
someone who can be bought if the check's got enough zeros
on it. I'd underestimated her reach.

I shoved the pages into my purse. Jocelyn's house was thirty minutes away, but today, I covered it in half that time, pounding the steering wheel and screaming at every red light, my entire body on fire.

The reporters had disappeared, apparently chasing a new scandal. I punched in the numbers, but the iron doors didn't budge. I tried again. Still nothing. She'd changed the key code.

Shaking with rage, I yelled through the intercom. "Okay, you've got my attention. Open the damn gate." When nothing happened, I repeated myself, this time holding down the button so it squealed. Jocelyn must have realized she couldn't sit in her fairy-tale castle and ignore me indefinitely because I finally heard a click and the lock sprang open. One last time, I drove up the curved driveway and skirted the ceramic fountain. Jocelyn stood at the front door, her face an angry mask. Hank, her gardener, was strategically positioned beside her. That was a good call on her part because if we'd been alone, I'd have slapped her.

"You got my note, I see." Her words were clipped and curt. "Should we have a seat like civilized adults and discuss our next steps?"

I pushed past her into the house. "She isn't part of this. You had no right to involve her."

"Hank, you can leave us now. I can handle this." The gardener backed out of the foyer and headed to the patio. Once he was out of earshot, Jocelyn shot back. "You play with fire, innocent bystanders can get burned. It's all part of the game."

My pulse shot through the roof. "This isn't a game, goddamn it. I can't believe you'd destroy my mother over something that happened twenty years ago."

She smirked. "Why not? You're doing that to me. There's a delicious irony to all this, isn't there?"

"Cut the crap, okay? There's a gigantic difference between your outright plagiarism and my mother's treatment for depression."

She didn't even flinch. "And yet, they have one thing in common. Both will spread like wildfire over the internet, leaving a woman's scorched reputation in the wake. Don't call my bluff."

I had no idea what had caused my mother's hospitalization, but I instinctively knew she wouldn't want it exposed. After all, she'd kept it hidden from me all my life. The campaign was at a crucial stage. Any scandal might tip the scales, and everything she'd worked for, everything she'd sacrificed, would be in jeopardy. "What in the hell do you want?"

"Kill the story." There was a silent *or else* hidden behind her words.

"I can't. It's with my editor. As soon as their legal team vets it, it goes to press."

"Pull it back. Say you got your facts wrong. You have a history of doing that, don't you?"

The balls on this woman. I'd told her that in confidence, and now she was throwing it in my face. God, she was a monster. "I'm not the only reporter around. Dragan will just contact another newspaper."

"Then make up a story that gets her to back off. You're clever, Megan. I have faith in your ingenuity. All you needed was a little incentive, and now I've given you that."

She was a master manipulator. I was way out of my league. "And if I can't?"

Her eyes never left my face. They reminded me of a raptor. The same intensity, the same unfiltered cruelty. "Abner Lynch is a friend of mine. He's ruthless, and he plays to win. His candidate's behind in the polls, and the election is less than two weeks away. He'd love to get his hands on that report."

"I need time." Time to talk to my mother and Dragan. Time to think this through.

"It's Monday. I'll give you until Thursday," she said.

Pull off a miracle in three days? And to think, when I first learned the truth, I'd pitied Jocelyn. Now I hated her. I wanted to yank her off that pedestal so badly I could taste it. If I let the story stand, my byline would appear in every news feed imaginable, and I'd be famous as the reporter who exposed the great Jocelyn Jones. But I'd have to sacrifice my mother in the process. And that wasn't who I was.

"If I can kill the story, I need your word on two points: you'll destroy all the evidence you've gathered, and you'll never tell a soul what you found."

"You have my word."

"Swear on the soul of Robert."

Her nostrils flared. "How dare you—"

I had her in my crosshairs and pressed my advantage.

"Swear or I'll call Dragan and have her contact her local newspaper." Which she'd do anyway once I pulled out, but I had no control over that.

"I promise." Her voice had softened. "On the soul of Robert."

"Then we're done here." I was halfway to the foyer when she spoke again.

"Wait." She closed the distance between us and touched my arm. "I don't know why I even care, but for some reason, I want you to understand." She hesitated, her breath ragged and shallow. "I wasn't all that different from you when I started out as a reporter. Determined to right wrongs. Convinced I could save the world. But once my career took off, the need to score the next big story became insatiable, like a giant mouth I had to feed or I'd lose my place at the table. Look at it from my perspective."

Her speech was a mass of platitudes, her attempt to justify her behavior. That day at the rally, I'd dreamed of someday being like Jocelyn. Now I prayed I never would be. "You still don't think you did anything wrong, do you? Not in Bosnia, and not now."

"I know you're angry, and I regret the necessity of involving your family. I only wish you'd agreed to help me because we're friends, not because I threatened you."

Friends. What an odd word for her to use.

A friend is someone you trust. Someone who'd never knowingly hurt you, never talk about you behind your back or date your ex or use a secret she knew against you.

Never threaten someone you loved.

Heat pulsed through my body as I spat out the words. "We were never friends."

I slammed the solid oak door behind me. Still seething, I popped open the trunk of my car, hoisted out a lug wrench, and marched to the stately ceramic fountain a few feet away. Pulling back my arm and marshalling all my strength, I gave it a ferocious *whack*.

The lion's head split into pieces and sank beneath the water.

THIRTY-TWO

I left a message for my mother the moment I got in the car. After thirty minutes, I tried again. Still nothing. I sent her a text saying it was urgent and to contact me when she got my message, and in the meantime, I paced the apartment, my nerves on fire. Why hadn't she returned my call? Her phone must be off. Then I realized, with the election looming, she must be booked solid with appearances.

Thinking she might be home, I drove there, but her car wasn't in the garage. I let myself in and grabbed a notepad and pencil off the fridge. *CALL ME, IT'S URGENT!* I underlined it three times and propped it against her coffee mug on the kitchen table.

Should I wait here? No, she might be gone all day. All I could think about was Jocelyn, sitting at her desk in the library, flipping through her Rolodex, calling sources, researching via the internet, her adrenaline spiking with each new lead she uncovered. She'd given me until Thursday, but I didn't trust her. She could use the information she'd found any time she wanted. All it would take was one press conference, hell, one phone call, and my mother's secret would be exposed.

I sat on the couch and cleared my brain. Where was she? I googled a list of her appearances on my phone but realized there was a quicker way.

"Watkins' campaign headquarters. Vote for a Change."

"Can you tell me where the candidate is speaking today?"

The guy rattled off her itinerary, including a rally that evening at seven o'clock at my old high school. "Want to make a donation? We accept Visa and Mastercard."

————— • —————

When I arrived, I was blown away by how many people had shown up. The line already snaked around the building, folks chatting with their neighbors as they inched forward. Luckily, I'd thought ahead and brought my old press pass, so I skirted around the crowd. Once I reached the front, I tucked my credentials into my pocket.

Peeking inside, I saw the event had all the trappings of political rallies I'd attended as a journalist: a raised platform at one end of the school gymnasium, a huge American flag mounted on the wall, and red, white, and blue balloons floating in clusters on the ceiling. It was surreal, seeing my mother's face multiplied dozens of times on the signs her supporters waved back and forth. Folding chairs lined the gym floor as people made their way inside, filling the bleachers, bopping in their seats as "Stars and Stripes Forever" pulsed at mega-decibels through the overhead speakers.

I'd done research when Mom first announced she was running. The ninth district had been a Democratic stronghold for years, and Underhill, a well-known Arlington Heights business owner, was their golden boy. He'd easily won his party's primary, but questions about his corporate tax returns had surfaced, and now my mother, with her squeaky-clean record, conservative platform, and financial support from well-heeled Republicans, held a slight lead.

The chanting grew louder as strobe lights played across the crowd. "Watkins! Watkins! Watkins!" A slew of reporters and cameramen clustered on one side of the stage apron. Any one of them would jump at the chance to publish what Jocelyn had found. And once the whiff of scandal attached to my mom, this enthusiastic crowd could just as quickly turn on her.

Scanning the area, I homed in on the double doors on each side of the podium leading to the hallway by the cafeteria. That's where she'd be, waiting for the bleachers to fill up before making her grand entrance. I needed to get back there.

"Can I help you find a seat?" a volunteer asked.

"Where's the restroom?"

"Back out into the lobby area and around the corner to your right."

I sailed past the lavatory, down the familiar hall. I passed my old, dented locker, sporting a shiny new lock. A colorful handmade poster about an upcoming pep rally hung beside a glass case packed with athletic trophies.

"Where do you think you're going, miss?" A security

guard stepped in front of me and blocked my way. A baton hung from his belt, and his face was the opposite of friendly.

"My mother's the candidate. I'm meeting her backstage."

"I'll need to see your ID."

I whipped out my driver's license and handed it over.

"Sorry, miss. Name's not a match. Turn back around and be on your way."

"No, I swear, I'm her daughter." I grabbed my phone, hit grid view, and swiped through my photos. Finally, I found a selfie from three Christmases ago of the two of us in front of the tree, goofy grins on our faces and arms around each other. The caption read *Rockin' with Mom for the holidays*. I held out the screen.

He glared at me and back at the photo. "Okay. But next time, get an official pass."

I hustled past my old social studies classroom and rounded the corner. A wall of noise thundered from the crowd inside—chanting voices, shrill whistles, pounding feet. I caught a glimpse of my mother as she pulled open a door and disappeared into the gym. Gavin lingered nearby, talking with a short, heavyset woman who scribbled notes on a pad of paper as if he were reciting the Sermon on the Mount.

I approached him, tucking my phone inside my purse.

"What the hell are you doing here?"

"My mother's a hard person to get a hold of these days. There's something I need to tell her."

He turned to the other woman. "Jan, would you brief Ted about those stats? He's at the table at the far end."

She scurried away, and Gavin addressed me, his tone hardened. "The last thing we need right now is a reporter cornering you. It's crunch time, and having the candidate's disapproving daughter show up out of nowhere would be a serious distraction."

"That's not what the polls say. Actually, I believe the voters are grumbling about why I'm not campaigning for her."

His face flashed crimson. "Who told you that?"

I knew it was petty, but I liked seeing him flustered. "Look, I'm not here to interfere with your strategy. All I want is an hour with my mother to discuss a personal matter." What I actually wanted to do was get in his face and tell him all his hard work wouldn't count for shit if I didn't find a way to deal with Jocelyn's blackmail threat. That I was all that stood between him and a defeat at the polls.

In the gym, my mother's voice reverberated through the speakers, and the clamor inside escalated. I glanced at the clock across the way. Candidates usually spoke no more than fifteen minutes at rallies like this, so she'd be finishing up soon. Gavin ordered me to wait and disappeared into the cafeteria, huddling with two other staffers. Every once in a while, they glanced in my direction, lowered their heads, and continued talking.

A loud cheer rose from the crowd inside. The door from the stage opened, and my mother emerged, her face flushed with excitement and adrenaline. She stopped short when she saw me.

"Meggie. You're the last person I expected to see tonight. What in the world are you doing here?"

THIRTY-THREE

I waited in a corner of the cafeteria while my mother shook hands and posed for photos.

Gavin pulled me to one side, a deep blue vein pulsing on his forehead as he ranted. "So are you showing up at all the rallies from now on? Should I schedule media interviews and shoehorn you into ads after I've worked my ass off all summer downplaying your existence?"

I didn't take the bait. "Relax. Nothing's changed. As soon as my mother and I talk, she's all yours again."

"Do me one favor. Don't end up in any pictures." He retreated to the other end of the room.

A few minutes later, Mom pried herself loose from her supporters and the two of us left out the back exit. But we hadn't gone far before several people spotted us and insisted on shaking Mom's hand. A reporter even snapped a picture of the two of us together in the middle of the crowd before I could stop him. I smirked, picturing Gavin's face when he found out.

After twenty long minutes, we made it out of the parking lot. I drove down side streets and eventually turned into the entrance to Dawes Park. I wasn't sure why I hadn't taken her straight home. I guess I hoped she'd drop her guard if I picked a place that held good memories for both of us.

"Why are we stopping here?" Mom asked.

"Remember the concerts and craft fairs here in the summer? Let's go and sit out on the pier like we used to."

She let out a sigh. "It's been a long day. We can talk at my house. Besides, I'm sure the park is closed."

"Nope." I pointed at a sign. "We've got another hour."

She peered out the windshield. "But it's getting dark. We'll hurt ourselves traipsing around."

"Stop being so stubborn." I opened the glove compartment and found a flashlight, then sprang out of the car and poked my face through the window. "I'm going, and I've got the keys. Please, Mom. Walk with me."

She wrapped a scarf around her neck, and we stumbled forward, lighting the path with the beam until we found Lake Michigan. I took hold of her hand, and together we made it to the end of the pier, where we took off our shoes and socks and dangled our feet off the side.

Traffic sounds from the freeway echoed off the water. The lake was smooth as glass, and a cool breeze tickled the back of my neck. Overhead, a full moon shone through wisps of roving clouds, the sky a deep velvet-blue.

"When I was young, I'd sit in this same spot and fantasize about far-off lands."

Mother grinned. "Where did you want to go?"

"Africa. Australia. Somewhere. Anywhere away from here."

"Away from me, you mean."

I shot her a glance. "Doesn't every little girl dream of exploring the world on her own?"

Mother's shoulders relaxed. She rested her hands on the dock and leaned back. "I suppose. But then life happens. You get married, have a child, and those dreams fade away."

We sat for a few minutes, each with our own thoughts, until the croaks of a family of frogs near the water's edge broke the stillness. "And now you're this close to your new dream, right? Congresswoman Watkins."

She touched the campaign button on her coat's lapel. "We'll see."

It couldn't wait any longer. "There's been a new development with the plagiarism rumor." I shared with her what Jocelyn had done in Bosnia, about our search for Dragan, and about the article I'd written.

Her eyes widened. "She had the gall to steal someone else's work? That's awful." She squinted at me. "How are you coping with all this? You must have been devastated when you learned the truth."

She'd warned me early on not to fall under Jocelyn's spell, but I hadn't listened. It was nice of her not to say she told me so. "I'm a journalist. My job is to report the facts, no matter who gets hurt."

"Even so. I know how much you admired her. What did she say when you told her what you'd found?"

"She made excuses, said exposing the prison camp

atrocities took precedence over who got credit for the story. Said she had the platform to make sure the world paid attention."

"That's all true, I suppose."

"But that doesn't justify what she did. She saw a chance to enhance her reputation, and she took it. And it worked. She got away with it for twenty years. Nobody even suspected until Dragan posted those tweets." I shifted my weight and faced her. "But that's not why I'm telling you all this. Jocelyn's threatened me. She says if I don't kill the story, she'll reveal what she knows."

Mom's nostrils flared. "She's resorting to blackmail? The nerve. You can't let her get away with that." She blew on her hands and tucked them into her pockets.

My insides were tied in knots. "I'm not sure you'll feel that way once I tell you what she's found out."

"It's something you don't want anyone else to know?"

The words caught in my throat. "The secret's not about me, Mom. It's about you."

Her body stiffened. "Me? I've never even met the woman. What could she possibly know about me that's got you so upset?"

I hesitated. There was no way to finesse this, so I blurted it out. "What happened in 1998? Why did you check yourself into Lake View Institute in Green Bay?"

She gasped, then lowered her head and squeezed her eyes shut. A full minute went by where neither of us said anything. Eventually, I laid my hand on her arm. "Talk to me. What's this about?"

Her eyes flew open, and they blazed. "Those are *my* health records. There's no way Jocelyn should have been able—"

"Agreed. But she did. Not everything, though. Not yet. But we shouldn't underestimate her. She'll dig further if I don't pull the story. Tell me. What are we dealing with here?"

She didn't move. When she did speak, her voice was so low I barely caught the words. "I was going to tell you once you got older, but it never seemed to be the right time." She sniffed and wiped her nose on her sleeve.

"I'm sorry to push you, but if I'm going to stop her, I need to know."

She ran her hands nervously over her legs and gazed out across the lake. In the distance, muted music filled the air, vestiges of a late-night party nearby. Her shoulders stiffened, and her voice, when she spoke, sounded robotic, as though she were reading from a teleprompter.

"It happened the summer before you started first grade." She paused and stared up at the sky, but eventually went on. "Your father landed an important case, a big antitrust lawsuit. The trial was in California, and he spent a month out there while you and I stayed behind." She turned to me. "Do you remember any of that?"

"I'm not sure." The acrid smell of burning leaves nearby made my eyes tear up.

"I bought you a bike with training wheels and taught you to ride. And we wrote a play together—what was it called— *The Perils of Jimmy the Who*, that was it." She grabbed my hand. "We went for a swim every day in the neighborhood pool, rode the train downtown to the zoo, and planted a vegetable garden." She focused back on the water. "But after three weeks, I needed a break, so I sent you to stay with my parents for a few days."

A memory surfaced. "I think I remember fishing with Grandpa. I caught a perch."

"And I treated myself to a Saturday in downtown Chicago. Shopped for shoes at Marshall Field's, took in a matinee performance of *Cabaret*, had dinner at the Palmer House. It felt great being on my own—no husband, no child—like when I was single."

Where was this going? Had my mother met someone during this bachelorette weekend? Had she had an affair? And what did any of this have to do with her stay at Lake View? She squeezed my hand so tight it pulsed, but I didn't dare interrupt.

"On the train ride home, I noticed a young man smiling at me. College-age. Wearing a letterman jacket. At first, I thought I recognized him as somebody's son from church or from the neighborhood. I smiled back, and he put his fingers to his forehead, as though he was saluting. I kept reading my book, but every time I glanced up, he was staring. And the more time that went by, the more I realized I didn't know him after all. I got more and more uncomfortable, and eventually I switched cars." She scrounged in her purse, found a tissue, and blew her nose.

"He followed you?"

"No. But he got off at the same stop I did. He didn't say anything, just strolled by and headed in the opposite direction. I remember laughing at myself for thinking he'd been flirting with me—I mean, I was a good ten years older than him. But even so, I hung around the station like I was waiting for my ride until I saw him drive away."

Her hand trembled in mine. "He must have waited around the corner until he saw me get in my car and followed me home. The garage door opener had been on the fritz, so I parked in the driveway." Her voice broke. "As soon as I got out, he grabbed me. Held a knife to my throat and dragged me into the bushes by the side of our house."

My heart cracked open, and I grabbed hold of her. "God, you could have been killed. Why didn't you ever tell me any of this?" I hugged her hard, rubbing her back. We sat like that for a few minutes. Finally, I let go, and she continued, her tone as flat as ever.

"After it was over, he didn't say anything, just got in his car and drove away. He'd ripped all the buttons off my blouse, and my slacks were torn. I lay still, too scared to move. Finally, after maybe a half hour, I stumbled into the house, locked all the windows, dead-bolted the doors, and threw myself in the shower. I scrubbed my skin raw, trying to wash him off my body. I collapsed on the shower floor. My teeth wouldn't stop chattering."

I squeezed my eyes shut and tried to block out the image. When I brushed my hand over my face, it came back wet.

"The hot water eventually ran out, and I threw on my robe. That's when I realized he knew where I lived. What if he came back? I crept into the kitchen, grabbed a butcher knife from the drawer, and flipped on every light in the house. I wedged a dining room chair under my bedroom door and sat up in bed all night."

"Why didn't you call the police?"

"This was almost twenty years ago. You know why." She dropped her head in her hands. "I was ashamed. Who would believe me? They'd say I provoked him. What was I thinking anyway, going downtown on my own? How many drinks had I had? Did I encourage the boy, stare at him a little too long on the train?"

"God, Mom, you didn't do anything wrong. None of it was your fault."

"I know. But that first morning? All I wanted was to forget. When your father came home a week later, I picked you up at my parents' and acted like nothing had happened. I pushed the whole incident away. But when I threw up one morning a month later, I knew. The doctor confirmed it. I was six weeks pregnant."

"That's when you told Dad what happened."

She shook her head. "I know it sounds absurd, but I thought he'd divorce me if he knew. I told him I was pregnant but not about the rape. I arranged for an abortion, and when it was over, I told him I'd had a miscarriage."

"Holy shit, Mom."

My mind rushed back. I'd been playing in my room when I'd heard a whimper, followed by two more short ones. They came from my parents' bathroom, so I tiptoed closer and listened. Silence. When I opened the door a sliver, I saw my mother crouched on the floor by the toilet.

It was the scene I'd recalled that night in the bathroom with Becca.

Another memory surfaced. Mom sobbing at the kitchen table. And another of her curled up on the couch, facing away from me when I came home from school. Not talking. That time, I'd been so scared I'd called Dad at work.

"I remember you cried a lot back then."

Her eyes filled, and a shudder ran through her body. "I'd fallen into a well and I couldn't find my way out. I didn't sleep. I lost twenty pounds. I wandered through the house in a fog, sometimes forgot to pack your lunch. Grief followed me around, clung to me like an extra layer of skin."

She clutched her coat tighter around her. "Your father finally arranged for me to stay at Lake View. I went on antidepressants, met with a therapist every day, and when I felt better, I came home and life went on."

"It must have been hard, asking for help."

"Thank God I did. That place saved my life. And your father stood by me all that time, even though he was grieving the loss of what he thought was his child. But I hadn't told him the truth, and it drove a wedge between us."

"He still doesn't know?"

"It's what I regret most. The assault colored my relationship with him. And with you." She finally made eye contact. "I became the worst kind of helicopter parent. Every time you wanted to stay overnight with friends or go on a road trip, all I could think was how I had to protect you. Make sure the same thing didn't happen to you."

All these years and I'd never sensed the sorrow my mother carried around, never realized her hovering hid a deep, personal wound. I wished there was something profound I could say to comfort her. Hot tears pricked my eyes. "I love you," I whispered, putting my arm around her. She leaned in, and I brushed a few loose strands of hair back from her face.

As I held her, I realized all Jocelyn knew was my mother had spent time in a psychiatric facility. But if she researched long enough, she might unearth the fact that Helen Watkins, a leader in the pro-life movement, had gotten an abortion.

I didn't hesitate. No scoop was worth this. "Listen, any newspaper in the country will leap at the chance to print this story. I'll tell my editor I got the facts wrong and withdraw the article. Dragan can work with another reporter."

Because there was no way I'd stand by and let Jocelyn destroy my mother.

THIRTY-FOUR

After what my mother had shared with me, I didn't want to leave her alone, so I stayed in my old bedroom at her house that night. I didn't sleep well, my mind fixated on what I'd tell Diaz. What I'd tell Dragan. Most importantly, what I'd tell Jocelyn.

When I came downstairs the next morning, my eyes gritty and my head throbbing, Mother was already dressed. "Don't call your editor until tomorrow, okay? There has to be another way we can handle this without you giving up your byline."

There wasn't. But Diaz still hadn't gotten the go-ahead from the lawyers, so waiting one more day to tell him wouldn't change anything. She snatched up her briefcase and headed for the door.

I stopped her. "Are you okay? Call Gavin and tell him you need a day off."

She scoffed at my suggestion. I should have known better. She was the queen of compartmentalizing, and this morning was no exception. "Nonsense. I've got a pancake breakfast with Rotary this morning, and then I'm speaking at the Women's Club at noon. I left the address on the fridge. I'd like you to come."

"Gavin doesn't want me at your events."

"I'm the candidate, not him, and I want you there. It's important."

My mother rarely asked me for favors, and after last night's revelation, I'd do anything to lend her moral support. "If it means that much to you, of course I'll come. But don't ask me to say anything."

She patted my shoulder. "Don't worry. I'll be doing all the talking."

—————•—————

The parking lot at the Women's Club was nearly full when I arrived, and I rushed up the stairs, barging into the second-floor ballroom after the program had already begun. My mother was seated at the head table, and when she spotted me, she gave a slight wave. I leaned against the back wall in the corner, making myself as small and inconspicuous as possible. After a brief introduction from the program coordinator, Mother approached the microphone.

She cleared her throat. "Today, as I look around the room, I see so many friendly faces. Many of you have marched on picket lines with me. You've canvassed on my behalf, stuffed envelopes, and raised money for my campaign. Which is why I picked today's luncheon for a major announcement."

Goosebumps rose on my arms. There was a new tension in the room, an atmosphere of attentiveness tinged with apprehension. Women turned and whispered to their neighbors, wary expressions on their faces. Eventually, the noise level died down.

"As most of you know, I've been a leader in the pro-life movement most of my adult life. In fact, I suspect that's the main reason my party asked me to run for Congress, since abortion in this country has become such a bedrock issue for many voters. So what I'm sharing with you today will come as a shock, given my history. It's a secret I've kept for a long time, partly to protect my family, but mostly out of shame."

I snapped to attention and held my breath. A photographer near the front rushed forward, lifted his camera, and snapped her picture. Mom looked straight at him.

"I know it's your job, but I'd appreciate it if you'd hold off until after I've finished my speech. Don't worry, you can take all the shots you want later. But not now."

He tucked his camera by his side and backed off.

She squared her shoulders and went on, but her voice tremored. "When I was twenty-eight, married with a young child, I had an abortion." Mother paused, letting her words sink in.

My body went cold and my mind shut down for several moments before slipping back into gear. It was like watching a train wreck in slow motion. My mother had lost the election before my eyes.

Because of me.

The silence was so absolute that when a woman at the back gasped, the sound echoed off the walls. Chairs scraped against the floor as a swarm of buzzing murmurs began. One woman seated near the front threw her napkin on the floor and left the room. Two others followed.

When the noise level died down, Mother continued. "I don't intend to share the details as to why I made that decision. The reasons are private, and, while I have shared them with my daughter and my former husband, I won't discuss them in a public forum. What I will say is I quickly spiraled into a profound depression, bruised inside in a deep way I couldn't articulate. I felt I had sinned in the eyes of God and sought forgiveness the only way I knew how. I joined the pro-life movement. I hoped to convince other women not to make the same mistake I had."

My stomach clenched as I watched the audience. A few heads nodded, but most of the women sat stone-cold sober, shock etched across their faces.

Mom closed her eyes for a beat. When she opened them, she stared hard at the audience. "I grew up in Green Bay in a middle-class family. My mother always told me to listen twice as much as I talk, and I still think that's sound advice. So when I agreed to run for Congress, I vowed to add a level of civility to the discourse. I've worked hard to listen to the opinions of those who agree with me, but also those who don't."

I'd watched a few of Mom's speeches on YouTube, so I'd heard much of this rhetoric before. The fact she came from a small town and had an upbringing much like theirs appealed to her base. But today, her words were more polished, more nuanced. She'd dropped a bombshell, and she knew she had to reassure her supporters she was still someone they could trust. Had she stayed up all night calibrating her words? Much of what she was saying was true, but there were parts that were spin. Her depression hadn't been a result of her abortion so much as the fact she'd been raped.

"Unfortunately, politics at both the national and the state level has devolved into a cesspool. We aren't having a conversation about abortion but a shouting match, and the candidate with the largest Twitter following or the catchiest sound bite wins. And I've realized something else. Like it or not, our current government is controlled by men, and at a fundamental level, men can't understand the sadness and the guilt and the fear many women go through when dealing with this life-changing decision."

Her hand trembled as she took a sip of water from a glass on the table. "Let me be clear. I have not changed my position on abortion."

A woman muttered "Thank God" under her breath.

"Based on what I went through two decades ago, I still believe terminating a pregnancy is a sin. That belief is at the core of who I am, and it always will be. If my daughter came to me today and sought my guidance about whether she should terminate a pregnancy, I would implore her not to. But I've also come to believe it's morally wrong for any politician to take that decision out of her hands."

I'd always seen my mother as weak, a woman who cooked and cleaned and decorated the house. A woman who lived in the shadow of her husband and was content in that role. A woman who basked in her daughter's accomplishments because she had none of her own. She was not a role model, not a person I admired, not someone who could teach me how to navigate the world.

It took this confession and her vulnerability today for me to realize my mother wasn't any of those things. All that I'd viewed as meek had been the mask. She'd latched on to that persona to keep herself safe. To keep me safe.

Despite our difficulties through the years, I'd always loved my mother. But now I felt something different. Respect. She'd called Jocelyn's bluff to help my career, but deep down, I believed she'd also done it for herself. Because she was tired of hiding who she was.

She scanned the room, making eye contact with many of the women there. "I challenge you today to reexamine your beliefs on this issue. Ask your daughters, your mothers, your best friends how they feel, and listen, really listen to their answers. See if you come away with a different perspective on this hot-button issue which is more moderate, more nuanced. And regardless of where you stand, regardless of whether I've lost your support because of what I've shared today, I urge you in ten days, as a citizen of this great country, to make your voice heard. Go to the polls. Vote with your conscience."

Three women at a table in the middle stood and clapped. Within seconds, they were joined by the majority of the attendees, although a good half dozen remained firmly planted in their seats. I rushed toward the front, dodging a parade of women who'd come forward to shake my mother's hand, and pulled her aside. "I never meant for you to—"

"My life. My decision."

"You did it for me."

"Partly. Mainly for me. The weight I've carried for years is gone, and I'm free. Besides, I *have* changed my mind, and I knew revealing details of my experience would lend my announcement the weight it deserved."

"You said Dad didn't know. Please don't let him hear about it through the media."

"We talked last night after you went to bed. It was a hard conversation, and we both did some crying. But we got closure."

"I should call him."

"You should, but not yet. This is a lot for him to process. He'll reach out when he's ready."

"What happens next?"

Her eyes blazed as she put her arm through mine. "I field a dozen questions from reporters, get a blistering lecture from the RNC, and deal with a campaign manager who's probably having heart palpitations right about now." She paused, then added, "And you let Jocelyn know her little blackmail scheme didn't work. Nobody messes with us Barnes girls."

"Women," I said.

She looked as though she was seeing me for the first time. "Yes." She nodded. "Women."

"Candidate Watkins, can I get that picture you promised?" It was the photographer from before, who'd been joined by a reporter from ABC News.

"Into the breach," Mother whispered and squeezed my elbow. "We'll catch up later." She turned to face a barrage of questions and flashbulbs.

I texted Jocelyn as I made my way to my car. *Helen Watkins, breaking news. Google it.*

And in case she didn't get the message.

Pawn takes Queen. Checkmate.

THIRTY-FIVE

I bustled around the kitchen, humming Taylor Swift's "Delicate," bopping my head to the rhythm. The paper's legal team had vetted my article, and it was slotted for the front page in the Sunday edition. Three days had passed since Mother's revelation, and from what her team could tell, she had gained as many moderate and undecided votes as she'd lost from the hard-liners. I felt sure that after the election, Diaz would offer me a staff position. My life was back on track.

I poured three eggs and a mix of red and orange peppers, onions, and shitake mushrooms into a pan and lit the one burner. A few minutes later, Nick joined me, his hair still damp from the shower. He poured each of us a mug of coffee while I divided the omelet and put two pieces of wheat bread in the toaster.

"Dragan must be happy the story's finally going to press," Nick said.

"I keep calling her, but she's not picking up. I hope her

mother hasn't taken a turn for the worse." The toast popped up, and I slathered on orange marmalade and gave each of us a slice. I'd only taken a couple of bites when my cell chirped.

It was Diaz. "What's Jocelyn doing on TV?" he blurted. Before I could make sense of what he'd asked, I heard muffled voices in the background, and when he came back on the line, he said, "Aw, cripes. This can't be good. She's on Channel Five. I'll call back after."

I wasn't sure what was going on, but Nick and I both grabbed our plates and plunked down in the living room in front of the television. Sure enough, there Jocelyn sat on a white leather couch, leaning against two colorful throw pillows. A blowup of her book cover, *On the Front Lines*, was prominently displayed behind her. Beneath the makeup, she looked older. Hardened. Across from her sat Diane Ackroyd, chirpy morning host of the NBC affiliate in Chicago. They seemed to be joking around while the pre-show music played over the intro credits. There was a bitter taste in my mouth.

"What's she up to?" Nick said.

My voice cracked. "Nothing good."

"Good morning, Chicago!" Diane stared into the camera, a practiced smile plastered across her face. She addressed the studio audience. "Today's something of a coup for us here at *The Morning Brew*. As most of you know, Jocelyn Jones, beloved news reporter and anchorwoman, has recently been accused of plagiarism via Twitter. Well, we're delighted to welcome her here today so she can give us her side of the story. So, without further introduction, let's hear from Jocelyn Jones." She faced her guest, and the camera followed. "This all started in early September, right?"

"That's right, Diane," Jocelyn began. "And I'll be honest. At first, I had no idea the tweets were even meant for me. But when the third one posted and called me out by name, I made the connection. I got in touch with my publicity team first thing and told them to locate @freethetruth, hoping I'd found Mak Petrovic's family and I could make this right."

An outright lie. My pulse pounded in my ears like one of Nick's drum solos.

"Give our studio audience a brief rundown if you would. Who is Mak Petrovic?"

Jocelyn filled in Mak's history, how he'd left his family back in Sarajevo, showed up in Manjaca after she'd already embedded herself there, and how they'd worked together, gathering evidence about what was happening.

That much was true. Where was this going?

"So you're saying this Bosnian reporter collaborated with you on the article about the Manjaca prison camp. The same series of articles which won you the Pulitzer back in 1995."

Jocelyn sat up straighter. Her answer was quick, too quick, but Diane didn't react. "We were in a war zone. Unsure who we could trust. Mak and I decided we'd keep our collaboration secret. I was a reporter for *The New York Times* at the time. I had a worldwide audience, so obviously, I'd file the story, but we agreed we'd share the byline."

"How much of the story did he write versus you?"

It was a crucial question, and I gave Diane credit for asking it.

"Oh, that's impossible to parse out." Jocelyn shot a huge smile at the audience. "We traded copy back and forth—what we observed firsthand and what others told us—but I remember him telling me several key anecdotes I used in the story."

"And he was killed days before the exposé broke, isn't that right?"

"Tragically, it's true."

"The obvious question is why didn't you give him credit anyway, particularly when your reporting garnered so many accolades?"

Good for you, Diane. Hold her accountable. Why *hadn't* Jocelyn shared the byline with Mak? There's no way she could get around that fact. But Jocelyn wasn't thrown by the question. If anything, it seemed as though she'd anticipated it.

"I had a good reason, and thankfully I can now share it with the world. My managing editor had reserved prime space on the front page, and I'd pulled back to Sarajevo and begun the final edits on the story. That's when I learned Mak had been killed."

She turned away from the camera and wiped her eyes, truly an Oscar-level performance. "My sources told me he'd been targeted. The Serbian military had labeled him a spy, accused him of feeding information to the rebels hiding in the hills. I heard rumors his family had been targeted as well, as a warning to others not to help the opposition. Several of his friends begged me not to mention him. They planned to smuggle his wife and child out of the country. So, despite the fact that it flew in the face of all my journalistic principles, I did what they asked and removed his name from the report."

"What a crock!" I yelled.

"This must be hard to watch," Nick began. "She's acting as if—"

"Shh. I need to hear this." I couldn't take my eyes off the screen. Jocelyn's story was so plausible, even I would have bought it, except there was a gaping hole in the logic. Why hadn't Jocelyn come forward once Dragan and her mother were safely out of the country? Chirpy Diane wasn't such an airhead after all. She'd spotted the hole too and asked about it.

"The situation in Bosnia at the time was total chaos," Jocelyn answered. "Constant fighting, explosions, fires. People disappeared. Homeless children begged in the streets for food. After my report, the United Nations called for an immediate investigation of the prison camp. I even received death threats."

Diane addressed the audience. "History is repeating itself—journalists across the globe are in fear for their lives right now as well." She turned back to Jocelyn. "What happened next?"

"My paper redeployed me to Iraq, and I lost track of my contacts in Sarajevo. A few years later, I hired a private detective to search for the Petrovic family, but the trail was cold. I didn't even know if they'd made it out of Bosnia, and if they had, whether they'd changed their name or been rerouted to another country after England."

Another lie. God, how could she keep them all straight?

"You put the whole incident behind you and moved on?" Diane asked.

At least Jocelyn had the decency to stare at the floor, even if she'd practiced the gesture ahead of time. "I'm ashamed to admit I did. The war heated up in the Middle East, and then 9/11, and after that . . ." She stopped herself and stared straight into the camera. "No. No more excuses. I should have made a point of finding out whether they were safe and got Mak the recognition he deserved. I'm truly sorry I didn't."

"And now you've been given another chance."

Jocelyn's face gave nothing away. "Unbelievably, I have. You know, it never crossed my mind the tweets referred to Mak until the word plagiarism surfaced. Of course, I wanted to be sure it wasn't a hoax, so I had my staff investigate. And I'm happy to report we found the messages had indeed been posted by someone in his family. His daughter."

Diane addressed the audience, her arms flung wide. "And that young woman is in the studio with us today. Please put your hands together for Dragan Petrovic." The sound stage erupted with applause, and Dragan materialized from behind a curtain.

So that's why she hadn't returned any of my phone calls. I couldn't take my eyes off the screen. The girl we'd met in St. Louis had disappeared. She had on just enough makeup to register under the studio lights but still seem innocent and natural. Her blond hair fell in soft curls around her face. She'd traded in her grungy T-shirt and leggings for a gray suede pencil skirt, a burgundy sweater set, and a paisley silk scarf, items she'd probably purchased solely for this appearance. Not a vicious troll seeking revenge, but a calm, even-keeled daughter whose sole goal was getting her father the recognition he deserved. She sat beside Jocelyn, hands clasped together in her lap, her legs primly crossed at the ankles.

"This must be a thrill, having your father's contribution to such an amazing story acknowledged after all these years," Diane said.

Dragan tucked a stray hair behind her ear. "I'm just glad my mum lived long enough to see this. That's what's important." She waved at the camera in what looked like a spontaneous gesture, and her tone softened. "Hi, Mum. We did it."

Then her expression changed, as though she was parroting lines from a script someone else had written. "And I'm doubly grateful to Jocelyn, who has promised she'll contact the Pulitzer committee right away and make sure my father's name is added to the record. It's such a gracious gesture on her part."

Another emotion crossed Dragan's face, so quickly I almost missed it. Was it anger? Fear? She pasted on a smile as Jocelyn patted her hand, and I saw what must have happened. Jocelyn hadn't only dug up dirt on *my* family. She'd done the same with Dragan. Or perhaps she'd threatened to call in markers and ruin her consulting business. Whatever it was, Dragan must have weighed the consequences, realized Jocelyn's version of the facts accounted for the notebook and the tape, and decided this was a fight she couldn't win.

Besides, her goal had never been to destroy Jocelyn, but to vindicate her father. And she'd accomplished that.

"A happy ending all the way around." Diane flashed her best toothpaste grin at her guests.

The camera zoomed in on Jocelyn as the smile gradually left her face and her voice turned serious. "And I hope your viewers will take away a message from this story. We should all do what's right the first time. Because sometimes we don't get a second chance."

The show cut to commercial, and I turned off the TV.

"She's a total imposter," Nick said. "Why did Dragan agree to lie?"

"It doesn't matter. Did you see the audience? They ate it up."

"What does this mean for your article?"

That I'm screwed. "It means Jocelyn owns the news cycle. She's concocted a narrative which dovetails with the known facts, and there's no way I can prove she's lying. It's my word against hers, and without Dragan's support, the media would paint me as a disgruntled former employee with an ax to grind."

"So she gets away with it?"

I hated it, but there wasn't any other way this could play out. By the time the Sunday edition rolled off the press, my article would be as stale as day-old bread. This wasn't how the story should end. The good guys were supposed to win.

My cell rang ten minutes later. It was Diaz. He was sorry, but he had no choice.

He'd killed my story.

THIRTY-SIX

T he turnout on Election Day was twice what the polls predicted. In my district alone, the line at midday wrapped around the building. I handed over my driver's license, and the silver-haired woman behind the table cross-referenced my name and address.

"I've never seen people so pumped up about an election," I remarked.

"It's been like this all day. We had to call in extra workers," she said. "Here's your slip, miss. Take it over to those folks and they'll get you set."

I presented my number, and a young volunteer handed me a ballot.

"There's pencils in the booth. Make sure you fully connect both sides of the arrow or your vote won't count." He pointed at eight identical cubicles lining the wall with three-sided white panels emblazoned with the word *Vote* beneath the image of an American flag flapping in the breeze. I chose a booth at the far end.

I'd voted in every election since I was eighteen. And in every case, I'd voted straight Democrat. This time, I paused over the House seat in the ninth district.

Gripping the pencil, I considered the choices. Edward Underhill, Democrat. Helen Watkins, Republican. If I cast my vote for Underhill, it would send a clear message to Washington that we needed a change.

But the other candidate was my own mother. She was a good person, although her beliefs and mine were miles apart. She would represent her constituency in Congress and vote her beliefs on crucial legislation, but I also knew she would reach across the aisle and compromise. I'd been adamant that first day—I would not campaign for her, and she would not get my vote.

I marked my ballot, fed it into the machine, and drove away from the polls.

I'm still not sure I made the right decision.

———————•———————

Mother lost the election, a casualty of the blue wave that swept through the country and flipped the House to the Democrats. After she called Underhill and conceded, I stood beside her as she thanked her supporters in the hotel ballroom. We went back to her suite and helped the staff dispose of the pizza boxes, half-filled flutes of champagne, and deflated balloons scattered around the space.

Gavin hovered in the doorway. His suit was rumpled as usual, his right shoe was untied, and there were purple bags under his eyes. "We should have bought more TV ads. Pulled in the governor at the rally last week. Or used what we knew about Underhill after all."

"I'm not sure any of that would have done any good." Mother gestured at the scroll on the TV screen. "Looks like the governor's in trouble, too." She gave Gavin a brief hug. "We could play Monday morning quarterback all night long. The bottom line is we both did all we knew how to do. If anyone's to blame, it's me. Given the current political climate, my message obviously didn't resonate with voters."

"We'll win next time."

She gave a light laugh. "We both know there's not going to be a next time. This was my shot. And you know what? That's okay. I won't mind being out of the public eye. I'll enjoy not having reporters hounding my every step, sticking microphones in my face. And thank goodness, no more reading vicious posts concerning my private life on social media. I'm not sure I have the stomach to play in this sandbox."

"Is there anything else I can do for you before I turn in?" Gavin asked. "I'm flying back home tomorrow evening. I hope my wife and kids recognize me."

"I'm fine. Megan's here to keep me company. Get some sleep. We'll touch base before you leave."

Gavin put his hand on my arm. "I know I gave you a hard time at first, but thank you for your support this last week. The exit polls showed it helped."

"I'm sorry I didn't step up sooner, but—"

He waved away my comment. "Water under the bridge."

He turned to my mother. "You would have made a great congresswoman."

She gave him a wan smile. "If only I didn't have to win an election to get the job."

"You should seriously consider their offer."

Once he left, we watched Underhill give his victory speech. Abner Lynch stood off to one side, a shit-eating grin on his face. Had he recognized me from the book party? Had he told Jocelyn who my mother was early on, and had she tucked that fact away, keeping it in reserve in case she needed it? Was Lynch the person who found out my mother's secret? Not that it mattered now, but I hated loose ends.

The newly elected congressman droned on and on. Outside our room, two men chanted, "Underhill! Underhill!" as they made their way down the hall. I'd gotten an adjoining room, thinking we'd stay up until the wee hours celebrating. "Ready to call it a night?" I asked.

"I'm way too keyed up for bed. Keep me company for a while."

"Okay. What did Gavin mean by that last remark? What offer?"

She sipped some champagne. "Seems I made a strong enough impression on the party's power brokers that they've asked me to move to Washington and take a staff position."

My breath caught. "And are you going to?"

"I'm not sure yet. Maybe."

We watched television for another hour as election results poured in from across the country. The pundits had a field day dissecting the trends, but my mind wandered.

"Meggie? You're off in your own little world. You haven't responded to anything I've said in the last five minutes."

"Oh, sorry." I sat up straighter and rubbed my eyes. "There's something I've kept from you, and I think it's time to come clean."

"Out with it." Mom readjusted the pillows behind her back. "After what we've been through these last few weeks, there's nothing you can't share with me, you know that."

It was such a relief to finally say it. "I saw Dad and Suzanne coming out of a restaurant a year before he left us." I swallowed hard. "He was sneaking around behind your back, and I should have told you. I should have." I squeezed my eyes shut. "I chose his side, and I'm sorry."

Mother's tone softened. "And you've carried this guilt around all this time?" She stroked my hair. "You always worshipped your father. It must have been devastating when you found out he was only human. But even if you'd told me back then, it wouldn't have made a difference."

"It might have. If you'd known, you could have done something. Talked to him. Gone to counseling."

She kissed the top of my head. "Oh, sweetheart. Your father and I were in couples therapy for years. Suzanne wasn't the reason he left. She was only the catalyst. Our marriage was over long before she came along. When he told me he'd fallen in love with someone else, I was hurt and angry. No, make that furious. I begged him not to leave. But deep down, I understood why." She poured herself another flute of champagne. "Tell me, how's that kid from your building doing?"

In other words, let's change the subject.

"Mateo? He's good. His father's getting out of the service any day now, and they're moving into their own place. I'll miss him."

"He seems like a bright young boy. Happy."

"Yeah, but that's kids, right? I mean, all they have to do is go to school, do homework, and stay up late texting friends. Life's way more complicated when you're a grown-up and out on your own."

"Wait until *you've* got kids. Talk about complicated."

I jabbed her lightly in the ribs. "Is that your subtle way of telling me I was a handful?"

She grinned. "A handful, yes. But also a joy. Do you remember the year when you went around the house shouting, 'Jubilee!' at the top of your lungs because you said it made your mouth happy? You were what, three, four? And oh, the questions. God, you drove me crazy with your questions." Her voice held a touch of sadness around the edges. "We were so close back then. I knew you loved tapioca pudding and white daisies and your favorite song was 'Hakuna Matata.' When you got nervous, you twirled the ends of your hair, and when you got excited, you stuck out your tongue. You were a book I'd read so many times, I'd memorized every page."

"And then I rebelled and pushed you away and you didn't know what to do." I looped my arm through hers. "I formally apologize for being such a shit."

She laughed. "Apology accepted." She reached for a piece of cheese. "I remember when you were a teenager,

I'd tried to imagine what my life would be like after you left. Because I knew you would. That's a mother's job, of course—preparing the person you love most in the world to leave you."

My chest filled, like a sail catching the wind. My mother was sharing her feelings with me again. "And then I did leave. Moved in with Becca, and later moved to New York."

"And made it clear I should butt out of your life, thank you very much. But you know what surprised me? How free I felt once you'd gone. I'd begun to pull away from you too. Begun carving out a new life for myself which didn't involve being your mother. And that seemed like a betrayal. Like breaking the promise I'd made when the nurse first put you in my arms."

"What promise?"

"To always put you first."

I took hold of her hand. "We've lost a lot of time, haven't we?"

"Let's change that." She slipped off her shoes. "How about we play the game from when you were a little kid. *What's My Secret?* Remember?"

Tell me something you never told me. A memory. An idea. A dream you had.

And that night, I told her the real story of what happened with Luke. About being fired from my job. I told her about Nick, said I thought I loved him.

And she told me she'd had doubts over moving to DC if she'd won the election. About a Buddhist retreat she'd gone to the year before when her life got too frantic. About a divorced man she'd dated for three months last fall until they parted ways.

"What happened?" I asked.

"He was a successful businessman, owned a large distribution company in the western suburbs. But as time went on, I realized he wanted a trophy wife—someone to stand beside him at business events, serve on charitable boards, and host dinner parties for his clients."

"And you didn't want that?"

"God, no. I'd already lived that life. I wanted to get out in the world and have adventures, do something meaningful with my life. I couldn't stand the idea of someone clipping my wings before I'd had a chance to see how far I could fly. Make sense?"

It made perfect sense. In fact, it sounded like something I would say.

THIRTY-SEVEN

The Monday after the election, Diaz offered me a job covering local politics, and I took it. It wasn't long before I'd immersed myself in the world of city councils, school boards, and special elections. I put the whole experience with Jocelyn out of my mind, even though I couldn't help feeling I'd ignored a detail that might have turned the entire narrative on its head. But after obsessing for days, I moved on and life got back to a new normal.

Becca and Sam had reconciled and were planning a spring wedding, with me as her maid of honor. Nick and I still spent several nights a week together, either at my place or his, and I'd adopted a cute little Sheltie from the pound who I named Gloria. Mom took the job in Washington but promised she'd come back every few months for a visit.

Even though everyone important in my life was doing well, it still bugged the hell out of me that Jocelyn hadn't been held accountable for what she'd done. If anything, she was a bigger celebrity than she'd been before the scandal. Her book was headed for the best seller list, and she was jetting around the country, giving keynote speeches and appearing on one talk show after another.

The second week in January, I was in the middle of transcribing an interview with the new mayor of Skokie when I heard a loud *whoop* from Jasmine Lennox, the staff reporter whose cubicle abutted mine. I swiveled around in my chair. "What are you going on about?"

"Bad Boy Tom-Tom's up to his old tricks." When I shot her a quizzical look, she pointed at a half-blurred photo on her computer screen. "That sleazebag guy Sugar Cube married last month?" Jasmine spent a lot of time on social media, monitoring the comings and goings of her favorite celebrities. "Says here he's already stepping out on her. Didn't even bother hiding it—hooked up with a female rocker at the Next Door Lounge last night. What'd he think, no one would notice?" She jabbed her finger at his image. "News flash, dude. Everyone and his cousin's got a camera." She turned back to me. "Once a cheater, always a cheater, I say. Leopards don't change their damn spots."

Simon had used the same phrase when he'd told me of Jocelyn's cheating scandal in high school. I couldn't stop myself. I replayed those last few weeks, step by step.

And this time I spotted it. The key to the entire story had been lying in plain sight all along, and I'd missed it.

I pulled out my phone and scrolled through my photos where I'd stored screenshots of Twitter responses to

Dragan's posts. Luckily, I'd never bothered to delete them. If others had been burned by Jocelyn, it made sense they might have left comments on @freethetruth's feed.

It wasn't long before I found the lead I was after. Someone by the name of @comradeinarms posted after all three of Dragan's entries. They offered support and encouragement and stopped just short of saying, "It happened to me too." After a half hour of digging around in their profile, I'd seen enough.

I bolted into Diaz's office without bothering to knock.

"It wasn't the only time."

He glanced up, glasses perched on the end of his nose. "Hell of an opening, but I've got no idea what you're talking about."

"Jocelyn."

He sighed. "Let it go, Barnes. It's over."

"No, it isn't." I hopped from one leg to the other. "Hear me out."

"You're making me nervous. Sit."

Before my butt hit the chair, the words tumbled out. "Something's always bugged me about the conversation I had with Jocelyn after that third tweet. I'd swear she had no idea who was behind it. But don't you see? That doesn't fit. If the only time she plagiarized a story was back in Bosnia, why didn't she connect the tweet to Mak? The logical reason was—"

"She'd done it before."

"Maybe. Or maybe it was the first time. He'd been killed. He wasn't there to raise a stink. So she copied his words, pretended they were her own, and held her breath. When no one caught on and she won the Pulitzer, she got cocky. Thought, why not try it again?"

"Jones has been a journalist for over four decades. If she were stealing stories, someone would have noticed."

"Where have you been? People in power protect their own. Besides, I'm not saying she stole all the time. She's too clever for that. But every once in a while when a cub reporter turned up a particularly juicy story . . ."

Diaz filled in the blank. "She'd take the credit."

"Why work her ass off when she could climb to the top on the backs of the poor schlubs who were starting out?"

"You think she had a pattern."

"I think she did it enough times that when she read the tweet accusing her of plagiarism, she literally had no idea who was behind it. That's why she didn't connect Dragan's accusations to Mak. It could have been any one of the dozens of reporters she'd shafted through the years. Let me dig around. I bet I can find two or three other sources who'll come forward."

When he hesitated, I leaned over the desk and got in his face. "This is about our sacred trust as journalists. We can't let her get away with it."

He fiddled with his pen. "Even if I buy your theory, how do you propose to find these people and convince them to turn whistleblower?"

"I've already got a lead. Someone with the handle @comradeinarms replied to each of Dragan's posts and then started a thread themselves focusing on intellectual property, examples of other plagiarists through history, and fake news."

"Your theory is this @comradeinarms is someone who got burned by Jocelyn?"

"I think it's worth digging into. Even if they don't have any hard evidence, they might lead me to others. People talk to each other, particularly people who've been betrayed. And if that's a dead end, I'll start from scratch. Dig into the archives, find other people who worked with Jocelyn through the years. There's something there—I can smell it."

This wasn't the first time I'd been obsessed with a story, but this time it was personal. Jocelyn had played me, played my mother. Hell, she'd even played Dragan. And gotten away with it.

But I'd outsmart her. Outthink her. She wouldn't have stolen from her peers. Too chancy. She'd have targeted people with no power, people who'd be flattered when a big-deal broadcaster like Jocelyn Jones took an interest in them. She'd have turned on that charm, pretended to care for them as a person, even offered to help their career. I knew what that felt like.

I held my breath, waiting for his answer.

"I'm going to need hard evidence." He wagged his finger. "Triple-check your facts. Document everything. And no anonymous sources. They'll need to go on the record."

"Got it." It sounded like I was winning him over, but he still hadn't given me the go-ahead.

He leaned back in his chair and stared at the ceiling, his jaw clenched. Finally, he stood, perched on the side of his desk, a slight crease between his eyes. He examined my face for a good minute.

We both knew it was risky. We'd be taking on powerful people. But I believed it was our moral obligation to ferret out the truth. And so did he.

"I'll give you one day a week. No more, you hear me? And don't tell anybody what you're working on. Management would ream me out if they knew."

"They'll give you a raise once I break the story. Don't worry. I'll keep a low profile." I sprang to my feet. "Thanks, boss. I owe you one."

"No giving up. Right, Bull Dog?" he called after me.

"Damn straight," I yelled back as I headed back to my desk.

BOOK CLUB DISCUSSION QUESTIONS:

If you'd like Maggie to speak to your book club, either in person or via Zoom, please go to https:// maggiesmithwriter.com/book-clubs/ for information.

1. Several characters in the novel have secrets they are keeping. Do you believe there's a difference between lying and keeping a secret?

2. What were your first impressions of Maggie? Of Helen? Of Jocelyn? How did these impressions change over time?

3. Megan sees her mother as overprotective. Have you known parents who stifled their children's growth with their helicopter parenting? Or conversely, gave their children so much space they ran wild and got in trouble? What do you think is the right balance between protecting your children and giving them enough freedom to develop maturity?

4. The plagiarism accusation spreads rapidly, primarily because of the wide reach of social media. What have we gained and what have we lost with our increased

BOOK CLUB DISCUSSION QUESTIONS:

If you'd like Maggie to speak to your book club, either in person or via Zoom, please go to **https:// maggiesmithwriter.com/book-clubs/** for information.

1. Several characters in the novel have secrets they are keeping. Do you believe there's a difference between lying and keeping a secret?

2. What were your first impressions of Megan? Of Helen? Of Jocelyn? How did those impressions change over time?

3. Megan sees her mother as overprotective. Have you known parents who stifled their children's growth with their helicopter parenting? Or conversely, gave their children so much space they ran wild and got in trouble? What do you think is the right balance between protecting your children and giving them enough freedom to develop maturity?

4. The plagiarism accusation spreads rapidly, primarily because of the wide reach of social media. What have we gained and what have we lost with our increased

interconnectivity? Have you ever known someone who was adversely affected by an internet posting?

5. At one point, Jocelyn tells Megan that she can't possibly understand how older people feel because her life is all about want, whereas as you grow older, it's all about fear. Does this ring true to you? Do you think as we grow older, we begin to hold tight to what we have instead of pursuing new dreams?

6. There is a generational gap theme running through the novel. Are you a boomer or a millennial or somewhere in between, and how do you feel about each generation's worldview?

7. Why do you think Helen decided to finally reveal her secret even though she must have known it would hurt her chances in the election? Were you surprised by her actions?

8. Initially, Megan views Jocelyn as a worthy role model. What signs were there early on that Jocelyn might not be who she seems? When did you first start to doubt her?

9. At first, Becca decides not to tell Sam about her abortion, but after talking with Helen, she makes a different decision. Why do you think Megan's mother advised her daughter's friend to tell the truth about what happened when she herself had kept a similar secret from her own husband for twenty years?

10. Did you understand what might have motivated Jocelyn to do what she did? After learning the story of what happened with her father and with Robert, did you sympathize more with her?

11. Until the last few pages, it seems as though Jocelyn has succeeded in switching the story around by presenting an alternative interpretation of the facts. Did this bother you? If the book had ended with that resolution, would you have felt cheated?

12. As the story unfolds, Helen and Megan learn, little by little, to connect as adults as opposed to parent and child. In your own life, have you had to make this type of transition, and what made it harder or easier?

13. Who do you think Megan voted for and why?

14. Helen shares her view of romantic love with Megan during an evening together. What did you think of her explanation, and how does it differ from your own viewpoint?

15. There are two examples of close friendships in the novel—Megan/Becca and Jocelyn/Rhoda. What did you think of each, and have you ever had a best friend where the relationship fell apart due to life situations, distance, or disagreements?

16. What did you think of Megan? How does she grow and change during the course of the novel?

17. What do you think the future holds for Megan? For Helen? For Jocelyn?

ACKNOWLEDGEMENTS

Writing can be a lonely endeavor. We sit alone for hours with nothing but the germ of an idea, a loose outline, and a set of characters we made up, trying to weave them together into a story worth telling. If we're lucky, we find a network of friends and colleagues who become our lifeline when we write ourselves into blind alleys, doubt our talent, or consider giving up. And now's my chance to thank those who helped me get here. Think of it as my Oscar speech, minus the glitz and the fancy ballgown.

I cannot say enough good things about the staff of Ten16 Press and their fearless leader, Shannon Ishizaki. Kaeley Dunteman listened to my ideas and worked tirelessly to create the perfect cover design, and no author could hope for a better editor than Lauren Blue, who read the manuscript with laser vision and saved me from several embarrassing errors. Ten16 may be small, but they're mighty, and I am privileged to count myself among their authors.

To Barbara Solomon Josselsohn and Patricia Friedrich, my early critique partners. This story is light-years from the one you read five years ago, but your encouragement and support gave me the incentive to keep at it. To Laura Broullire for her advice on how a modern pressroom operates. To Kathryn Craft, who had the insight to tell me this was Megan's story and to keep the focus on her. To the writing coaches who took a fledgling author and taught her how to get better: Donald Maass, Steven James, Robert Dugoni, Margie Lawson, Lisa Cron, Jennie Nash, S.J. Rozan, and Tim Storm. You are marvels.

Special thanks to the insightful Jess Moore, my developmental editor, who worked tirelessly to make *Truth and Other Lies* the story she believed it could be. From our first exchange of emails, I sensed she was a woman who would push me to go further and work harder. My story is richer for her astute and thoughtful editorial suggestions.

A special thanks to Red Oak Writing in Milwaukee, my first in-person writer's group, spearheaded by the fabulous Kim Suhr. Walking into a room with twelve strangers and sharing your pages out loud can be an intimidating experience. Thanks for making it a safe haven instead.

To WFWA for providing an online writing community I could turn to for information, support, and celebration. My selection as a finalist in your Rising Star contest was confirmation of the worthiness of my tale, and the chance to host your podcast these last four years has been a joy.

To the best book club friends any writer could wish for: Rochelle, Judy, Cathy, Patti, Barb, Dorothy, Marianne, Sue,

Toni, Laurel, Jane, and the incomparable Dianne Ostrowski, who was an early reader. Your constant friendship and encouragement has been a godsend.

To my best gal pals: Judi Strout, Margie Mahlberg, and Barb Hansen. We started out as singles buddies and have endured through ten years of ups and downs. Thanks for reminding me that there is life outside the writing world and for always being there with moral support. You keep me grounded.

I am blessed to know so many funny, intelligent, warm, and creative authors whose friendships I cherish: Michelle Cox, Della Leavitt, Lainey Cameron, Kristin Oakley, Samantha Hoffman, Alison Hammer, Linda Rosen, Jennifer Klepper, Therese Walsh, and Joan Fernandez. You are more than colleagues—you are sisters. Meeting wonderful writers like you has been the best part of this journey.

A special shout-out to two very special women who have encouraged me from the beginning. Barbara Linn Probst is my wise and savvy friend. Not only does she provide a sounding board about all things writerly, but she braved the debut waters two years before me and has generously shared her sage advice on everything from querying and publishers to blurbs and marketing. And then there's Jennifer Rupp, with her unflagging enthusiasm, generous spirit, and wise editorial advice. The first time you praised my writing, I felt like I'd won the Booker. You are a great friend as well as an awesome talent.

To the bookstore owners, bloggers, bookstagrammers, book clubs, librarians, podcasters, and readers who have embraced this novel. No writer can succeed without people like you spreading the word through word of mouth, author interviews, social media posts, and online reviews. The folks at Kaye Publicity deserve special kudos for helping me bring my baby into the world, as does Amy McFadden for bringing my characters to life through audio. Thanks to all of you for your support.

Grateful hugs all around to the best family a woman could wish for. Lee, you welcomed me into the fold, and I've felt I belonged ever since. Jordan, Spencer, and Francesca, you are the best and brightest millennials I know. Follow your dreams and never take no for an answer.

To my best friend and husband Scott, who makes me laugh every day. The journey has not always been smooth, but it's never been boring. You keep our household running and surprise me in delightful ways. Thank you for your unfailing support and for not freaking out when I decided to sell my company and become a full-time writer. Nora Ephron had it right: if you want a happy life, marry an Italian.

And finally to all those reporters and journalists out there who work tirelessly to give us the real and unadulterated facts. Your commitment to publishing the truth, no matter what the personal or professional cost, is a continuing inspiration.

In a career that's included forays into journalism and psychology (both great jobs for gathering fictional material), as well as a stint as CEO of a national art consulting company, Maggie Smith now adds novelist to her resume with the publication of her debut. In addition to her creative writing, she hosts the weekly podcast *Hear Us Roar*, blogs monthly for Rocky Mountain Fiction Writers, serves on the board of the Chicago Writers Association, and is Managing Editor of *The Write City Magazine*. A connoisseur of smooth wine and rich chocolate, she's an avid fan of the Green Bay Packers, classic noir films, reading late at night, and that moment between daylight and evening when the world slows down. She favors VRBO over hotels, dogs over cats, and jeans over dresses, and the last thing on her to-do list is always house cleaning.

 https://maggiesmithwriter.com

@maggiesmithwrites

CPSIA information can be obtained
at www.ICGtesting.com
Printed in the USA
LVHW040131160222
711209LV00002B/4